FALLING ANGEL

FALLING ANGEL

WILLIAM HJORTSBERG

For Bruce, Jada, Ellen, and Nick,
"Boys and girls together . . .
On the sidewalks of New York."

Alas, how terrible is wisdom when it brings no profit to the man that's wise.

Sophocles
Oedipus the King

The signatures of the seven demons

Left to right and top to bottom, they are Lucifer, Beelzebub, Satan, Astoroth, Leviathan, Elimi, and Baalbarith. They are found in a pact drawn up in 1616 between Lucifer and Urbain Grandier, the minister of St. Peter in Loudon, France.

1

IT WAS FRIDAY THE THIRTEENTH and yesterday's snowstorm lingered in the streets like a leftover curse. The slush outside was ankle-deep. Across Seventh Avenue a treadmill parade of lightbulb headlines marched endlessly around Times Tower's terra cotta façade: . . . HAWAII IS VOTED INTO UNION AS SOUTH STATE: HOUSE GRANTS FINAL APPROVAL, 232 TO 89; EISENHOWER'S SIGNATURE OF BILL ASSURED . . . Hawaii, sweet land of pineapples and Haleloki; ukeleles strumming, sunshine and surf, grass skirts swaying in the tropical breeze.

I spun my chair around and stared out at Times Square. The Camels spectacular on the Claridge puffed fat steam smoke rings out over the snarling traffic. The dapper gentleman on the sign, mouth frozen in a round O of perpetual surprise, was Broadway's harbinger of spring. Earlier in the week, teams of scaffold-hung painters transformed the smoker's dark winter homburg and chesterfield overcoat into seersucker and panama straw; not as poetic as the Capistrano swallows, but it got the message across. My building was built before the turn of the century; a four-story brick pile held together with soot and pigeon dung. An Easter bonnet of billboards flourished on the roof, advertising flights to Miami and various brands of beer. There was a cigar store on the corner, a Pokerino parlor, two hot dog stands, and the Rialto Theatre, mid-block. The entrance was tucked between a peep-show bookshop and a novelty place, show windows stacked with whoopee cushions and plaster dog turds.

My office was two flights up, in a line with Olga's Electrolysis, Teardrop Imports, Inc., and Ira Kipnis, C.P.A. Eight-inch gold letters gave me the edge over the others: CROSSROADS DETECTIVE AGENCY, a name I bought along with the business from Ernie Cavalero, who took me on as his legman back when I first hit the city during the war.

I was about to go out for coffee when the phone rang. "Mr. Harry Angel?" a distant secretary trilled. "Herman Winesap of McIntosh, Winesap, and Spy calling."

I grunted something pleasant and she put me on hold.

Herman Winesap's voice was as slick as the greasy kid stuff hair oil companies like to warn you about. He introduced himself as an attorney. That meant his fees were high. A guy calling himself a lawyer always costs a lot less. Winesap sounded so good I let him do most of the talking.

"The reason I called, Mr. Angel, was to ascertain whether your services were at present available for contract."

"Would this be for your firm?"

"No. I'm speaking in behalf of one of our clients. Are you available for employment?"

"Depends on the job. You'll have to give me some details."

"My client would prefer to discuss them with you in person. He has suggested that you have lunch with him today. One o'clock sharp at the Top of the Six's."

"Maybe you'd like to give me the name of this client, or do I just look for some guy wearing a red carnation?"

"Have you a pencil handy? I'll spell it for you."

I wrote the name LOUIS CYPHRE on my desk pad and asked how to pronounce it.

Herman Winesap did a swell job, rolling his *r*'s like a Berlitz instructor. I asked if the client was a foreigner?

"Mr. Cyphre carries a French passport. I am not certain of his exact nationality. Any questions you might have no doubt he'll be happy to answer at lunch. May I tell him to expect you?"

"I'll be there, one o'clock sharp."

Attorney Herman Winesap made some final unctuous remarks before signing off. I hung up and lit one of my Christmas Montecristos in celebration.

2

666 FIFTH AVENUE WAS AN unhappy marriage of the International Style and our own homegrown tailfin technology. It had gone up two years before between 52nd and 53rd streets: a million square feet of office space sheathed in embossed aluminum panels. It looked like a forty-story cheese grater. There was a waterfall in the lobby, but that didn't seem to help.

I took an express elevator to the top floor, got a number from the hatcheck girl, and admired the view while the maître d' gave me the once-over like a government meat inspector grading a side of beef. His finding Cyphre's name in the reservation book didn't exactly make us pals. I followed him back through a polite murmuring of executives to a small table by a window.

Seated there in a custom-made blue pin-stripe suit with a blood-red rosebud in his lapel was a man who might have been anywhere between forty-five and sixty. His hair was black and full, combed straight back on a high forehead, yet his square-cut goatee and pointed moustache were white as ermine. He was tanned and elegant; his eyes a distant, ethereal blue. A tiny, inverted golden star gleamed on his maroon silk necktie. "I'm Harry Angel," I said, as the maître d' pulled out my chair. "A lawyer named Winesap said there was something you wanted to speak to me about."

"I like a man who's prompt," he said. "Drink?"

I ordered a double Manhattan, straight up; Cyphre tapped his glass with a manicured finger and said he'd have one more of the same. It was easy to imagine those pampered hands gripping a whip. Nero must have had such hands. And Jack the Ripper. It was the hand of emperors and assassins. Languid, yet lethal, the cruel, tapered fingers perfect instruments of evil.

When the waiter left, Cyphre leaned forward and fixed me with a conspirator's grin. "I hate to bother with trivialities, but I'd like to see some identification before we get started."

I got out my wallet and showed him my photostat and honorary chiefs button. "There's a gun permit and driver's license in there, too."

He flipped through the celluloid card holders and when he handed back the wallet his smile was ten degrees whiter. "I prefer to take a man at his word, but my legal advisors insisted upon this formality."

"It usually pays to play it safe."

"Why, Mr. Angel, I would have thought you were a gambling man."

"Only when I have to be." I listened hard for any trace of an accent, but his voice was like polished metal, smooth and clean, as if it had been buffed with banknotes from the day he was born. "Suppose we get down to business," I said. "I'm not much good at small talk."

"Another admirable trait." Cyphre withdrew a gold and leather cigar case from his inside breast pocket, opened it, and selected a slender, greenish panatela. "Care for a smoke?" I declined the proffered case and watched Cyphre trim the end of his cigar with a silver penknife.

"Do you by any chance remember the name Johnny Favorite?" he asked, warming the panatela's slim length in the flame of his butane lighter.

I thought it over. "Wasn't he a crooner with a swing band back before the war?"

"That's the man. An overnight sensation, as the press agents like to say. Sang with the Spider Simpson orchestra in 1940. Personally, I loathed swing music and can't recall the titles of his hit recordings; there were several, in any case. He created a near-riot at the Paramount Theatre two years before anyone ever heard of Sinatra. You should remember that, the Paramount's over in your part of town."

"Johnny Favorite's before my time. In 1940, I was just out of high school, a rookie cop in Madison, Wisconsin."

"From the Midwest? I would have taken you for a native New Yorker."

"No such animal, at least not above Houston Street."

"Very true." Cyphre's features were shrouded in blue smoke as he puffed his cigar. It smelled like excellent tobacco, and I regretted not taking one when I had the chance. "This is a city of outsiders," he said. "I'm one myself."

"Where are you from?" I asked.

"Let us say I'm a traveler." Cyphre waved away a wreath of cigar smoke, flashing an emerald the Pope himself would have kissed.

"Fine with me. Why did you ask about Johnny Favorite?"

The waiter set our drinks on the table with less intrusion than a passing shadow.

"A pleasant voice, all things considered." Cyphre raised his glass to eye level in a silent European toast. "As I said, I could never stomach swing music; too loud and jumpy for my taste. But Johnny sounded sweet as a caroler when he wanted to. I took him under my wing when he was first getting started. He was a brash, skinny kid from the Bronx. Mother and father both dead. His real name wasn't Favorite, it was Jonathan Liebling. He changed it for professional reasons; Liebling wouldn't have looked nearly as good in lights. Do you know what happened to him?"

I said I had no idea whatsoever.

"He was drafted in January '43. Because of his professional talents, he was assigned to the Special Entertainment Services Branch and in March he joined a troop show in Tunisia. I'm not certain of the exact details; there was an air raid one afternoon during a performance. The Luftwaffe strafed the bandstand. Most of the troupe was killed. Johnny, through some quirk of fortune, escaped with facial and head injuries. *Escaped* is the wrong word. He was never the same again. I'm not a medical man, so I can't be very precise about his condition. Some form of shell shock, I suppose."

I said I knew something about shell shock myself.

"Really? Were you in the war, Mr. Angel?"

"For a few months right at the start. I was one of the lucky ones."

"Well, Johnny Favorite was not. He was shipped home, a total vegetable."

"That's too bad," I said, "but where do I fit in? What exactly do you want me to do?"

Cyphre stubbed out his cigar in the ashtray and toyed with the age-yellowed ivory holder. It was carved in the shape of a coiled serpent with the head of a crowing rooster. "Be patient with me, Mr. Angel. I'm getting to the point, however circuitously. I gave Johnny some help at the start of his career. I was never his agent, but I was able to use my influence in his behalf. In recognition of my assistance, which was considerable, we had a contract. Certain collateral was involved. This was to be forfeited in the event of his death. I'm sorry that I can't be more explicit, but the terms of our agreement specified that the details remain confidential.

"In any event, Johnny's case was hopeless. He was sent to a veteran's hospital in New Hampshire and it seemed as if he would spend the remainder of his life in a ward, one of the unfortunate discards of war. But Johnny had friends and money, a good deal of money. Although he was by nature profligate, his earnings for the two years prior to his induction were considerable; more than any one man could squander. Some of this money was invested, with Johnny's agent having power of attorney."

"The plot begins to grow complicated," I said.

"Indeed it does, Mr. Angel." Cyphre tapped his ivory cigar holder absently against the rim of his empty glass, making the crystal chime like distant bells. "Friends of Johnny's had him transferred to a private hospital upstate. There was some sort of radical treatment. Typical psychiatric hocus-pocus, I suppose. The end result was the same; Johnny remained a zombie. Only the expenses came out of his pockets instead of the government's."

"Do you know the names of these friends?"

"No. I hope you won't consider me entirely mercenary when I tell you that my continuing interest in Jonathan Liebling concerns only our contractual arrangement. I never saw Johnny again after he went away to war. All that mattered was whether he was alive or dead. Once or twice each year, my attorneys contact the hospital and obtain from them a notarized affidavit stating he is indeed still among the living. This situation remained unchanged until last weekend."

"What happened then?"

"Something very curious. Johnny's hospital is outside Poughkeepsie. I was in that vicinity on business and, quite on the spur of the moment, decided to pay my old acquaintance a visit. Perhaps I wanted to see what sixteen years in bed does to a man. At the hospital, I was told visiting hours were on weekday afternoons only. I insisted, and the doctor in charge made an appearance. He informed me that Johnny was undergoing special therapy and could not be disturbed until the following Monday."

I said: "Sounds like you were getting the runaround."

"Indeed. There was something about the fellow's manner I didn't like." Cyphre slipped his cigar holder into his vest pocket and folded his hands on the table. "I stayed over in Poughkeepsie until Monday and returned to the hospital, making certain to arrive during visiting hours. I never saw the doctor again, but when I gave Johnny's name, the girl at the reception desk asked if I was a relative. Naturally, I said no. She said only family members were permitted to visit with the patients."

"No mention of this the previous time around?"

"Not a word. I grew quite indignant. I'm afraid I made something of a scene. That was a mistake. The receptionist threatened to call the police unless I left immediately."

"What did you do?"

"I left. What else could I do? It's a private hospital. I didn't want any trouble. That's why I'm engaging your services."

"You want me to go up there and check it out for you?"

"Exactly." Cyphre gestured expansively, turning his palms upward like a man showing he has nothing to hide. "First, I need to know if Johnny Favorite is still alive—that's essential. If he is, I'd like to know where."

I reached inside my jacket and got out a small leather-bound notebook and a mechanical pencil. "Sounds simple enough. What's the name and address of the hospital?"

"The Emma Dodd Harvest Memorial Clinic; it's located east of the city on Pleasant Valley Road."

I wrote it down and asked the name of the doctor who gave Cyphre the runaround.

"Fowler. I believe the first name was either Albert or Alfred."

I made a note of it. "Is Favorite registered under his actual name?"

"Yes. Jonathan Liebling."

"That should do it." I put the notebook back and got to my feet. "How can I get in touch with you?"

"Through my attorney would be best." Cyphre smoothed his moustache with the tip of his forefinger. "But you're not leaving? I thought we were having lunch."

"Hate to miss a free meal, but if I get started right away I can make it up to Poughkeepsie before quitting time."

"Hospitals don't keep business hours."

"The office staff does. Any cover I use depends on it. It'll cost you money if I wait until Monday. I get fifty dollars a day, plus expenses."

"Sounds reasonable for a job well done."

"The job will get done. Satisfaction guaranteed. I'll give Winesap a call as soon as anything turns up."

"Perfect. A pleasure meeting you, Mr. Angel."

The maître d' was still sneering when I stopped for my overcoat and attaché case on the way out.

3

MY SIX-YEAR-OLD CHEVY WAS PARKED in the Hippodrome Garage on 44th, near Sixth Avenue. Only the name remained to mark the site of the legendary theater. Pavlova danced at the Hipp. John Philip Sousa led the house band. Now it stank of automobile exhaust, and the only music came from a portable radio in the office, between bursts of the Puerto Rican announcer's machine-gun Spanish.

By two o'clock I was heading north up the West Side Highway. The weekend exodus had yet to start, and traffic was light along the Saw Mill River Parkway. I stopped in Yonkers and bought a pint of bourbon for company. By the time I passed Peekskill it was half gone, and I filed it in the glove compartment for the return trip.

I drove in mellow silence through the snow-covered countryside. It was a nice afternoon, too nice to spoil with the car radio's hit parade lineup of adenoidal retards. After the yellow slush of the city, everything looked white and clean, like a Grandma Moses landscape.

I reached the outskirts of Poughkeepsie a little after three and found Pleasant Valley Road without spotting a single Vassar girl. Five miles out of town I came to a walled estate with an ornately arched wrought-iron gate and large bronze letters in the brickwork: EMMA DODD HARVEST MEMORIAL CLINIC. I turned off onto a graveled drive and meandered for half a mile or so through dense hemlocks, emerging in front of a six-story red-brick Georgian building that looked more like a college dormitory than a hospital.

Inside, the place was all hospital, walls a pale, institutional green and the gray linoleum floor clean enough to operate on. A glass-topped admissions desk was built into a recessed alcove along one wall. Across from it hung a large oil portrait of a bulldozer-faced dowager who I guessed was Emma Dodd Harvest without reading the little plaque screwed to the gilt frame. Straight ahead, I could see a gleaming corridor where a white-clad orderly pushing an empty wheelchair turned a corner and disappeared from view.

I've always hated hospitals, having spent too many months recovering in them during the war. There was something depressing about the efficient sterility of such places. The hushed tread of rubber soles down bright hallways reeking with Lysol. Faceless attendants anonymous in crisp, white uniforms. A routine so monotonous that even changing a bedpan takes on ritual importance. Memories of the ward rose in me with a choking horror. Hospitals, like prisons, are all the same from the inside.

The girl behind the admissions desk was young and homely. She was dressed in white and wore a small black nametag that said R. FLEECE. The alcove opened onto an office lined with filing cabinets. "May I help you?" Miss Fleece had a voice as sweet as angel's breath. Fluorescent light glinted on her thick, rimless glasses.

"I certainly hope so," I said. "My name is Andrew Conroy; I do field work for the National Institute of Health." I set my black calfskin attaché case on the glass-topped desk and showed her some fake I.D. in an extra wallet I carry as a dummy. I rigged it going down in the elevator back at 666 Fifth, changing the front card in the glassine window.

Miss Fleece regarded me suspiciously, her dim, watery eyes wavering behind the thick lenses like tropical fish in an aquarium. I could tell she didn't like my wrinkled suit or the soup stains on my tie, but the Mark Cross attaché case carried the day. "Is there anyone in particular you'd like to see, Mr. Conroy?" she asked, experimenting with a weak smile.

"Perhaps you'll know the answer to that." I slipped my dummy wallet back inside my jacket and leaned against the desk top. "The Institute is conducting a survey of incurable trauma cases. My job is to gather information about surviving victims currently in private hospitals. I understand you have a patient here fitting that description."

"What is the patient's name, please?"

"Jonathan Liebling. Any information you can provide will be kept strictly confidential. In fact, no names at all will be used in the official report."

"One moment, please." The homely receptionist with the heavenly voice retreated into the inner office and pulled out a lower drawer in one of the filing cabinets. It didn't take her long to find what she was looking for. She returned carrying an open manila folder and slid it across the glass top in front of me. "We did have such a patient at one time, but as you can see, Jonathan Liebling was transferred to the V.A. hospital up in Albany years ago. These are his records. Anything we'd have on him would be in there."

The transfer was duly recorded on the form, and beside it the date, 5/12/45. I got out my notebook and went through the motions of jotting down a few statistics. "Who was the physician attending this case, do you know?"

She reached over and turned the folder so she could read it. "It was Dr. Fowler." She tapped the name with her forefinger.

"He still work here in the hospital?"

"Why, of course. He's on duty right now. Would you like to speak with him?"

"If it's no trouble."

She made another attempt at a smile. "I'll call and see if he's free." She stepped to the switchboard and spoke quietly into a small microphone. Her amplified voice echoed down a distant corridor: "Dr. Fowler to the reception desk, please . . . Dr. Fowler to the reception desk."

"Were you working last weekend?" I asked as we waited.

"No, I was away for a few days. My sister got married."

"Catch the bouquet?"

"I'm not that lucky."

Dr. Fowler appeared as if out of nowhere, cat-silent on his crepe-soled shoes. He was a tall man, well over six feet, and walked with a stoop that made him look slightly hunchbacked. He wore a rumpled brown herringbone suit several sizes too large. I guessed him to be somewhere near seventy. What little hair he had left was the color of pewter.

Miss Fleece introduced me as Mr. Conroy and I fed him the line about the N.I.H., adding, "If there's anything at all you can tell me regarding Jonathan Liebling, I'd appreciate it very much."

Dr. Fowler picked up the manila folder. It might have been palsy that made his fingers tremble, but I had my doubts.

"So long ago," he said. "He was an entertainer before the war. Sad case. There was no physical evidence of neural damage, yet he didn't respond to treatment. There seemed no point in keeping him here, what with the expense and all, so we transferred him to Albany. He was a veteran and entitled to a bed for the rest of his life."

"And that's where he can be found, up in Albany?"

"I would imagine so. If he's still alive."

"Well, doctor, I won't take up any more of your time."

"That's quite all right. Sorry I couldn't be more help."

"Not at all, you've been very helpful." And he had. One look at his eyes told the whole story.

4

I DROVE BACK INTO POUGHKEEPSIE, stopping at the first bar and grill I came across. First, I called the V.A. hospital in Albany. It took a little time, but they confirmed what I already knew: there never was a transfer patient named Jonathan Liebling. Not in 1945; not anytime. I thanked them and let the phone dangle while looking up Dr. Fowler. I wrote the address and phone number in my notebook and gave the good doctor a call. No answer. I let it ring a dozen times before hanging up.

I had a quick drink and asked the bartender for directions to 419 South Kittridge Street. He drew a crude map on a napkin, remarking with studied indifference that it was a classy part of town. The bartender's cartography proved right on the money. I even got to see a few Vassar girls in the bargain.

South Kittridge was a pleasant, tree-lined street not many blocks from the campus. The doctor's house was a carpenter Gothic Victorian with a circular turret at one corner and quantities of elaborate scrollwork hanging under the eaves like lace on an old lady's collar. A wide veranda with Doric columns surrounded the building, and tall lilac hedges screened the yard on either side from the neighboring houses.

I drove slowly past, checking things out, and parked the Chevy around the corner in front of an ashlar-walled church. The sign out front announced this Sunday's sermon: SALVATION IS WITHIN YOU. I walked back to 419 South Kittridge Street carrying my black attaché case. Just another insurance salesman hunting a commission.

The front door framed a beveled-glass oval, allowing a glimpse of a dim, wainscoted hall and a set of carpeted steps leading up to the second floor. I rang the bell twice and waited. No one came. I rang again and tried the door. It was locked. The lock was at least forty years old and I had nothing to fit it.

I went along the side veranda trying each window without success. Around back, there was a lean-to cellar door. It was padlocked, but the unpainted wooden frame was soft and old. I got a jimmy out of my attaché case and pried off the hasp.

The steps were dark, festooned with cobwebs. My penlight flash kept me from breaking my neck. A coal furnace crouched in the center of the cellar like a pagan idol. I found the stairs and started up.

The door at the top was unlocked, and I stepped into a kitchen that would have been a modern miracle during the Hoover administration. There was a gas range with tall curving legs and a refrigerator whose circular motor perched on top like a hatbox. If the doctor lived alone, he was a tidy man. The breakfast dishes were washed and stacked on the drainboard. The linoleum floor was waxed. I left my case on the oilcloth-covered kitchen table and cased the rest of the house.

The dining room and front parlor looked never used. Dust powdered dark, ponderous furniture arranged with showroom precision. Upstairs were three bedrooms. The closets in two were empty. The smallest, with a single iron bed and plain oak dresser, was where Dr. Fowler lived.

I had a look through his dresser, not finding anything other than the usual round of shirts, handkerchiefs, and cotton underwear. Several musty woolen suits hung beside a shoe rack in the closet. I felt the pockets without knowing why and didn't turn up a thing. There was a .455-caliber Webley Mark 5 revolver in his bedside table lying next to a small leather-bound Bible. This was the sidearm issued to British officers in World War I. Bibles were optional. I checked the breakfront action, but the Webley wasn't loaded.

In the bathroom I got lucky. A sterilizer was steaming on the washstand. Inside, I found a half-dozen needles and three syringes. The medicine cabinet yielded nothing more than the standard array of aspirin and cough syrup bottles, toothpaste tubes and eye drops. I examined several vials containing prescription capsules, but they all seemed legit. None was narcotic.

I knew it had to be somewhere, so I went back downstairs and had a look in the old-fashioned fridge. It was on the same shelf with the milk and eggs. Morphine; at least twenty 50-cc bottles at rough count. Enough to keep a dozen junkies stoned for a month.

5

IT GREW DARK OUTSIDE BY degrees, the bare trees in the front yard becoming silhouettes against a cobalt sky before merging altogether into blackness. I chain-smoked, piling a pristine ash tray with spent butts. A few minutes before seven, the headlights of an automobile turned into the driveway and went out. I listened for the doctor's footsteps on the porch but didn't hear a thing until his key turned in the lock.

He switched on an overhead lamp and a rectangle of light pierced the dark parlor and illuminated my outstretched legs as far as my knees. I made no sound other than exhaling, but expected he would smell the smoke. I was wrong. He hung his overcoat on the banister and shuffled off toward the kitchen. When he turned on the lights, I started back through the dining room.

Dr. Fowler seemed not to notice my attaché case sitting on the table. He had the refrigerator door open and was bent over, poking around inside. I leaned against the arched dining room entrance and watched him.

"About time for your evening fix?" I said.

He spun around clutching a milk carton to his shirt front with both hands. "How did you get in here?"

"Through the mail slot. Why don't you sit down and drink your milk and we'll have a nice, long talk."

"You're not with N.I.H. Who are you?"

"The name is Angel. I'm a private investigator from the city," I pulled out one of the kitchen chairs and he sat down wearily, holding the milk as if it was all he had left in the world.

"Breaking and entering is a serious crime," he said. "I suppose you know you'd lose your license if I were to call the police."

I turned a chair around across the table from him and straddled it, folding my arms on the bentwood frame. "We both know you're not calling the law. Too embarrassing if they found the opium den in the icebox."

"I'm a medical man. It's perfectly within my rights to store pharmaceuticals at home."

"Come off it, doc, I saw your works cooking in the bathroom. How long have you been hooked?"

"I'm not . . . an addict! I will not stand for such an inference. I have severe rheumatoid arthritis. Sometimes, when the pain is overwhelming, I employ a mild narcotic analgesic. Now I suggest you get out of here or I truly will call the police."

"Go ahead," I said. "I'll even dial them for you myself. They'll get a kick out of seeing your Nalline test."

Dr. Fowler sagged within the folds of his oversized suit. He seemed to be shrinking before my eyes. "What do you want with me?" He pushed the milk carton to one side and propped his head in his hands.

"Same thing I was after back at the hospital," I said. "Information about Jonathan Liebling."

"I've told you everything I know."

"Doc, let's not kid around. Liebling was never transferred to any V.A. hospital. I know because I called Albany myself and checked it. Not smart making up a story as thin as that." I shook a cigarette out of the pack and stuck it in my mouth but didn't light it. "The second mistake you made was using a ballpoint pen to record the fake transfer on Liebling's chart. Ballpoints weren't such a hot item in 1945."

Dr. Fowler groaned and cradled his head in his arms on the tabletop. "I knew it was all over when he finally had a visitor. In almost fifteen years there were never any visitors, not one."

"Sounds like a popular guy," I said, thumbing my Zippo and tilting the cigarette into the flame. "Where is he now?"

"I don't know." Dr. Fowler pulled himself upright. It seemed to take all he had in him to get the job done. "I haven't seen him since he was my patient during the war."

"He must have gone someplace, doctor."

"I have no idea where. Some people came one night long ago. He got into a car with them and drove away. I never saw him again."

"Into a car? I thought he was supposed to be a vegetable."

The doctor rubbed his eyes and blinked. "When he first came to us he was in a coma. But he responded well to treatment and within a month was up and around. We used to play table tennis in the afternoons."

"Then he was normal when he left?"

"Normal? Hateful word, normal. No meaning whatsoever." Dr. Fowler's nervous, drumming fingers clenched into fists on the faded oilcloth. On his left hand he wore a gold signet ring engraved with a five-pointed star. "To answer your question, Liebling was not the same as you or me. After recovering his senses, his speech and sight and so on, the use of his limbs, he continued to suffer from acute amnesia."

"You mean he had no memory?"

"None whatsoever. He had no idea who he was or where he came from. Not even his name meant anything to him. He insisted he was someone else and would eventually remember. I said he left with friends; I have only their word for it about that. Jonathan Liebling didn't recognize them. They were strangers as far as he was concerned."

"Tell me more about these friends. Who were they? What were their names?"

The doctor closed his eyes and pressed his trembling fingers to his temples. "It's been so long. Years and years. I've done my best to forget it."

"Don't you go pleading amnesia on me, doc."

"There were two of them," he said, speaking very slowly, the words dragged out of the distance and filtered through layers of regret. "A man and a woman. I can't tell you anything about the woman; it was dark and she stayed in the car. In any case, I'd never seen her before. The man was familiar to me. I'd met him several times. He was the one who made all the arrangements."

"What was his name?"

"He said it was Edward Kelley. I have no way of knowing if that was the truth or not."

I made a note of the name in my little black book. "What about the arrangements you mentioned? What was the deal there?"

"Money." The doctor spat the word out as if it were a piece of rotten meat. "Isn't every man supposed to have his price? Well, I certainly had mine. This fellow Kelley came to see me one day and offered money—"

"How much money?"

"Twenty-five thousand dollars. Perhaps that doesn't seem like such a vast sum now, but during the war it was more than I'd ever dreamed of."

"It still might make for some sweet dreams today," I said. "What did Kelley want for the money?"

"What you probably already suspect; discharge Jonathan Liebling without keeping a record. Destroy any evidence of his recovery. Most important, I was to maintain the pretense that he was still a patient at Emma Harvest."

"Which is just what you did."

"It wasn't very difficult. Aside from Kelley and Liebling's theatrical agent, or manager, I forget which, he never had any visitors."

"What was the agent's name?"

"I think it was Wagner; I can't recall his first name."

"Was he in on the arrangement with Kelley?"

"Not to my knowledge. I never saw them together, and he didn't seem to know that Liebling had gone. He called every few months for a year or so to ask if there was any improvement, but never came up to visit. After a while, he stopped calling."

"What about the hospital? Didn't the administration suspect they were missing a patient?"

"Why should they? I kept his charts up to date, week by week; and every month a check came from Liebling's trust fund to cover his expenses. As long as the bills are paid, no one is going to ask too many questions. I made up some sort of story to satisfy the nurses, but they had other patients to worry about, so it wasn't very hard, really. As I said, there were never any visitors. After a while, all I had to do was fill out a legal affidavit which arrived every six months, regular as clockwork, from a law firm in New York."

"McIntosh, Winesap, and Spy?"

"That's the one." Dr. Fowler raised his haunted eyes from the tabletop and met my gaze. "The money wasn't for me. I want you to know that. My wife, Alice, was alive then. She had carcinoid syndrome and needed an operation we couldn't afford. The money paid for that, and a trip to the Bahamas, but she died anyway. Didn't take a year. You can't buy off pain. Not with all the money in the world."

"Tell me about Jonathan Liebling."

"What do you want to know?"

"Anything at all; little things, habits, hobbies, how he liked his eggs. What color were his eyes?"

"I can't remember."

"Give me what you can. Start with a physical description."

"That's impossible. I have no idea what he looked like."

"Don't crap around with me, doc." I leaned forward and blew a stream of smoke into his watery eyes.

"I'm telling the truth," the doctor coughed. "Young Liebling came to us following intensive facial restoration."

"Plastic surgery?"

"Yes. His head was swathed in bandages for his entire stay. I wasn't the one who changed the dressings and so had no opportunity to see his face."

"I know why they call it 'plastic' surgery," I said, fingering my boiled-potato nose.

The doctor studied my features professionally. "Wax?"

"A war souvenir. It looked fine for a couple years. The guy I worked for had a summer place on the Jersey shore down at Barnegat. I fell asleep on the beach there one August and when I woke up it had melted inside."

"Wax is no longer used for that procedure."

"So I'm told." I stood up and leaned against the table. "Give me what you can about Edward Kelley."

"It's been a long time," the doctor said, "and people change."

"How long, doc? What was the date of Liebling's departure from the clinic?"

"It was 1943 or '44. During the war. I can't remember more precisely."

"Having another amnesia attack?"

"It's been more than fifteen years. What do you expect?"

"The truth, doc." I was beginning to grow impatient with the old man.

"I'm telling the truth, as best as I can recall."

"What did this Edward Kelley look like?" I growled.

"He was a young man then, mid-thirties, I would guess. Be in his fifties now, in any case."

"Doc, you're stalling me."

"I only met the man on three occasions."

"Doc." I reached down and took hold of the knot in his necktie, pinching it between my forefinger and thumb. Not much of a grip, but when I lifted he came up to meet me as easily as an empty husk. "Save yourself some trouble. Don't make me squeeze the truth out of you."

"I've told you all I can."

"Why are you shielding Kelley?"

"I'm not. I hardly knew him. I—"

"If you weren't such an old fart, I'd bust you up like a soda cracker." When he tried to pull away, I jerked the knot in his tie a touch tighter. "Why wear myself out when there's an easier way?" Dr. Fowler's bloodshot eyes broadcast his fear. "You're in a cold sweat, aren't you, doc? Can't wait to get rid of me so you can mainline the junk in your fridge?"

"Everyone needs something to help him forget," he whispered.

"I don't want you to forget. I want you to remember, doc." I took him by his arm and steered him from the kitchen. "That's why we're going upstairs to your room where you can lie down and think things over while I go out and grab a bite to eat."

"What do you want to know? Kelley had dark hair and one of those thin moustaches Clark Gable made popular."

"Not good enough, doc." I bullied him up the stairs by the collar of his tweed jacket. "A couple hours' cold turkey should refresh your memory."

"Always expensively dressed," Dr. Fowler pleaded. "Conservative suits; nothing flashy."

I pushed him through the narrow door of his spartan room and he fell forward onto the bed. "You think it over, doc."

"Had perfect teeth. The most engaging smile. Please don't go."

I closed the door behind me and turned the long-handled key in the lock. It was the kind of key grandmother used to keep her secrets. I dropped it in my pocket and went down the carpeted stairs, whistling.

6

IT WAS AFTER MIDNIGHT WHEN I got back to Dr. Fowler's place. A single light burned in the bedroom upstairs. The doc wasn't getting much sleep tonight. It didn't trouble my conscience. I devoured an excellent mixed grill and sat through half a double-feature without a pang of remorse. It's a heartless profession.

I let myself in the front door and walked back through the dark hall to the kitchen. The refrigerator purred in the shadows. I took a bottle of morphine off the top shelf to bait the hook and started upstairs, guided by my penlight. The bedroom door was locked up tight.

"Be right with you, doc," I called, fumbling in my pockets for the key. "I brought you a little taste."

I turned the key and opened the door. Dr. Albert Fowler didn't say a word. He was propped against the pillows on his bed, still wearing the brown herringbone suit. The framed photograph of a woman was clutched to his chest in his left hand. In his right he held the Webley Mark 5. He was shot through the right eye. Thickened blood welled in the wound like ruby tears. Concussion drove the other eye halfway out of its socket, giving him the goggling stare of a tropical fish.

I touched the back of his hand. It was cold as something hanging in a butcher shop window. Before I touched anything else, I opened my attaché case on the floor and put on a pair of latex surgeon's gloves I took from the snap-front pocket inside the lid.

Something was wrong with the whole setup. Shooting yourself through the eye seemed an odd way to go about it, but presumably medical men are more informed in these matters. I tried to picture the doc holding his Webley upside down with his head bent back as if he were administering eye drops. It didn't add up.

The door was locked, and I had the key in my pocket. Suicide was the only logical explanation. "If thine eye offend thee," I muttered, trying to put my finger on what was out of place. The room looked exactly the same, military hairbrush and mirror at attention on the bureau, an undisturbed assortment of socks and underwear in the drawers.

I picked the leather-bound Bible off the bedside table and an open box of cartridges tumbled out onto the throw rug. The book was hollow inside, a dummy. I was the dummy for not finding the bullets earlier. I picked them off the floor, groping under the bed for strays, and put them back inside the empty Bible.

I went over the room with my handkerchief, wiping everything I had touched during my initial search. The Poughkeepsie police wouldn't exactly be charmed by the idea of an out-of-town private eye bullying one of their prominent citizens into suicide. I told myself if it was suicide they wouldn't look for prints and kept on wiping.

I cleaned the knob and the key and closed the door, leaving it unlocked. Downstairs, I emptied the ashtray into my jacket pocket, carried it to the kitchen and washed it, stacking it with the dishes on the drainboard. I put the morphine and the milk carton back in the icebox and went over the kitchen carefully with my handkerchief. Backtracking through the cellar, I wiped the banisters and doorknobs. There was nothing I could do about the hasp on the lean-to door. I set it in place and pushed the screws into the spongy wood. Anyone doing his job would spot it right away.

The drive back to the city provided plenty of time for thinking.

I didn't like the idea that I had hounded an old man to his death. Vague feelings of sorrow and remorse troubled me. It was a bad mistake locking him up with a gun like that. Bad for me because the doc had a lot more to tell.

I tried to fix the scene in my mind like a photo. Dr. Fowler stretched on the bed with a hole in his eye and his brains spread across the counterpane. There was an electric lamp burning on the bedside table next to the Bible. Inside the Bible were bullets. The framed photograph from up on the bureau was locked in the doctor's cooling grip. His finger rested on the revolver's trigger.

No matter how many times I went over the scene there was something missing, a piece gone out of the puzzle. But which piece? And where did it fit? I had nothing to go on but my instincts. A nagging hunch that wouldn't let go. Maybe it was just because I didn't want to face my own guilt, but I was sure Dr. Albert Fowler's death was not suicide. It was murder.

7

MONDAY MORNING WAS FAIR AND cold. What was left of the snowstorm had been hauled off and dumped in the harbor. After a swim at the "Y" across the street from my place in the Chelsea Hotel, I drove uptown, parked the Chevy at the Hippodrome Garage and walked to my office, stopping to buy a copy of yesterday's *Poughkeepsie New Yorker* from the out-of-town newsstand at the north corner of Times Tower. No mention anywhere of Dr. Albert Fowler. It was a little after ten when I unlocked the inner-office door. The usual bad news across the street: . . . NEW IRAQ ATTACK ON SYRIA ALLEGED . . . GUARD WOUNDED IN BORDER INCURSION BY BAND OF THIRTY . . . I phoned Herman Winesap's Wall Street law firm, and the machine-tooled secretary put me straight through without delay.

"And what might I do for you today, Mr. Angel?" the attorney asked, his voice smooth as a well-oiled hinge.

"I tried calling you over the weekend but the maid said you were out at Sag Harbor."

"I keep a place there where I can relax. No phone. Has something important come up?"

"That information would be for Mr. Cyphre. I couldn't find him in the phone book either."

"Your timing is perfect. Mr. Cyphre is sitting across the desk from me this very moment. I'll put him on."

There was the muffled sound of someone speaking with his hand over the receiver and then I heard Cyphre's polished accent purring on the other end. "So good of you to call, sir," he said. "I'm anxious to know what you found out."

I told him most of what I'd learned in Poughkeepsie, leaving out the death of Dr. Fowler. When I finished, I heard only heavy breathing on the other end. I waited. Cyphre muttered, "Incredible!" through tightly clenched teeth.

I said: "There are three possibilities: Kelley and the girl wanted Favorite out of the way and took him for a ride, in which case he's long gone. It could be they were working for someone else with the same result. Or Favorite was faking amnesia and engineered the whole setup himself. In any case, it adds up to a perfect disappearing act."

"I want you to find him," Cyphre said. "I don't care how long it takes or how much it costs, I want that man found."

"That's a pretty tall order, Mr. Cyphre. Fifteen years is a long time. Give a guy that kind of lead and the trail is bound to be cold as ice. Your best bet would be the Missing Persons Bureau."

"No police. This is a private matter. I don't want it dragged out in the open by involving a lot of nosy civil servants." Cyphre's voice was acid with patrician scorn.

"I suggested it because they've got the manpower for the job," I said. "Favorite could be anywhere in the country, or abroad. I'm just one man on my own. I can't be expected to accomplish the same results as an organization with an international information network."

The acid in Cyphre's voice grew more corrosive. "What it boils down to, Mr. Angel, is simply this: Do you want the job or not? If you are not interested, I will engage someone else."

"Oh, I'm interested all right, Mr. Cyphre, but it wouldn't be fair to you as my client if I underestimated the difficulty of the project." Why did Cyphre make me feel like a child?

"Of course. I appreciate your honesty in the matter, as I do the enormity of the undertaking." Cyphre paused, and I heard the flick of a lighter and the intake of his breath as he set fire to one of his expensive panatelas. He resumed, sounding somewhat mellowed by fine tobacco. "What I want you to do is get started right away. I'll leave the approach up to you. Do whatever you think best. The key to the whole operation, however, must remain discretion."

"I can be discreet as a father confessor when I try," I said.

"I'm sure you can, Mr. Angel. I'm instructing my attorney to make you out a check for five hundred dollars in advance. That will go in the mail today. Should you need anything more for expenses, please contact Mr. Winesap."

I said that five hundred would certainly take care of things, and we hung up. The urge to crack the office bottle for a self-congratulatory toast was never stronger, but I resisted and lit up a cigar instead. Drinking before lunch was bad luck.

I started by calling Walt Rigler, a reporter I knew over at the *Times*. "What can you tell me about Johnny Favorite?" I asked, after the prerequisite snappy patter.

"Johnny Favorite? You must be kidding. Why don't you ask me the names of the other guys who sang with Bing Crosby in the A&P Gypsies?"

"Seriously, can you dig anything up on him?"

"I'm sure the morgue has a file. Give me five or ten minutes and I'll have the stuff ready for you."

"Thanks, buddy. I knew I could count on you."

He grunted goodbye and we hung up. I finished my cigar while sorting the morning mail, mostly bills and circulars, and closed up the office. The fire stairs are always quicker than the coffin-sized self-service elevator, but I was in no hurry, so I pushed the button and waited, listening to Ira Kipnis, C.P.A., rattle off figures next door on his adding machine.

The Times Building on 43rd Street was just around the corner. I walked there, feeling prosperous, and took the elevator to the newsroom on the third floor after exchanging frowns with the statue of Adolph Ochs in the marble lobby. I gave Walt's name to the old man at the reception desk and waited a minute or so until he appeared from the back in shirt sleeves with his necktie loosened, like a reporter in the movies.

We shook hands and he led me into the newsroom where a hundred typewriters filled the cigarette haze with their staccato rhythms.

"This place has been gloomy as hell," Walt said, "ever since Mike Berger died last month." He nodded at an empty desk in the front row where a wilted red rose stood in a glass of water on the shrouded typewriter.

I followed him through the clatter of the rewrite bank to his desk in the middle of the room. A fat manila folder sat in the top wire basket of the desk tray. I picked it up and glanced at the yellowed clippings inside. "Okay if I hang onto some of this stuff?" I asked.

"House rules say no." Walt hooked a forefinger into the collar of the worsted jacket draped over the back of his swivel chair. "I'm going out to lunch. There're some 8-by-12 envelopes in the bottom drawer. Try not to lose anything and my conscience'll be clean."

"Thanks, Walt. If I can ever do you a favor—"

"Yeah, yeah, yeah! For a guy who reads the *Journal-American* you come to the right place for your research."

I watched him slouch between the rows of desks, trading wisecracks with the other reporters and waving to one of the editors in the bullpen on his way out. Seated at his desk, I had a look through the Johnny Favorite folder.

Most of the old clippings were not from the *Times*, but from other New York dailies and a selection of national magazines. Mainly, they were about Favorite's appearances with the Spider Simpson band. A few were feature stories, and I read through these with care.

He was an abandoned child. A cop found him in a cardboard box with only his name and "June 2, 1920," the date of his birth, pinned in a note to his receiving blanket. His first few months were spent at the old Foundling Hospital on East 68th Street. He was raised in an orphanage in the Bronx and was on his own at sixteen, working as a busboy in a series of restaurants. Within a year, he was playing piano and singing in roadhouses upstate.

He was "discovered" by Spider Simpson in 1938 and soon was headlining with a fifteen-piece orchestra: He set an attendance record for a week's engagement at the Paramount Theatre in 1940 that wasn't equaled until the Sinatra craze of '44. In 1941, his records sold over five million copies, and his income was said to be better than $750,000. There were several stories about his injury in Tunisia, one reporting that he was "presumed dead," and that was the end of it. There was nothing about his hospitalization or return to the States.

I sorted through the rest of the material, making a small pile of the stuff I wanted to keep. Two photos, one a studio glossy of Favorite in a tuxedo, his Vaseline-bright hair pomaded into a frozen black wave. The agent's name and address were rubber-stamped on the back: WARREN WAGNER, THEATRICAL REPRESENTATIVE, 1619 BROADWAY (THE BRILL BUILDING). WYNDHAM 9-3500.

The other glossy showed the Spider Simpson orchestra in 1940. Johnny stood to one side with his hands folded like a choirboy. The names of all the sidemen were written in beside them on the print.

I borrowed three other items, clippings that caught my attention because they didn't feel like part of the package. The first was a photo from *Life*. It was taken at Dickie Wells's bar in Harlem and showed Johnny leaning against a baby grand, holding a drink in one hand and singing along with a Negro piano player named Edison "Toots" Sweet. There was a piece from *Downbeat*, dealing with the singer's superstitions. The story claimed he went out to

Coney Island once a week whenever he was in town and had his palm read by a gypsy fortune-teller named Madame Zora.

The last item was a squib in Walter Winchell's column dated 11/20/42 announcing that Johnny Favorite was breaking off his two-year engagement to Margaret Krusemark, daughter of Ethan Krusemark, the shipping millionaire.

I shuffled all of this stuff together, got a manila envelope out of the bottom drawer, and stuffed it inside. Then, on a hunch, I dug out the glossy of Favorite, and called the number in the Brill Building stamped on the back.

"Warren Wagner Associates," answered a perky female voice.

I gave her my name and made an appointment to see Mr. Wagner at noon.

"He has a luncheon engagement at twelve-thirty and can only give you a few minutes."

"I'll take them," I said.

8

"WHEN YOU'RE NOT ON BROADWAY, everything is Bridgeport." This blue-ribbon wisecrack was made to George M. Cohan in 1915 by Arthur "Bugs" Baer, whose column in the *Journal-American* I read every day for years. It might have been true in 1915. I can't say, not having been there. That was the era of Rector's and Shanley's and the New York Roof. The Broadway I knew was Bridgeport; a carnie street of shooting galleries and Howard Johnson's; Pokerino parlors and hot dog stands. Two old dowagers, Times Tower and the Astor Hotel, were all that remained from the golden age "Bugs" Baer remembered.

The Brill Building was on 49th and Broadway. Walking up from 43rd, I tried to remember how the Square looked the night I saw it for the first time. So much had changed. It was New Year's Eve of '43. An entire year of my life had vanished. I was fresh out of an army hospital with a brand-new face and nothing but loose change in my pockets. Someone had lifted my wallet earlier in the evening, taking all I owned: driver's license, discharge papers, dog-tags, the works. Caught up in the vast crowd and surrounded by the electric pyrotechnics of the spectaculars, I felt my past sloughing away like a shed snakeskin. I had no identification, no money, no place to live, and knew only that I was heading downtown.

It took an hour to move from in front of the Palace Theatre

to the center of the Square, between the Astor and Bond Clothes, home of the "two-trouser suit." I stood there at midnight and watched the golden ball drop on top of Times Tower, a landmark I didn't reach for another hour. That was when I saw the lights in the Crossroads office and played a hunch which led me to Ernie Cavalero and a job I've never left.

In those days, a pair of mammoth nude statues, male and female, bookended the block long waterfall on the roof of Bond Clothes. Today, gigantic twin Pepsi bottles loomed in their place. I wondered if the plaster statues were still there, trapped inside the sheet-metal bottles like caterpillars slumbering within the confines of their chrysalides.

Outside the Brill Building, a tramp in a tattered army greatcoat paced back and forth, muttering, "Scumbag, scumbag" to all who entered. I checked the directory at the end of the narrow T-shaped lobby and located Warren Wagner Associates, surrounded by dozens of songpluggers, prizefight promoters, and fly-by-night music publishers. The creaking elevator took me to the eighth floor, and I prowled a dim hallway until I found the office. It was in a corner of the building, several rabbit-warren cubicles with interconnecting doors.

The receptionist was knitting when I opened the door. "You Mr. Angel?" she asked, forming her words around a wad of gum.

I said that I was and got a card out of my dummy wallet. It had my name on it but said I was a representative of the Occidental Life and Casualty Corp. A friend with a print shop in the Village made them up for me in a dozen professions. Everything from ambulance chaser to zoologist.

The receptionist pincered the card between fingernails as green and glossy as beetle wings. She had large breasts and slim hips and emphasized them with a pink angora sweater and a tight black skirt. Her hair was on the brassy side of platinum. "Wait here a minute, wouldja please," she said, smiling and chewing at the same time. "Have a seat or something."

She sidled past me, tapped once with her knuckle on a door marked PRIVATE, and stepped inside. Across from where she entered stood an identical door equally private. In between, the walls were hung with hundreds of framed photographs, the faded smiles preserved like moths under glass. I looked around and found the same 8-by-10 glossy of Johnny Favorite that I carried in the manila envelope under my arm. It was high on the left-hand wall, flanked by photos of a female ventriloquist and a fat man playing the clarinet.

The door behind me opened and the receptionist said: "Mr. Wagner will see you right away."

I said thanks and went in. The inner office was half the size of the cubbyhole outside. The pictures on the walls seemed newer, but the smiles were just as faded. A cigarette-scarred wooden desk took up most of the floor space. Behind it, a young man in shirt-sleeves was shaving with an electric razor. "Five minutes," he said, holding up his hand, palm outward so I could count his fingers.

I sat my attaché case on the worn green rug and stared at the kid as he finished shaving. He had curly, rust-colored hair and freckles. Beneath his horn-rimmed glasses, he couldn't have been much more than twenty-four or twenty-five.

"Mr. Wagner?" I asked when he switched off the razor.

"Yes?"

"Mr. Warren Wagner?"

"That's right."

"Surely you're not the same man who was Johnny Favorite's agent?"

"You're thinking about Dad. I'm Warren junior."

"Then it's your father I'd like to speak to."

"You're out of luck. He's been dead four years."

"I see."

"What's this all about?" Warren Jr. leaned back in his leatherette chair and clasped his hands behind his head.

"Jonathan Liebling is named a beneficiary in a policy owned

by one of our customers. This office was given as his address." Warren Wagner, Jr. started to laugh.

"There's not a great deal of money involved," I said. "The gesture of an old fan, perhaps. Can you tell me where I can find Mr. Favorite?"

The kid was laughing like crazy now. "That's terrific," he snorted. "Really terrific. Johnny Favorite, the missing heir."

"Quite frankly, I fail to see the humor in all this."

"Yeah? Well, lemme draw you a picture. Johnny Favorite is flat on his back in a nut hatch upstate. He's been a turnip for nearly twenty years."

"Say, that's a wonderful joke. Know any other good ones?"

"You don't understand," he said, taking off his glasses and wiping his eyes. "Johnny Favorite was Dad's big score. He sank every penny he had in the world into buying his contract from Spider Simpson. Then, just as he was riding high, Favorite got drafted. There were movie deals and everything in the works. The army sends a million-dollar property to North Africa and three months later ships home a sack of potatoes."

"That's too bad."

"Damn right it's too bad. Too bad for my pop. He never got over it. For years he thought Favorite might someday get well, make a big comeback, and land him on Easy Street. Poor sucker."

I stood up. "Can you give me the name and address of the hospital where Favorite is a patient?"

"Ask my secretary. She must have it tucked away some place."

I thanked him for his time and left. In the outer office I went through the motions of having the receptionist locate and write down the address of the Emma Dodd Harvest Memorial Clinic.

"You ever been up to Poughkeepsie?" I asked, tucking the folded slip of paper into my shirt pocket. "It's a lovely town."

"Are you kidding? I never even been to the Bronx."

"Not even to the zoo?"

"The zoo? What do I need with a zoo?"

"I don't know," I said. "Try one on for size some time. Might be a good fit."

My last shot of her as I went out the door was an open red mouth round as a hula hoop framing a shapeless wad of gum atop her pink tongue.

9

THERE WERE TWO BARS ON the ground floor of the Brill Building, facing Broadway on either side of the entrance. One was Jack Dempsey's, watering hole for the prizefight crowd. The other, the Turf, on the corner of 49th, was a hangout for musicians and songwriters. Its façade of blue mirrors made it seem as cool and inviting as a grotto in Capri.

Inside, it was just another gin mill. I made a circuit of the bar and found the very man I had in mind, Kenny Pomeroy, an accompanist and arranger since before I was born. "Whaddya say, Kenny," I whispered as I climbed on an adjacent stool.

"Well, well, Harry Angel, the famous shamus. Long time no see, pardner."

"It's been a while. Your glass looks empty, Kenny. Sit still and I'll buy you a refill." I signaled the bartender and ordered a Manhattan and another round for Kenny.

"Skoal, kiddo," he said, lifting his glass when the drinks were set in front of us. Kenny Pomeroy was a bald fat man with a light-bulb nose and a set of chins stacked one on top of the other like replacement parts. His mode of dress ran to hound's-tooth jackets and star sapphire pinkie rings. The only place I'd ever seen him outside of a rehearsal hall was at the bar in the Turf.

We jawed for a bit about old times before Kenny asked: "So

what brings you to this end of the street? The pursuit of evil-doers?"

"Not exactly," I said. "I'm working on a job you might be able to help me with."

"Anytime, anyplace."

"What can you tell me about Johnny Favorite?"

"Johnny Favorite? Talk about Memory Lane."

"Did you know him?"

"Nah. Caught his act a few times before the war. Last time was at the Starlight Lounge in Trenton, if I remember it right."

"Haven't seen him around anyplace, say in the last fifteen years or so?"

"Are you kidding? He's dead, ain't he?"

"Not exactly. He's in a hospital upstate."

"Well, if he's inna hospital, how am I supposed to see him around?"

"He's been in and out," I said. "Listen, take a look at this." I slid the photo of the Spider Simpson orchestra out of the manila envelope and passed it to him. "Which one of those guys is Simpson? It doesn't say on the picture."

"Simpson's the drummer."

"What's he doing now? Still leading a band?"

"Nah. Drummers never make good front men." Kenny sipped his drink and looked thoughtful, furrowing a brow that ran without interruption onto the top of his head. "Last I heard he was doing studio work out on the Coast. You might try calling Nathan Fishbine in the Capitol Building."

I made a note of the name and asked Kenny if he knew any of the sidemen.

"I worked a gig in Atlantic City with the trombone player once years ago." Kenny pointed a pudgy finger at the photo. "This guy, Red Diffendorf. He's blowing corn with Lawrence Welk now."

"What about any of the others? Know where I can find them?"

"Well, I recognize a lot of the names. They're still in the business, but I can't tell you who with. You'd have to ask around the street, or call the union."

"How about a Negro piano player named Edison Sweet?"

"Toots? He's the greatest. Got a left hand like Art Tatum. Very tasty. You won't have to look far for him. He's been playing uptown at the Red Rooster on 138th Street for the last five years."

"Kenny, you're a fund of useful information. How about some lunch?"

"Never touch the stuff. But I wouldn't say no to one more seven-and-seven."

I ordered us both another drink and a cheeseburger with fries for myself and while waiting I found a pay phone and called Local 802 of the American Federation of Musicians. I said I was a free-lance journalist working on assignment for *Look* and I wanted to interview the surviving members of the Spider Simpson orchestra.

They connected me with the girl in charge of membership records. I gift-wrapped it by promising to plug the union in my article and gave her the names of the band members on the photo, together with the instruments they played.

I held the line for ten minutes while she looked it up. Of the original fifteen musicians four were deceased and six had been dropped from the union membership rolls. She gave me the addresses and telephone numbers of the others. Diffendorf, the trombonist with Lawrence Welk, lived in Hollywood. Spider Simpson also had a place in the L.A. area, over in the Valley in Studio City. The others were here in town.

There was an alto player named Vernon Hyde in the "Tonight" show house band, address c/o NBC Studios; and two hornmen, Ben Hogarth, trumpet, with an address on Lexington Avenue, and another trombone, Carl Walinski, who lived in Brooklyn.

I got it all down in my notebook, thanked the girl from the bottom of my heart, and called the local numbers without success. The hornmen weren't home, and the best I could do with the switchboard at NBC was leave my office number.

I was beginning to feel like the sucker in a snipe hunt. The guy who waits all night in the woods holding the empty sack. There was less than one chance in a million that any of Johnny Favorite's former bandmates had run across him since he went away to war. These were the only odds in town, and I was stuck with them.

Back at the bar, I ate my sandwich and nibbled a few wilted french fries. "It's a great life, ain't it, Harry," Kenny Pomeroy said, rattling the ice in his empty glass.

"The best and only."

"Some poor stiffs've got to work for their living."

I scooped my change off the bar. "Don't drum me out of the club if I start working for mine."

"You ain't leaving, are you Harry?"

"Got to do it, old friend, much as I'd like to stay and poison my liver with you."

"Next thing I know, you'll be punching a time-clock. You know where to find me, should you have further need of my expertise."

"Thanks, Kenny." I pulled on my overcoat. "Does the name Edward Kelley mean anything to you?"

Kenny corrugated his Vista-Dome forehead in concentration. "There was a Horace Kelly back in K.C.," he said. "About the time Pretty Boy Floyd bumped off those G-men at Union Station. Horace played piano at the Reno Club on 12th and Cherry. Made a little book on the side. This any relation of his?"

"I hope not," I said. "See you around."

"Make that a promise and I'll frame it."

10

I RODE THE SEVENTH AVENUE IRT one stop to Times Square to save shoe leather and let myself into the office as the phone was ringing. I grabbed it mid-ring. It was Vernon Hyde, Spider Simpson's sax player.

"Very good of you to call," I said, unreeling the *Look* assignment line. He swallowed it all, and I suggested we get together for a drink at his convenience.

"I'm at the studio now," he said. "We start rehearsal in twenty minutes. I won't be free until four-thirty."

"That would be fine with me. If you can spare a half-hour, why don't we get together then. What street is your studio on?"

"On 45th Street. The Hudson Theater."

"Okay. The Hickory House is only a couple blocks away. How about meeting me at quarter to five?"

"Sounds boss. I'll have my axe along so you won't have any trouble spotting me."

"A man with an axe stands out in a crowd," I said.

"No, man, no, you don't get it. An axe is like an instrument, you dig?"

I dug and said so, and we both hung up. After struggling out of my overcoat, I sat down behind the desk and took a look at the photos and clippings I'd been lugging around. I arranged them on the blotter like a museum exhibit and stared at Johnny Favorite's smarmy smile until I could no longer stomach it. Where do you search for a guy who was never there to begin with?

The Winchell column was as brittle with age as the Dead Sea Scrolls. I reread the item about the end of Favorite's engagement and dialed Walt Rigler's number over at the *Times.*

" 'lo, Walt," I said, "it's me again. I need to know some stuff about Ethan Krusemark."

"The big-shot shipowner?"

"The very same. I'd like whatever you've got on him plus his address. I'm especially interested in his daughter's broken engagement to Johnny Favorite back in the early forties."

"Johnny Favorite again. He seems to be the man of the hour."

"He's the star of the show. Can you help me out?"

"I'll check with the Woman's Department," he said. "They cover society and all its dirty doings. Call you back in a couple minutes."

"My blessings be upon you." I dropped the receiver back in the cradle. It was ten minutes shy of two o'clock. I got out my notebook and placed a couple long-distance calls to L.A. There was no answer at Diffendorf s number in Hollywood, but when I tried Spider Simpson I connected with the maid. She was Mexican, and although my Spanish was no better than her English, I managed to leave my name and office number along with the general impression that it was a matter of importance.

I hung up and the phone rang again before I lifted my hand. It was Walt Rigler. "Here's the poop," he said. "Krusemark's very top-drawer now; charity balls, Social Register, all that sort of thing. Has an office in the Chrysler Building. His residence is Number Two, Sutton Place; phone number's in the book. You got that?"

I said it was all down in black and white, and he went on. "Okay. Krusemark wasn't always so upper-crust. He worked as a merchant seaman in the early twenties, and it's rumored he made his first money smuggling bootleg hootch. He was never convicted of anything, so his record's clean even if his nose isn't. He started putting his own fleet together during the Depression, all Panama registry, of course.

"He first made it big building concrete hulls for the war effort. There were accusations that his firm used inferior construction material, and many of his Liberty Ships broke apart when the weather got rough, but he was cleared by a congressional investigation and nothing more was said about it."

"What about his daughter?" I asked.

"Margaret Krusemark; born 1922; father and mother divorced in 1926. The mother committed suicide later that same year. She met Favorite at a college prom. He was singing with the band. Their engagement was the society scandal of 1941. Seems that he was the one who broke things off, though no one knows why any more. The girl was generally regarded as something of a crackpot, so maybe that was the reason."

"What sort of crackpot?"

"The kind with visions. She used to tell fortunes at parties. Went every place with a pack of tarot cards in her purse. People thought it was cute for a while, but it got too rich for their blue blood when she started casting spells in public."

"Is this on the level?"

"Absolutely. She was known as the 'Witch of Wellesley.' It was quite the gag among young Ivy League nabobs."

"Where is she now?"

"No one I talked to seemed to know. Society editor says she doesn't live with her father, and she's not the type who gets invited to the Peacock Ball at the Waldorf, so we haven't got anything on her over here. The last mention she got in the *Times* was on her departure for Europe ten years ago. She may still be there."

"Walt, you've been a big help. I'd start reading the *Times* if they ran comic strips."

"What's all this about Johnny Favorite? Anything in it for me?"

"I can't open yet, buddy, but when the time comes, you'll get it all first."

"Much obliged."

"Me, too. See you around, Walt."

I got the phone book out of the desk and ran my finger down a page in the K section. There was a listing for a Krusemark, Ethan and a Krusemark Maritime, Inc., as well as a Krusemark, M., Astrological Consultations. This one seemed worth a try. The address was 881 Seventh Avenue. I dialed the number and let it ring. A woman answered.

"I got your name through a friend," I said. "Personally, I don't put much stock in the stars, but my fiancée is a true believer. I thought I'd surprise her and have both our horoscopes done."

"I charge fifteen dollars per chart," the woman said.

"Fine by me."

"And I don't do any consulting over the phone. You'll have to make an appointment."

I said that was also fine and asked if she had an opening today.

"My desk calendar is completely clean for the afternoon," she said, "so whatever is convenient for you."

"How about right away? Say in half an hour?"

"That would be wonderful."

I gave her my name. She thought my name was wonderful, too, and told me her apartment was in Carnegie Hall. I said I knew where to find it and hung up.

11

I TOOK THE UPTOWN BMT to 57th Street and climbed the exit stairs that let me out on the corner by the Nedick's in Carnegie Hall. A bum shuffled up and tapped me for a dime as I headed for the Studio entrance. Across Seventh Avenue one block down, a picket line paraded in front of the Park Sheraton. The lobby of the Carnegie Hall Studios was small and barren of decoration. Two elevator doors stood on the right, flanking a mailbox fed by a glass chute. There was a back entrance to the Carnegie Tavern around the corner on 56th and a wall directory. I looked for Krusemark, M., Astrological Consultations, and found her listed on the eleventh floor.

The brass indicator over the left-hand elevator described a descending arc through a semicircle of floor numbers like a clock running backward. The arrow paused at 7 and again at 3 before coming to rest horizontally. A large Great Dane was first off, tugging a stout woman in a fur coat. They were followed by a bearded man carrying a cello case. I got in and gave the floor number to an ancient operator who resembled a Balkan army pensioner in his ill-fitting uniform. He looked at my shoes and said nothing. After a moment, he shoved the metal gate closed and we started up.

There were no stops until I got off at eleven. The hallway was long and wide and as drab as the lobby downstairs. Folded canvas firehoses hung at intervals along the walls. Several pianos debated dissonantly behind closed doors. In the distance, I heard a soprano warming up, trilling through the scales.

I found M. Krusemark's apartment. Her name was painted on the door in gold letters, and beneath it an odd symbol which looked like the letter *M* with an upturned arrow as a tail. I rang the bell and waited. High-heeled footsteps tapped on the floor inside, a lock was turned, and the door opened to the limit of the police chain securing it.

An eye regarded me out of the shadows. The voice that went with it asked, "Yes?"

"I'm Harry Angel," I said. "I called earlier about an appointment."

"Why, of course. Just a minute, please." The door closed, and I heard the chain sliding free. When the door reopened, the eye was one of a cat-green pair set in a pale, angular face. They burned within discolored hollows beneath dark, heavy brows. "Do come in," she said, standing aside for me to enter.

She was dressed all in black, like a weekend bohemian in a Village coffeehouse; black wool skirt and sweater, black stockings, even her thick, black hair was held in a bun with what looked to be a pair of ebony chopsticks. Walt Rigler indicated she was about thirty-six or thirty-seven years old, but without any makeup she looked much older. She was very thin, almost gaunt, her meager breasts barely discernible beneath the heavy folds of her sweater. Her only ornament was a gold medallion hanging around her neck on a simple chain. It was an upside-down five-pointed star.

Neither of us said a word, and I found myself staring at the dangling medallion. "Go, and catch a falling star . . . " The opening line of the Donne poem echoed through my mind, accompanied by an image of Dr. Albert Fowler's hands. For an instant, I saw the golden ring on his drumming fingers. A five-pointed star was engraved on the ring that Dr. Albert Fowler was no longer wearing when I found his body locked in the upstairs bedroom. Here was the missing piece in the puzzle.

The revelation hit me like an ice-water enema. A cold chill ascended my spine and raised the hackles along the back of my neck. What happened to the doctor's ring? It might have been in his pocket; I didn't go through his clothes; but why would he take it off before blowing his brains out? And if he didn't remove it, who did?

I felt the woman's fox-fire eyes focused on me. "You must be Miss Krusemark," I said to break the silence.

"I am," she answered without smiling.

"I saw your name on the door but didn't recognize the symbol."

"My sign," she said, closing and relocking the door. "I'm a Scorpio." She stared at me for a long moment, as if my eyes were peepholes revealing some interior scene. "And you?"

"Me?"

"What's your sign?"

"I don't really know," I said. "Astrology's not one of my strong points."

"When were you born?"

"June 2,1920." I gave her Johnny Favorite's birth date just to try her out, and for a split second I thought I caught a faraway flicker in her intense, emotionless stare.

"Gemini," she said. "The twins. Curious, I once knew a boy born the very same day."

"Really? Who was that?"

"It doesn't matter," she said. "It was a long, long time ago. How rude of me to keep you standing here in the hall. Please come in and have a seat."

I followed her out of the murky hall into a spacious, high-ceilinged studio living room. The furniture was a nondescript collection of early Salvation Army brightened by paisley-print spreads and quantities of embroidered throw pillows. The bold geometry of several fine Turkestan rugs offset the thrift shop decor. There were ferns of all descriptions and palms towering to the ceiling. Greenery dangled from hanging planters. Miniature rain forests steamed within enclosed glass terrariums.

"Beautiful room," I said, as she took my overcoat and folded it over the back of a couch.

"Yes, it's wonderful, isn't it? I've been very happy here." She was interrupted by a sharp whistling in the distance. "Would you like some tea?" she asked. "I just put the kettle on when you arrived."

"Only if it's no trouble."

"No trouble at all. The water's already boiling. Which would you prefer, Darjeeling, jasmine or oolong?"

"You decide. I'm not a connoisseur of tea."

She gave me a wan half-smile and hurried off to deal with the insistent whistling. I took a closer look around.

Exotic knick-knacks crowded every available surface. Things like temple-flutes and prayer-wheels, Hopi fetishes and papier-mâché avatars of Vishnu ascending out of the mouths of fishes and turtles. An obsidian Aztec dagger carved in the shape of a bird glittered on a bookshelf. I scanned the haphazard volumes and spotted the *I Ching,* a copy of *Oaspe,* and several of the Evan-Wentz Tibetan series.

When M. Krusemark returned carrying a silver tray and tea set, I was standing by a window thinking about Dr. Fowler's missing ring. She placed the service on a low table by the couch and joined me. Across Seventh Avenue, a Federal-style mansion with white Doric columns sat on the roof of the Osborne Apartments like a hidden crown. "Somebody buy the Jefferson place and have it moved?" I quipped.

"Earl Blackwell's. He gives wonderful parties. Fun to watch anyway."

I followed her back to the couch. "That's a familiar face." I nodded at an oil portrait of an aging pirate in a tuxedo.

"My father, Ethan Krusemark." Tea swirled into translucent china cups.

There was the hint of a roguish smile on the determined lips, a glint of ruthlessness and cunning in eyes as green as his daughter's. "He's the shipbuilder, isn't he? I've seen his picture in *Forbes.*"

"He hated the painting. Said it was like having a mirror that got stuck. Cream or lemon?"

"I'll take it straight, thanks."

She handed me the cup. "It was done last year. I think it's a wonderful likeness."

"He's a good-looking man."

She nodded. "Would you believe he's over sixty? He always looked ten years younger than his age. His sun is in trine with Jupiter, a very favorable aspect."

I let the mumbo-jumbo pass and said that he looked like a swashbuckling captain in the pirate movies I saw as a kid.

"Very true. When I was in college all the girls in the dorm thought he was Clark Gable."

I sipped my tea. It tasted like fermenting peaches. "My brother knew a girl named Krusemark when he was at Princeton," I said. "She went to Wellesley and told him his fortune at a prom."

"That would have been my sister, Margaret," she said. "I'm Millicent. We're twins. She's the black witch in the family; I'm the white one."

I felt like a man waking from a dream of riches, his golden treasure melting like mist between his fingers. "Does your sister live here in New York?" I asked, keeping up the banter. I already knew the answer.

"God, no. Maggie moved to Paris over ten years ago. Haven't seen her in an age. What's your brother's name?"

The entire charade hung limply over me like the skin of a deflated balloon. "Jack," I said.

"I don't remember Maggie ever mentioning a Jack. Of course, there were so many young men in her life in those days. I need for you to answer some questions." She reached for a leather pad and pencil set on the table. "So I can do your chart."

"Fire away." I flipped a cigarette from the pack and stuck it in my mouth.

Millicent Krusemark waved her hand in front of her face like a woman drying her nails. "Please don't. I'm allergic to smoke."

"Sure." I tucked the butt back behind my ear.

"You were born on June 2, 1920," she said. "There's quite a bit I know about you from that fact alone."

"Tell me all about myself."

Millicent Krusemark fixed me with her feline stare. "I know that you're a natural actor," she said. "Playing roles comes easily. You switch identities with the instinctive facility of a chameleon changing color. Although you are deeply concerned with discovering the truth, lies flow from your lips without hesitation."

"Pretty good. Go on."

"Your role-playing ability has a darker side and presents a problem when you confront the dual nature of your personality. I would say that you were frequently the victim of doubt. 'How could I have done such a thing?' is your most constant worry. Cruelty comes easily to you, yet you find it inconceivable that you are so gifted at hurting others. On one hand you are methodical and tenacious, but by contrast you place great stock in intuition." She, smiled. "When it comes to women, you prefer them young and dark."

"A-plus," I said. "You were right on the money." And she was. She had it down pat. An analyst who could probe such secrets would be worth the twenty-five-bucks-an-hour couch fare. Only one problem: wrong birthday; she was telling my fortune with Johnny Favorite's vital statistics. "Do you know where I can meet some dark, young women?"

"I'll be able to tell a great deal more once I have what I need." The white witch scribbled on her notepad. "I can't guarantee the girl of your dreams, but I can be more specific. Here, I'm jotting down star positions for the month so I can see how they'll affect your chart. Not yours really, that boy I mentioned. Your horoscopes are undoubtedly similar."

"I'm game."

Millicent Krusemark frowned, studying her notes. "This is a period of great danger. You have been involved in a death quite recently, within a week at least. The deceased was not someone you knew well; nevertheless, you are deeply troubled by his passing. The medical profession is involved. Perhaps you will soon be in a hospital yourself; the unfavorable aspects are very strong. Beware of strangers."

I stared at this odd woman in black and felt invisible fear-tentacles encircle my heart. How did she know so much? My mouth was dry, my lips stuck as I spoke: "What's that ornament around your neck?"

"This?" The woman's hand paused at her throat like a bird resting in flight. "Just a pentacle. Brings good luck."

Dr. Fowler's pentacle didn't bring him much luck, but then he wasn't wearing it when he died. Or did someone take the ring after killing the old man?

"I need additional information," Millicent Krusemark said, her filigreed gold pencil poised like a dart. "When and where was your financée born. I need the exact hour and location. So I can determine longitude and latitude. Also, you haven't told me where you were born."

I ad-libbed some phony dates and places and made the ritual gesture of glancing at my wristwatch before placing my cup on the table. We rose together, as if on a lift. "Thanks for the tea."

She showed me to the door and said the charts would be ready next week. I said I'd call, and we shook hands with the mechanical formality of clockwork soldiers.

12

I FOUND THE CIGARETTE BEHIND my ear on the way down in the elevator and lit it as soon as I hit the street. The March wind felt cleansing. There was almost an hour before my meeting with Vernon Hyde, and I walked slowly down Seventh trying to make sense out of the nameless fear that seized me back in the astrologer's bosky apartment. I knew it had to be a con, verbal slight of hand, like encyclopedia salesmanship. Beware of strangers. That was the sort of bullshit you got for a penny along with your weight. She suckered me with her oracle's voice and hypnotic eyes.

Fifty-second Street looked down-at-the-heels. Two blocks east, "21" preserved elegant speakeasy memories, but a fantan chorus line of strip joints had replaced most of the jazz clubs. With the Onyx Club gone, only Birdland kept the temple fires of bop burning over on Broadway. The Famous Door had closed forever. Jimmy Ryan's and the Hickory House were the only survivors on a street whose brown-stones housed more than fifty blind pigs during Prohibition.

I walked east, past Chinese restaurants and petulant whores with zippered leatherette hatboxes. Don Shirley's trio was on deck at the Hickory House, but the music didn't start until hours later and the bar was quiet and dim when I entered.

I ordered a whisky sour and settled by a table where I could watch the door. Two drinks later, I spotted a guy carrying a saxophone case. He wore a brown suede windbreaker over a cream-colored Irish-knit turtleneck. His hair was salt-and-pepper gray and cut short. I waved and he came over.

"Vernon Hyde?"

"That's me," he said through a twisted grin.

"Park your axe and have a drink."

"Solid." He placed his saxophone case carefully on the table and pulled up a chair. "So you're a writer. What kind of thing is it you write?"

"Magazine work mostly," I said. "Profiles, personality pieces."

The waitress came over and Hyde ordered a bottle of Heineken's. We made small talk until she brought the beer and poured it into a tall glass. Hyde took a long sip and got down to business. "So you want to write about the Spider Simpson band. Well, you picked the right street. If cement could talk, that sidewalk'd tell you my life story."

I said: "Look. I don't want to lead you on. The story will mention the band, but I'm mainly interested in hearing about Johnny Favorite."

Vernon Hyde's smile twisted so far it became a frown. "Him? What'd you want to write about that prick for?"

"I take it he wasn't a pal of yours?"

"Besides, who remembers Johnny Favorite anymore?"

"An editor at *Look* remembers him well enough to have suggested the story. And your own memories seem sufficiently strong. What was he like?"

"The guy was a bastard. What he did to Spider was lower than Benedict Arnold's jockstrap."

"What did he do?"

"You got to understand that Spider discovered him, picked him up from some nowhere beer hall in the sticks."

"I know about that."

"Favorite owed Spider plenty. He was getting a percentage of the gate, too, not just a salary like the rest of the band, so I can't see that he had any complaints. His contract with Spider still had four years to run when he split. We had some heavy bookings canceled because of that little fade."

I got out my notebook and mechanical pencil and pretended to take notes. "Has he ever been in touch with any of the old Simpson sidemen?"

"Do ghosts walk?"

"Sorry?"

"The cat's croaked, man. Got bumped in the war."

"Is that right?" I said. "I heard he was in a hospital upstate."

"Could be, but I think I remember he was dead."

"I was told he was superstitious. Do you remember anything about that?"

Vernon Hyde smiled his bent smile again. "Yeah, he was always off in search of séances and crystal balls. Once, on the road, I think it was Cincy, we hired the hotel whore to make like she was a palm reader. She told him he was gonna get the clap, and he didn't so much as look at any frail until the end of the tour."

"He had a high-society girlfriend who was a fortune-teller, didn't he?"

"Yeah, something like that. I never met the chick. Johnny and I were on different orbits at the time."

"Spider Simpson's orchestra was segregated when Favorite sang with you, right?"

"We were all ofays, yeah. I think there was a Cuban on vibes one year." Vernon Hyde finished his beer. "Duke Ellington didn't break the color line back then either, you know."

"True." I scribbled in the notebook. "Getting together after hours must have been another story."

Hyde's smile lost most of its crookedness at the memory of those smoky rooms. "When Basie's band was in town, a bunch of us would get together and jam all night."

"Did Favorite make those sessions?"

"Nope. Johnny didn't care for spades. After a gig, the only black people he wanted to see were the maids in Park Avenue penthouses."

"Interesting. I thought Favorite was a friend of Toots Sweet."

"He might of asked him to shine his shoes one time. I'm telling you, Johnny Favorite had a thing about spades. I remember him saying Georgie Auld was a better tenor man than Lester Young. Imagine that!"

I said it was beyond comprehension.

"He thought they were bad luck."

"Tenor players?"

"Spades, man. To Johnny they were like black cats, no pun intended."

I asked him if Johnny Favorite had been close to anyone in the band.

"I don't think Johnny had a friend in the world," Vernon Hyde said. "And you can quote me if you like. He was a loner. Kept to himself most of the time. Oh, he'd joke with you and always had a big smile on his face, but it didn't mean a thing. Johnny was good at charm. He used it like a shield to keep you from getting too close."

"What can you tell me about his private life?"

"I never saw him except on the bandstand or riding through the night on some bus somewhere. Spider knew him best of all. He's the guy you should talk to."

"I have his number on the coast," I said. "We haven't connected yet. Another beer?"

Hyde said why not and a round was ordered. We spent the next hour swapping lies about 52nd Street in the old days, and Johnny Favorite's name was not mentioned again.

13

VERNON HYDE DEPARTED FOR POINTS unknown shortly before seven, and I walked two blocks west to Gallagher's and the best steak in town. I finished my cigar and second cup of coffee about nine, paid my check, and caught a cab on Broadway for the eight blocks down to my garage.

I drove uptown on Sixth, following the traffic north through Central Park, past the reservoir and Harlem Meer. I left the park by the Warrior's Gate at 110th and Seventh and entered a world of tenements and shadowy side streets. I hadn't been to Harlem since before they tore down the Savoy Ballroom last year, but it looked just the same. Park Avenue was under the New York Central tracks at this end of town, so Seventh, with its concrete center islands dividing the two-way traffic, became the street to be seen on.

Crossing 125th Street everything was bright as Broadway. Further along, Small's Paradise and Count Basie's place seemed alive and well. I found a parking spot across the avenue from the Red Rooster and waited out the light. A young coffee-colored man with a pheasant feather in his hat emerged out of a group loitering on the corner and asked if I wanted to buy a watch. He pushed up both sleeves of his natty topcoat and showed me a half-dozen timepieces on either arm. "Can make you a nice price, brother. Real nice."

I said I already had a watch and crossed on the green.

The Red Rooster was plush and dark. The tables around the bandstand were crowded with uptown celebrities, big spenders with their bare-armed ladies glittering beside them in a rainbow display of sequined, strapless evening gowns.

I found a stool at the bar and ordered a snifter of Remy Martin. Edison Sweet's trio was on deck, but from where I was sitting I saw only the piano player's back as he hunched over the keyboard. Bass and electric guitar were the other instruments.

The band was playing a blues, the guitar darting in and out of the melody like a hummingbird. The piano throbbed and thundered. Toots Sweet's left hand was every bit as good as Kenny Pomeroy had promised. The group had no need of a drummer. Above the moody, shifting bass rhythms Toots traced an intricate lament, and when he sang, his voice was bittersweet with suffering:

I got them voodoo blues,
Them evil hoo-doo blues.
Petro Loa won't leave me alone;
Every night I hear the zombies moan.
Lord, I got them mean ol' voodoo blues.

Zu-Zu was a mambo, she loved a hungan man;
Messin' with Erzuli wasn't part of her plan.
The spell of the tom-tom turned her into a slave,
And now Baron Samedi's dancin' on her grave.

Yeah, she's got them voodoo blues,
Them bad ol' hoo-doo blues . . . .

When the set ended, the musicians laughed and talked and wiped their sweating faces with large white handkerchiefs. After a while, they drifted in toward the bar. I told the bartender I wanted to buy the group a drink. He filled their orders and nodded in my direction.

The two sidemen picked up their drinks, shot me a glance, and moved off into the crowd. Toots Sweet took a stool at the end of the bar and leaned back so he could watch the house, his large, grizzled head resting against the wall. I collected my glass and made my way over to him.

"Just wanted to say thanks," I said, climbing on the next stool. "You're an artist, Mr. Sweet."

"Call me Toots, son. I don't bite."

"Toots it is, then."

Toots Sweet had a face as broad and dark and wrinkled as a slab of cured tobacco. His thick hair was the color of cigar ash. He filled a shiny blue serge suit to the bursting point, yet the feet encased in two-tone black-and-white pumps were as small and delicate as a woman's.

"I liked the blues you played at the end," I said.

"Wrote that one day in Houston, years ago, on the back of a cocktail napkin." He laughed. The sudden whiteness of his smile split his dark face like the end of a lunar eclipse. One of his front teeth was capped in gold. The white enamel underneath gleamed through a cutout shaped like an inverted five-pointed star. It was something you noticed right away.

"That your home town?"

"Houston? Lord, no, I was just visitin'."

"Where're you from?"

"Me? Why I'm a New Orleans boy, born and bred. You're lookin' at an amfropologist's dee-light. I played in Storyville crib-houses 'fore I was fo-teen. I knew all that gang, Bunk and Jelly and Satchelmouth. I went up 'de ribber' to Chicago. Haw, haw, haw." Toots roared and slapped his big knees. The rings on his stubby fingers flashed in the dim light.

"You're putting me on," I said.

"Maybe just a little bit, son. Maybe just a little bit."

I grinned and sniffed my drink. "Must be swell having so many memories."

"You writin' a book, son? I can spot me a book writer quick as a fox recognizes a hen."

"You're close, old fox. I'm working on a piece for *Look* magazine."

"A story 'bout Toots in *Look?* Right in there with Doris Day! Haw!"

"Well, I won't put you on, Toots. The story's going to be about Johnny Favorite."

"Who?"

"A crooner. Used to sing with Spider Simpson's swing band back in the early forties."

"Yeah. I remember Spider. He played the drums like two jackhammers fucking."

"What do you remember about Johnny Favorite?" I asked.

Edison Sweet's dark face assumed the innocence of an algebra student who doesn't know the answer. "I don't remember nothin' about him; 'cept maybe he changed his name and became Frank Sinatra. Vic Damone on weekends."

"Maybe I've got the wrong information," I said. "I figured you were pretty good pals."

"Son, he made a record of one of my songs way back when and I thank him for all the long-gone royalty checks, but that don't make us pals."

"I saw a picture of the two of you singing together. It was in *Life.*"

"Yeah. I remember that night. That was at Dickie Wells' bar. I seen him around once or twice, but he sure didn't come uptown to see me."

"Who did he come uptown to see?"

Toots Sweet ducked his eyes in mock coyishness. "You gettin' me to tell tales out of school, son."

"What does it matter after all these years?" I said. "I gather he was seeing a lady."

"She was every inch a lady, to be sure."

"Tell me her name."

"It ain't no secret. Anyone who was around fo' the war knows Evangeline Proudfoot was makin' the scene with Johnny Favorite."

"None of the downtown press seemed to know."

"Son, if you was crossin' the line in them days, it wasn't something you wanted to brag about."

"Who was Evangeline Proudfoot?"

Toots smiled. "A beautiful, strong West Indian woman," he said. "She was ten, fifteen years older than Johnny, but still such a fox that he was the one looked the fool."

"Know where I could get in touch with her?"

"Ain't seen Evangeline in years. She got ill. Store's still there, so maybe she is, too."

"What sort of store was that?" I did my best to keep any trace of cop out of my question.

"Evangeline had an herb shop over on Lenox. Stayed open till midnight every day 'cept Sunday." Toots gave me a theatrical wink. "Time to play some mo'. You gonna stick around for another set, son?"

"I'll be back," I said.

14

PROUDFOOT PHARMACEUTICALS WAS LOCATED ON the northwest corner of Lenox Avenue and 123rd Street. The name hung in the show-window in six-inch blue neon script. I parked half a block down and looked the place over. The window contained a dusty display bathed in vaporous blue light. Faded boxes of homeopathic cures sat on small, circular cardboard shelves arranged along either side. Stapled to the rear wall was a multicolored anatomical diagram of the human body, flesh and muscles peeled way to reveal a tangled visceral pudding. Each of the cardboard shelves was connected to the appropriate internal organ by a drooping length of satin ribbon. The stuff linked to the heart was called, "Proudfoot's Beneficial Belladonna Extract."

Over the back wall of the display, I could see into a portion of the store. Fluorescent lights hung from a pressed tin ceiling; old-fashioned glass-fronted wooden shelves ran along the far wall. The swinging of a clock pendulum seemed the only activity.

I went inside. A smell of burning incense stung the air. Bells tinkled above my head as I shut the door. I took a quick look around. On a revolving metal stand near the entrance a collection of "dream books" and pamphlets addressing the various problems of love competed for the customer's attention, in gaudy multilith jackets. There was a pyramid display of lucky powders packaged in tall cardboard cylinders. Sprinkle some of this stuff on your suit in the morning and the number you pick from your dream book will for sure pay off big.

I was examining the perfumed, colored candles guaranteed to bring good fortune with continued use when a lovely mocha-skinned girl came in from the back room and stood behind the counter. She wore a white smock over her dress and looked about nineteen or twenty. Her wavy, shoulder-length hair was the color of polished mahogany. A number of thin, silver hoops jingled on her fine-boned wrist. "May I help you?" she asked. Just beneath her carefully modulated diction lingered the melodic calypso lilt of the Caribbean.

I answered off the top of my head: "Have you got any High John the Conqueror root?"

"Powdered or entire?"

"I want the whole thing. Isn't the shape what makes the charm work?"

"We don't sell charms, sir. This is an herbal pharmacy."

"What do you call the stuff up front?" I asked. "Patent medicine?"

"We carry a few novelty items. Rexall's sells greeting cards."

"I was joking. Didn't mean to offend you."

"No offense. You tell me how much John the Conqueror you want, and I'll weight it out."

"Is Miss Proudfoot on the premises?"

"I'm Miss Proudfoot," she said.

"Miss Evangeline Proudfoot?"

"I'm Epiphany. Evangeline was my mother."

"You say was?"

"Mama died last year."

"I'm sorry to hear that."

"She'd been sick for a long time, flat on her back for years. It was best."

"She left you a lovely name, Epiphany," I said. "It fits you."

Beneath her coffee-and-milk complexion she flushed slightly. "She left me a good deal more than that. This store's been making a profit for forty years. Did you do business with mama?"

"No, we never met. I was hoping she might answer some questions for me."

Epiphany Proudfoot's topaz eyes, darkened. "What're you, some kind of cop?"

I smiled, the *Look* alibi engraved on my silver tongue, but I figured she was too smart to buy it, so I said: "Private license. I can show you a photostat."

"Never mind your dime-store photostat. Why did you want to talk to mama?"

"I'm looking for a man named Johnny Favorite."

She stiffened. It was as if someone touched the back of her neck with an ice cube. "He's dead," she said.

"No, he's not, although most people seem to think so."

"Far as I'm concerned he's dead."

"Did you know him?"

"We never met."

"Edison Sweet said he was a friend of your mother's."

"That was before I was born," she said.

"Did your mother ever talk to you about him?"

"Surely, Mr . . . whoever-you-are, you don't expect me to betray my mama's confidences. I clearly see you are not a gentleman."

I let that one pass. "Perhaps you can tell me if you or your mother ever saw Johnny Favorite in, say, the last fifteen years or so."

"I told you we never met, and I was always introduced to *all* mama's friends."

I got out my wallet, the one I carry cash in, and gave her my Crossroads card. "Okay," I said, "it was a long shot anyway. That's my office number on the bottom. I wish you'd call me if you think of anything or hear of anybody having seen Johnny Favorite."

She smiled, but there was no warmth in it. "What're you after him for?"

"I'm not 'after' him; I just want to know where he is."

She stuck my card in the glass of the ornate brass cash register. "And what if he's dead?"

"I get paid either way."

It was almost a real laugh this time. "I hope you find him six feet under," she said.

"That would be okay with me. Please hang on to my card. You never know what might turn up."

"That's true."

"Thanks for your time."

"You're not leaving without your John the Conqueror, are you?"

I straightened my shoulders. "Do I look like I need it?"

"Mr. Crossroads," she said, and her laughter was rich and full, "you look like you need all the help you can get."

15

BY THE TIME I GOT back to the Red Rooster I'd missed an entire set and Toots was sitting on the same stool at the bar. A glass of champagne fizzed at his elbow. I lit a cigarette as I edged through the crowd. "Find out what you were after?" Toots asked without interest.

"Evangeline Proudfoot is dead."

"Dead? Now that is a for-certain shame. She was one fine lady."

"I talked with her daughter. She wasn't much help."

"Maybe you better pick somebody else to write about, son."

"I don't think so. I'm just getting interested." The ash from my cigarette dropped onto my tie and left a smudge next to the soup stain when I brushed it off. "You seem to have known Evangeline Proudfoot pretty well. What more can you tell me about her affair with Johnny Favorite?"

Toots Sweet lumbered to his tiny feet. "I can't tell you nothin', son. I'm too big to go around hiding under beds. 'Sides, it's time fo' me to go back to work."

He flashed his star-studded grin and started for the bandstand. I tagged along like an eager newshound. "Perhaps you remember some of their other friends? People who knew them when they were together."

Toots settled on the piano bench and surveyed the room for

his tardy sidemen. He spoke to me while his eyes darted from table to table. "S'pose I pacify my mind with some music. Maybe something will come back to me."

"I'm in no hurry. I can listen to you play all night."

"Just sit out the set, son." Toots lifted the curved lid of the baby grand. A chicken foot lay on the keyboard. He slammed the lid shut. "Stop hangin' over my shoulder!" he growled. "I got to play now."

"What was that?"

"That was nothin'. Never you mind that."

But it was not nothing. It was the foot of a chicken, spanning an octave from the sharp yellow claw on the lizardlike toe to where it was cut off above the joint and, bleeding. Below a remaining tuft of white feathers a length of black ribbon was tied in a bow. It was considerably more than nothing.

"What's going on, Toots?"

The guitar player took his seat and switched on his amplifier. He glanced at Toots and fiddled with the volume. He was having feedback problems.

Toots hissed. "Nothin's going on you got to know about. Now I ain't talking to you no mo'. Not after the set. Not never!"

"Who's after you, Toots?"

"You git outta here."

"What does Johnny Favorite have to do with it?"

Toots spoke very slowly, ignoring the bass player who appeared at his shoulder. "If you don't get the hell out of here, an' I mean clean out onto the sidewalk, yo' gonna wish yo' lily-white ass never was born."

I met the bass player's implacable gaze and glanced around. There was a full house. I knew how Custer must have felt up on the hilltop at Little Big Horn.

"All I got to do," Toots said, "is say the word."

"You don't need to send a telegram, Toots." I dropped my butt onto the dance floor, ground it under my heel, and left.

My car was parked in the same spot across Seventh, and I headed for it when the light changed. The loiterers on the corner had moved on, their place taken by a thin, dark woman wearing a bedraggled fox fur. She swayed back and forth on her spike-heeled shoes, sniffing air rapidly through her nostrils like a coke fiend on a three-day blow. "Spo'tin', mister?" she asked as I passed. "Spo'tin'?"

"Not tonight," I said.

I got in behind-the wheel and lit another cigarette. The thin woman watched me for a while before weaving off down the avenue. It was not quite eleven.

Around midnight, I ran out of smokes. I figured Toots wasn't going to bolt until after work. There was all the time in the world. I walked a block and a half up Seventh to an all-night liquor store and bought two packs of Luckies and a pint of Early Times. On the way back, I crossed the avenue and lingered a moment by the entrance to the Red Rooster. Toots' blend of barrelhouse and Beethoven boomed inside.

It was a cold night, and every so often I ran the engine until the chill was off. I didn't want it warm. Too easy to fall asleep. By the time the last set ended at quarter to four, the dashboard ashtray was full and the Early Times empty. I felt fine.

Toots came out of the club about five minutes before closing time. He buttoned his heavy overcoat and joked with the guitar player. A passing cab squealed to a stop at his shrill, two-fingered whistle. I switched on the ignition and started the Chevy.

Traffic was sparse, and I wanted to give them a couple blocks, so I left the lights off and watched in the rearview as the cab made a U-turn on 138th Street and started back up Seventh in my direction. I let them get as far as the all-night liquor store before I switched on my lights and pulled away from the curb.

I tailed the cab to 152nd Street, where it turned left. Midway down the block it stopped in front of one of the Harlem River Houses. I continued on over to Macomb's Place, swung uptown, and circled back to Seventh at the upper end of the housing development.

Near the corner, I saw the cab waiting out front with the door open and the roof light off. No one was in the back seat. Toots was just running upstairs to get rid of his chicken foot. I turned my headlights off and double-parked where I could watch the cab. Toots was back down in minutes. He carried a red plaid canvas bowling-ball bag.

The cab took a left at Macomb's Place and continued downtown on Eighth Avenue. I stayed three blocks back and kept it in sight all the way to Frederick Douglass Circle where it swung east on 110th and followed the northern wall of Central Park to the point where St. Nicholas and Lenox Avenues have their bifurcated beginnings. As I drove past I saw Toots holding his wallet and waiting for change.

I hung a sharp left and parked around the corner on St. Nicholas, sprinting back to 110th in time to see the cab driving off and the retreating form of Toots Sweet, a shadow sliding into the shadow world of the dark and silent park.

16

HE KEPT TO THE PATH bordering the western rim of Harlem Meer, passing through the pooled light under a succession of lampposts like Jimmy Durante saying goodnight to Mrs. Calabash. I stayed off to one side in the shadows, but Toots never looked back. He hurried along the edge of the Meer and under the arch of Huddlestone Bridge. An occasional cab whizzed uptown on East Drive overhead.

Beyond the Drive was the Loch, the most remote section of Central Park. The path wound into a deep ravine crowded with trees and shrubs and completely cut off from the city. It was dark here and very still. For a moment I thought I lost Toots. Then I heard the drums.

Light glimmered like fireflies in the underbrush. I edged through the trees until I reached the cover of a large rock. Four white candles flickered on saucers set on the ground. I counted fifteen people standing in the dim light. There were three drummers, each playing an instrument of a different size. The largest looked like a conga. A lean, gray-haired man beat on it with one bare hand and a small wooden mallet.

A girl wearing a white dress and turban inscribed convoluted designs on the ground between the candles. She used handfuls of flour like a Hopi sand-painter, tracing the swirling figures around a circular hole dug into the packed earth. She turned and her face was illuminated by candle flame. It was Epiphany Proudfoot.

The onlookers swayed from side to side, chanting and clapping in time with the drumming. Several men shook gourd rattles, and one woman produced a frenzied staccato rhythm with a pair of iron clappers. I watched Toots Sweet wielding his maracas like Xavier Cugat fronting a rhumba band. The empty plaid bowling-ball bag sagged at his feet.

Epiphany was barefoot in spite of the cold and danced to the pulsing rhythm, twirling handfuls of Pillsbury's Best onto the ground. When the design was finished, she jumped back, reaching her ghost-white hands above her head like a cheerleader of doom. Her spastic shimmy soon had the whole crowd dancing.

Shadows shifted grotesquely in the uneven candlelight. The demonic heartbeat of the drums caught the dancers in its throbbing spell. Their eyes rolled back in their heads; spittle frothed on the chanting lips. Men and women rubbed together and moaned, pelvises thrusting in an ecstatic approximation of sex. The whites of their eyes gleamed like opals in their sweating faces.

I edged forward through the trees for a closer look. Someone played a pennywhistle. Shrill, piping notes stabbed into the night above the dissonant clangor of iron clappers. The drums growled and grumbled, the rhythm as insistent as a fever, delirious, entrancing. One woman fell to the ground and writhed like a snake, her tongue darting in and out with reptilian rapidity.

Epiphany's white dress clung to her wet, young body. She reached into a wicker basket, removing a leg-bound rooster. The bird held up his head proudly, his blood-red comb vivid in the candlelight. Epiphany rubbed the white plumage against her breasts as she danced. Weaving among the crowd, she caressed each of the others in turn. A piercing cockcrow silenced the drums.

Gliding gracefully, Epiphany bent to the circular pit and cut the rooster's jugular with a deft turn of a razor. Blood spouted into the dark hole. The rooster's defiant crow became a gargling scream. Its wings thrashed wildly as it died. The dancers moaned.

Epiphany placed the drained bird alongside the pit where it jerked and bucked, bound legs twitching in tandem, until the wings spread for a final shudder and slowly folded. One by one, the dancers swayed forward and dropped offerings into the pit. Scatterings of coins, handfuls of dried corn, assorted cookies, candies, and fruit. One woman poured a bottle of Coca-Cola over the dead chicken.

Afterward, Epiphany took the limp bird and hung it, upside down, from the branches of a nearby tree. Things began to break up about then. Several of the congregation stood whispering to the dangling rooster, heads bowed and hands clasped. Others packed up their instruments and they all slipped off into the darkness after shaking hands, first the right, then the left, arm over arm around the circle. Toots, Epiphany, and two or three others walked back along the path toward Harlem Meer. No one spoke.

I tailed them through the shadows, skirting the path and keeping out of sight among the trees. By the Meer the path divided. Toots turned left. Epiphany and the others took the righthand path. I tossed a mental coin, and it came up Toots. He headed toward the Seventh Avenue exit. If he wasn't going straight home, chances were good he'd be there before long. I planned on arriving first.

Ducking through the shrubbery, I scaled the rough stone wall and sprinted across 110th Street. When I reached the corner of St. Nicholas, I looked back and saw Epiphany in her white dress at the entrance to the park. She was alone.

I suppressed an urge to second-guess and ran for the Chevy. The streets were nearly empty, and I sped uptown on St. Nicholas, crossing Seventh and Eighth without missing a light. After turning onto Edgecomb, I followed Broadhurst along the edge of Colonial Park up to 151st Street.

I parked near the corner of Macomb's Place and walked the

rest of the way through the Harlem River Houses development. These were attractive four-story buildings arranged around open courts and malls. A Depression-era project, it was a far more civilized approach to public housing than the inhuman monoliths currently in municipal favor. I found the entrance to Toots' building on 152nd and looked for his apartment number on the row of brass mailboxes set into the brick wall.

The front door was no problem. I got it open with my penknife blade in less than a minute. Toots lived on the third floor. I climbed the stairs and checked out his lock. There was nothing I could do without my attaché case, so I sat on the steps leading up and waited.

17

I DIDN'T HAVE TO WAIT long. I heard him puffing up the stairs and stubbed out my butt against the bottom of my shoe. He didn't see me and set his bowling-ball bag down on the floor as he dug for his keys. When he had the door open, I made my move. He was reaching for the plaid bag as I caught him from behind, grabbing his coat collar with one hand and shoving him forward into the apartment with the other. He stumbled to his knees, the bag flung rattling into the darkness like a sackful of snakes. I switched on the ceiling light and closed the door behind me.

Toots huffed to his feet, panting like an animal at bay. His right hand plunged into his coat pocket and came out holding a straight razor. I shifted my weight. "I don't want to hurt you, old man."

He muttered something I didn't make out and lumbered forward, waving the razor. I caught his arm with my left hand and stepped in close, bringing my knee up hard, where it did the most good. Toots sagged and sat down with a soft grunt. I twisted his wrist a little and he dropped the razor on the carpet. I kicked it against the wall.

"Dumb, Toots." I picked up the razor, folded it, and put it in my pocket.

Toots sat, holding his belly with both hands as if something might come loose if he let go. "What you want with me?" he moaned. "You're no writer."

"Getting smarter. So save the bullshit and tell me what you know about Johnny Favorite."

"I'm hurt. I feel all busted up inside."

"You'll recover. Want something to sit on?"

He nodded. I dragged a red and black Moroccan leather ottoman over behind him and helped ease his bulk up off the floor. He groaned and clutched his middle.

"Listen, Toots," I said. "I saw your little shindig in the park. Epiphany Proudfoot's number with the chicken. What was going on?"

"Obeah," he groaned. "Voodoo. Not every black man is a Baptist."

"What about the Proudfoot girl? How does she fit in?"

"She's a mambo, like her mother was before her. Powerful spirits speak through that child. She been comin' to humfo meetin's since she was ten. Took over as priestess at thirteen."

"That when Evangeline Proudfoot got sick?"

"Yeah. Somethin' like that."

I offered Toots a smoke but he shook his head. I lit one myself and asked: "Was Johnny Favorite into voodoo?"

"He was runnin' 'round with the mambo, wasn't he?"

"Did he go to meetings?"

"Course he did. Lots of 'em. He was a hunsi-bosal."

"A what?"

"He'd been initiated, but not baptized."

"What do they call you when you're baptized?"

"Hunsi-kanzo."

"That what you are, a hunsi-kanzo?"

Toots nodded. "I been baptized a long time."

"When was the last time you saw Johnny Favorite at one of your chicken-snuffings?"

"I tol' you, I ain't seen him since fo' the war."

"What about the chicken foot? The one in the piano wearing a bowtie."

"Means I talk too much."

"About Johnny Favorite?"

"'Bout things in general."

"Not good enough, Toots." I blew a little smoke in his face. "Ever try to play piano with your hand in a cast?"

Toots started to rise, but sagged grimacing back onto the ottoman. "You wouldn't do that?"

"I'll do what I have to, Toots. I can break a finger easy as a breadstick."

There was considerable fear in the old piano player's eyes. I cracked the knuckles in my right hand for emphasis. "Ask me anything you want," he said. "I been telling you the truth right along."

"You haven't seen Johnny Favorite in the last fifteen years?"

"No."

"What about. Evangeline Proudfoot? She ever mention seeing him?"

"Not where I could hear it. Last time she spoke of him was eight, ten years ago. I recollect it 'cause it was the time some college professor come around wantin' to write somethin' in a book about Obeah. Evangeline told him white people weren't allowed in the humfo. I said, 'cept if they can sing, you know, pullin' her leg an' all."

"What did she say?"

"I'm comin' to it. She didn't laugh but she wasn't mad. She said, 'Toots, if Johnny was alive he'd be one plenty powerful hungan, but that don't mean I have to open the door to ev'ry pink pencil pusher takes a notion to pay a call.' See, far as she was concerned, Johnny Favorite was dead and buried."

"Toots, I'll take a chance and believe you. How come you wear a star on your tooth like that?"

Toots grimaced. The cutout star glinted in the overhead light.

"That's so folks be sure I'm a nigger. Wouldn't want 'em to make any mistakes."

"Why is it upside down?"

"Look nicer that way."

I placed one of my Crossroads cards on top of the TV. "I'm leaving a card with my number on it. If you hear anything, give me a call."

"Yeah, I ain't got enough troubles awready I got to start phonin' up mo'."

"You never know. You might need some help next time you get a special-delivery chicken foot."

Outside, dawn smudged the night sky like rouge on a chorus girl's cheek. Walking to the car, I dropped Toots' pearl-handled razor into a garbage can.

18

THE SUN WAS SHINING WHEN I finally hit the sack, but I managed to sleep until almost noon in spite of the bad dreams. I was haunted by nightmares more vivid than any "Late Show" horror feature. Voodoo drums throbbed as Epiphany Proudfoot cut the rooster's throat. The dancers swayed and moaned, only this time the bleeding didn't stop. A crimson fountain gushed from the thrashing bird, soaking everything like a tropical rain, dancers all drowning in a lake of blood. I watched Epiphany go under and ran from my hiding place, gore splashing at my heels.

Blind with panic, I ran through deserted nighttime streets. Garbage cans stacked in pyramids; rats the size of bulldogs watching from sewers. The air putrid with rot. I ran on, somehow becoming the pursuer instead of the quarry, chasing a distant figure down endless unknown avenues.

No matter how fast I ran, I couldn't catch up. The runner eluded me. When the pavement ended, the chase continued along the flotsam-strewn beach. Dead fish littered the sand. An enormous seashell, tall as a skyscraper, loomed ahead. The man ran inside. I followed him.

The interior of the shell was high and vaulted, like an opalescent cathedral. Our footsteps echoed within the twisting spiral. The passage narrowed, and I came around a final turn to find my adversary blocked by the enormous, quivering, fleshy wall of the mollusk itself. There was no way out.

I seized the man by his coat collar and spun him around, pushing him back into the slime. He was my twin. It was like looking in the mirror. He gathered me in a brother's embrace and kissed my cheek. Lips, eyes, chin; his every feature was interchangeable with mine. I relaxed, overwhelmed by a wave of affection. Then I felt his teeth. His fraternal kiss grew savage; strangler's hands found their way to my throat.

I struggled, and we went down together, my fingers groping for his eyes. We thrashed on the hard, nacreous floor. His grip relaxed as I gouged with my thumbs. He made no sound during the struggle. My hands sank deep into his flesh, familiar features oozing between my fingers like wet dough. His face was a shapeless pulp lacking bone or cartilage and when I pulled away my hands were mired there, like a cook caught in a suet pudding. I woke up screaming.

A hot shower settled my nerves. I was shaved, dressed, and driving uptown inside of twenty minutes. I dropped the Chevy off at my garage and walked to the out-of-town newsstand next to Times Tower. Dr. Albert Fowler's picture was on the front page of Monday's *Poughkeepsie New Yorker.* NOTED DOCTOR FOUND DEAD said the headline. I read all about it over breakfast at the Whelan's drugstore in the corner of the Paramount Building.

The cause of death was listed as suicide although there was no note found. The body was discovered Monday morning by two of Dr. Fowler's colleagues who grew worried when he didn't show up for work or answer his phone. The newspaper had most of the details right. The woman in the framed photograph clutched to the dead man's chest was his wife. No mention was made of the morphine or the missing ring. The contents of the dead man's pockets were not listed, so I had no way of knowing whether he had taken the ring off himself or not.

I had a second cup of coffee and headed for my office to check the mail. There was the usual third-class junk and a letter from a man in Pennsylvania offering a ten-dollar mail-order course in cigarette ash analysis. I swept the whole batch into the wastebasket and considered my options. I had planned on driving out to Coney Island to try to locate Madame Zora, Johnny Favorite's gypsy fortune-teller, but decided to play a long shot and go back up to Harlem first. There was a lot Epiphany Proudfoot hadn't told me last night.

I got my attaché case out of the office safe and was buttoning my overcoat when the phone rang. It was long-distance, person-to-person collect from Cornelius Simpson. I told the operator I would accept the charges.

A man's voice said: "The maid gave me your message. She seemed to think it was some kind of emergency."

"Are you Spider Simpson?"

"Last time I looked I was."

"I'd like to ask you some questions about Johnny Favorite."

"What kind of questions?"

"Have you seen him at all in the past fifteen years for starters?"

Simpson laughed. "Last time I saw Johnny was the day after Pearl Harbor."

"Why is that so funny?"

"It's not funny. Nothing about Johnny was ever very funny."

"Then how come all the laughter?"

"I always laugh when I think of how much money I lost when he walked out on me," Simpson said. "It's a whole lot less painful than crying. What's this all about, anyway?"

"I'm doing a story for *Look* on forgotten vocalists of the forties. Johnny Favorite is at the top of the list."

"Not my list, brother."

"That's fine," I said. "If I spoke to just his fans, I wouldn't get a very interesting story."

"The only fans Johnny had were strangers."

"What can you tell me about his affair with a West Indian woman named Evangeline Proudfoot?"

"Not a damn thing. This is the first I've heard of it."

"Did you know he was involved in voodoo?"

"Sticking pins in dolls? Well, it figures; Johnny was a weirdo. He was always into something strange."

"Such as what?"

"Oh, let's see; one time I saw him catching pigeons up on the roof of our hotel. We were out on the road someplace, I can't remember just where, and he was up there with a big net like some kind of Looney Tunes dog catcher. I thought maybe he didn't like the chow in the place, but later, after the show, I dropped by his room, and there he was with the damn pigeon all split open on the table, poking through the guts with a pencil."

"What was that all about?"

"That's what I asked him. 'What're you up to?' I said. He told me some fancy word I can't remember, and when I asked him to put it in English, he said he was predicting the future. He said it was what the priests in ancient Rome used to do."

"Sounds like that ol' black magic had him in its spell," I said.

Spider Simpson laughed. "You said it, brother. If it wasn't pigeon guts, it was some other damn thing, tea leaves, palm readers, yoga. He wore a heavy gold ring with Hebrew characters all over it. As far as I know, he wasn't Jewish."

"What was he?"

"Damned if I know. Rosicrucian, or some damn thing. He carried a skull in his suitcase."

"A human skull?"

"Once upon a time it was human. He said it came from the grave of a man who murdered ten people. Claimed it gave him power."

"Sounds like he was putting you on," I said.

"Could be. He used to sit and stare at it for hours before a performance. If that was a put-on, it was a damn good one."

"Did you know Margaret Krusemark?" I asked.

"Margaret who?"

"Johnny Favorite's fiancée."

"Oh, yeah, the debutante society girl. I met her a few times. What about her?"

"What was she like?"

"Very pretty. Didn't talk much; You know the type, lots of eye contact but no conversation."

"I heard somewhere she was a fortune-teller."

"That may be. She never told me mine."

"Why did they break up?"

"I wouldn't know."

"Can you give me the names of any of Johnny Favorite's old friends? People who might be able to help me out with the story."

"Brother, aside from bonehead in the suitcase, Johnny didn't have a friend on earth."

"What about Edward Kelley?"

"Never heard of him," Simpson said. "I knew a piano player named Kelly in K.C., but that was years before I ran into Johnny."

"Well, thanks for the information," I said. "You've been a big help."

"Anytime."

We both hung up.

19

I DODGED CHUCK-HOLES ON THE West Side Highway up to 125th and drove east along Harlem's Rialto, past the Hotel Theresa and the Apollo Theatre, over to Lenox Avenue. The neon sign was dark in the window of Proudfoot Pharmaceuticals. A long green shade reached all the way down behind the front door, and Scotch-taped to the glass was a cardboard sign that said CLOSED TODAY. The place was locked up tight.

I found a wall phone in a luncheonette in the next block and looked up the number. There was no listing for Epiphany Proudfoot, only one for the store. I tried but got no answer. Thumbing through the directory, I located Edison Sweet's number. I dialed the first four digits and hung up, deciding a surprise visit would be more effective. Ten minutes later, I was parked on 152nd Street across from his building.

At the entrance, a young housewife with two small children bawling underfoot was struggling with a shopping bag and fumbling in her purse for the key. I offered to help and held her bag as she opened the front door. She lived on the ground floor and thanked me with a weary smile when I handed back the groceries. The kids clung to her coat, snuffling runny noses, and stared up at me with wide, brown eyes.

I climbed the stairs to the third floor. There was no one else on the landing, and when I bent to check the make of the lock on Toots' apartment I found the door was not quite shut. I pushed it all the way open with my foot. A vivid red splash stained the opposite wall like a Rorschach test blot. It might have been paint, but it wasn't.

I closed the door behind me, leaning my back against it until the lock caught.

The room was a mess, furniture thrown about haphazardly on a carpet waved with wrinkles. Someone put up quite a fight. A shelf of flower pots lay overturned in the corner. The curtain-rod was bent in a V and the drapes sagged like the stockings of a hooker on a week-long drunk. Amid the wreckage the TV stood intact. The set was switched on and a soap opera nurse discussed adultery with an attentive intern.

I was careful not to touch anything as I stepped over the upended furniture. The kitchen showed no signs of struggle. A cold cup of black coffee sat on the Formica tabletop. It seemed very homey until I looked back into the living room.

Beyond the babbling TV, a short, dark hall led to a closed door. I got my latex surgeon's gloves out of the attaché case and rolled them onto my hands before turning the knob. One look in the bedroom made me want a drink badly.

Toots Sweet lay on his back on the narrow bed, his hands and feet bound to the posts with lengths of cotton clothesline. He would never get any deader. A crumpled, bloodsoaked flannel bathrobe draped his pot belly. Beneath his black body, the sheets were stiff with blood.

Toots' face and body were badly bruised. The whites of his open, bulging eyes were yellowed, like antique ivory cueballs, and stuffed into his gaping mouth was something resembling a fat, severed hunk of bratwurst. Death by asphyxiation. I knew that without waiting for the autopsy.

I took a closer look at what protruded from his swollen lips and suddenly one drink wasn't going to be enough. Toots had choked to death on his own genitalia. Outside, in the courtyard three flights down, I heard the happy laughter of children.

No power on earth could have made me lift that matted bathrobe. I knew where the murder weapon came from without peeking. On the wall above the bed, a number of childlike drawings had been daubed in Toots' blood: stars, spirals, long zigzag lines representing snakes. The stars, three of them, were five-pointed and upside down. Falling stars were getting to be a habit.

I told myself it was time to pack up and leave. No percentage in sticking around. But my snooper's instinct made me look through his dresser drawers and check out the closet first. It took ten minutes to go over the room, and I didn't find anything worth looking at twice.

I said goodbye to Edison Sweet and closed the bedroom door on the sightless stare of his bulging eyes. My tongue felt heavy and dry in my mouth when I thought of what was stuffed in his. I wanted to check out the living room before I left, but there was too much dirt strewn about and I was afraid of leaving heelprints. My business card was no longer on the TV. I hadn't turned it up among his things, and a fresh paper bag in the kitchen meant the trash went out earlier. I hoped my card went with it.

At the front door, I squinted through the peephole before letting myself out, I left the door open a crack, just the way I found it, and peeled off my rubber gloves, shutting them inside the calfskin case. I paused at the top of the landing and listened to the silence below. No one was using the stairs. The housewife on the first floor might remember me, but there was nothing I could do about that.

I made it down the stairs without being seen, and when I left the building, the only ones around were a group of small children playing hopscotch in the courtyard. They didn't look up as I passed.

20

THREE STRAIGHT SHOTS SETTLED MY nerves and put me in a philosophic frame of mine. It was a quiet neighborhood bar called Freddie's Place, or Teddy's Spot or Eddie's Nest, something along those lines, and I sat with my back to the TV and thought things over. Now I had two dead men on my hands. They both knew Johnny Favorite and wore five-pointed stars. I wondered if Toots' front tooth was missing like the doctor's ring, but didn't want to know badly enough to go back and look. The stars maybe were a coincidence; it's a common design. And maybe it was just by chance that a junkie doctor and a blues piano player both knew Johnny Favorite. Maybe. But deep down in my gut I had a feeling that it was tied in to something bigger. Something enormous. I scooped my change off the damp bar top and went back to work for Louis Cyphre.

The drive out to Coney Island was a pleasant distraction. Rush hour was still ninety minutes off and traffic moved freely along F.D.R. Drive and through the Battery Tunnel. I rolled down my window on the Shore Parkway and breathed the cold sea air blowing in through the Narrows. By the time I reached Cropsey Avenue the smell of blood was gone from my nostrils.

I followed West 17th Street down to Surf Avenue and parked beside a boarded-up bumper-car ride. Coney Island in the off-season had the look and feel of a ghost town. The skeletal tracks of the roller coasters rose above me like metal and timber spiderwebs, but the screams were missing and the wind moaned through the struts, lonesome as a train whistle.

A few odd souls wandered about Surf Avenue looking for something to do. Sheets of newspaper blew like tumbleweed down broad, empty streets. Overhead, a pair of sea gulls hovered, scanning the ground for discarded scraps. All along the avenue, cotton candy stands, fun houses, and games of chance were tightly shuttered, like clowns without makeup.

Nathan's Famous was open for business as always, and I stopped for a hot dog and a cardboard cup of beer under the boldly lettered billboard facade. The counterman looked like he'd been around since the days of Luna Park, and I asked if he'd ever heard of a fortune-teller named Madame Zora.

"Madame who?"

"Zora. She was a big attraction here back in the forties."

"Beats me, bud," he said. "I only had this job less'n a year. Ask me something about the Staten Island Ferry. I ran the night food concession on the *Gold Star Mother* fifteen years. Go on, ask me something."

"Why'd you quit?"

"Can't swim."

"So?"

"Afraid of gettin' drowned. Din't wanna press my luck." He smiled, showing me four missing teeth. I stuffed the last of the hot dog into my face and wandered off, sipping beer.

The Bowery, situated between Surf Avenue and the Boardwalk, was more a circus midway than a street. I strolled past the silent amusements and wondered what to do next. The gypsy community was more clannish than all the Ku Kluxers in Georgia, and I knew I would get no help from that direction. Leg work. Pound the pavement until someone turned up who remembered Madame Zora and was willing to talk about it.

Danny Dreenan seemed like a good place to start. He was a

retired bunco-steerer who operated a run-down wax museum near the corner of 13th Street and the Bowery. I met him in '52 when he was fresh out from a four-year stretch in Dannemora. The Feds tried to make him on a stock-option swindle, but he was just the fall guy for a pair of Wall Street shysters named Peavey and Munro. I was working for a third party who was also a victim of their grift and had a hand in cracking the case. Danny still owed me for that one, so he put me wise when I needed some knock-down on the q.t.

The Wax Gallery was housed in a narrow, one-story building sandwiched between a pizza stand and a penny arcade. Out in front, in foot-high crimson letters, it said:

SEE:
HALL OF AMERICAN PRESIDENTS
FIFTY FAMOUS MURDERS
ASSASSINATION OF LINCOLN AND GARFIELD
DILLINGER IN MORGUE
FATTY ARBUCKLE ON TRIAL

EDUCATIONAL! LIFELIKE! SHOCKING!

A henna-haired harpy not a day older than President Grant's widow sat in the ticket booth, playing solitaire like one of the mechanical fortune-tellers in the penny arcade next door.

"Danny Dreenan around?" I asked.

"Out back," she grunted, sneaking the jack of clubs from the bottom of the deck. "He's working on a display."

"Mind if I go in and talk to him?"

"Still gonna cost you two bits," she said, nodding her ancient head at a cardboard placard: ADMISSION . . . 25¢

I dug a quarter out of my trousers, slid it under the barred window, and went inside. The place smelled like a backed-up sewer. Large, rust-colored stains blotched the sagging cardboard ceiling.

Warped wooden flooring creaked and groaned. In glass-fronted display windows along either wall, wax mannequins stood stiffly at attention, an army of cigar-store Indians.

The Hall of American Presidents came first: identically featured chief executives dressed in the discards of a vaudeville costume shop. After F.D.R. it was all murderer's row. I walked through a maze of mayhem. Hall-Mills, Snyder-Gray, Bruno Hauptmann, Winnie Ruth Judd, the Lonely Hearts killers; all were there, wielding sashweights and meat saws, stuffing dismembered limbs into trunks, adrift in oceans of red paint.

In the back I found Danny Dreenan on his hands and knees inside a show window. He was a small man wearing a faded blue workshirt and salt-and-pepper wool slacks. A turned-up nose and sparse blond mustache gave him the expression of a frightened hamster. His habit of blinking his eyes rapidly when he spoke didn't help any.

I tapped on the glass and he looked up at me and smiled around a mouthful of carpet tacks. He mumbled something unintelligible, put down his hammer, and slipped out through a small crawl-space in the back. He was working on the barber shop slaying of Albert Anastasia, Lord High Executioner of Murder, Inc. Two masked killers pointed revolvers at the sheet-draped figure in the chair, while the barber stood calmly in the background waiting for another customer.

"Hiya, Harry," Danny Dreenan called cheerfully, coming up behind me where I didn't expect him. "Whaddya think of my latest masterpiece?"

"Looks like they've all got rigor mortis," I said. "Umberto Anastasia, right?"

"Give the man a free cigar. Can't be too bad if you guessed it right off."

"I was over by the Park Sheraton yesterday, so it's fresh on my mind."

" 'S gonna be my big new attraction for the season.

"You're a year late. The headlines are as cold as the corpse."

Danny blinked nervously. "Barber chairs are expensive, Harry. I couldn't afford no improvements last season. Say, that hotel sure is good for business. Didja know Arnold Rothstein got knocked off there back in twenty-eight? Only it was called the Park Central in them days. Come on, I got him up front; I'll show you."

"Some other time, Danny. I see enough of the real thing to keep me satisfied."

"Yeah, I guess you do at that. So what brings you out to this neck of the woods, as if I didn't know already."

"You tell me, since you know all about it."

Danny's eyes were going like insane semaphores. "I don't know beans about it," he stammered. "But I figger, if Harry comes to see me, he's gonna want some info."

"You figured it just right," I said. "What can you tell me about a fortune-teller named Madame Zora? She worked the midway here back in the early forties."

"Aw, Harry, you know I can't help you there. I had a Florida real estate scam going in them days. It was Easy Street for Danny Dreenan back then."

I shook a cigarette from my pack and offered one to Danny who wagged his head negatively. "I didn't think you could finger her for me, Danny," I said, lighting up. "But you've been around a while now. Tell me who the old-timers are. Put me wise to someone who knows the score."

Danny scratched his head to show me he was thinking. "I'll do what I can. Problem is, Harry, most everybody who can afford it is off in Bermuda or someplace. I'd be lying on a beach myself if I wasn't up to my neck in bills. I ain't complaining; after the joint, Brighton Beach looks good as Bermuda any day."

"There must be someone around. You're not the only one open for business."

"Yeah, now you mention it, I know just the people to send you to. There's a freak show over on 10th Street near the Boardwalk.

Ordinarily, most of the oddities would be working the circus this time of year, but these are old people. Semiretired, you might say. They don't take vacations. Going out in public is not their idea of a lot of laughs."

"What's the name of this place?" I asked.

"Walter's Congress of Wonders. Only it's run by a gent named Haggarty. You can't miss him. He's all covered with tattoos like a road map."

"Thanks, Danny. You're a fund of valuable information."

21

WALTER'S CONGRESS OF WONDERS STOOD on 10th Street near the ramp leading up to the Boardwalk. More than any of the surrounding attractions, it had the look of an old-time carnie midway. The front of the low building was festooned with bunting, below which hung large primitive paintings of the exhibits inside. Simple as cartoons, these vast canvases depicted human deformity with an innocence that belied their inherent cruelty.

MY IS SHE FAT! read the caption under the picture of a woman big as a blimp holding a tiny parasol above her pumpkin-sized head. The tattooed man—BEAUTY IS ONLY SKIN DEEP—was flanked by portraits of Jo-Jo, the Dog-faced Boy, and Princess Sophia, the Bearded Lady. Other crude portraits showed an hermaphrodite, a young girl entwined by snakes, the seal man, and a giant wearing evening clothes.

OPEN SAT. & SUN. ONLY, a sign announced in the empty ticket booth by the entrance. A chain hung across the open doorway like the velvet ropes in nightclubs, but I ducked underneath and went inside.

The only illumination came from a dingy skylight, yet it was sufficient to reveal numbers of flag-draped platforms arranged along both sides of the deserted room. A smell of sweat and sadness hung in the air. At the far end, a line of light showed under a closed door. I went over and knocked.

"It's open," a voice called.

I turned the knob and looked into a large, bare room, made homelike by several sagging secondhand couches and gay circus posters brightening the mildewed walls. The fat lady filled a couch like it was an armchair. A diminutive woman with a black curling beard spread across her demure pink bodice sat engrossed in a half-assembled jigsaw puzzle. Under a dusty fringed lampshade, four curious misshapen humans engaged in the familiar ritual of draw poker. A man with no arms or legs perched Humpty Dumpty-fashion on a large cushion and held his cards in hands growing directly out of his shoulders like flippers. Next to him sat a giant, playing cards reduced to postage stamps in his massive fingers. The dealer had a skin condition which made his cracked complexion look like the hide of an alligator.

"You in or out?" he demanded of the player on his left, a wizened leprechaun wearing a tank-top undershirt. His neck, shoulders, and arms were so heavily tattooed that he appeared to have on some exotic skin-tight garment. Unlike the gaudy epidermal artwork pictured on the canvas poster outside, he was bleached and faded, a blurred carbon of what was advertised.

The tattooed man eyed my attaché case. "Whatever you're selling, we don't want any," he barked.

"I'm not a salesman," I said. "No insurance or lightning rods today."

"Then what the hell're you after, a free show?"

"You must be Mr. Haggarty. A friend of mine thought someone here might be able to help me out with some information."

"And just who might this friend be?" the multicolored Mr. Haggarty demanded.

"Danny Dreenan. He runs the wax museum around the corner."

"Yeah, I know Dreenan, a two-bit con man." Haggarty hacked up a wad of phlegm and spat into a wastebasket at his feet. Then he smiled to show he didn't mean it. "Any friend of Danny's is jake with me. Tell me what you need to know. I'll give you the straight dope if I can."

"Mind if I sit down?"

"Be my guest." Haggarty pushed an unoccupied folding chair away from the card table with his foot. "Park it there, pal."

I sat between Haggarty and the giant, scowling above us like Gulliver among the Lilliputians. "I'm looking for a gypsy fortune-teller named Madame Zora," I said, setting my case between my feet. "She was a big attraction before the war."

"Can't place her," Haggarty said. "What about you fellas?"

"I remember a tea-reader named Moon," piped the man with flippers in place of arms.

"She was Chinese," the giant growled. "Married an auctioneer and moved to Toledo."

"Why're you looking for her?" the alligator-skinned man wanted to know.

"She used to know a guy I'm trying to find. I was hoping she could help me out."

"You a shamus?"

I nodded. Denying it now would only make things worse.

"Gumshoe, eh?" Haggarty spit into the wastebasket again. "I don't hold it against you. We all gotta earn a living."

"Me, I could never stomach a peeper," grumbled the giant.

I said: "Eating detectives gives you indigestion, right?"

The giant grumped. Haggarty laughed and pounded the card table with his red-and-blue-embroidered fist, upsetting careful stacks of chips all around.

"I knew Zora." It was the fat lady who spoke, her voice delicate as bone china. Magnolias and honeysuckle bloomed in her melodic accent. "She was no more a gypsy than you are," she said.

"You sure of that?"

" 'Course I am. Al Jolson wore blackface, but it didn't make him a nigger."

"Where can I find her now?"

"I couldn't tell you. I lost track of her after she folded her mitt camp."

"When was that?"

"Spring of forty-two. One day she just wasn't there any more. Walked away from her racket without a word to anyone."

"What can you tell me about her?"

"Not a whole lot. We'd have a cuppa java together once in a while. Jaw about the weather and stuff like that."

"Did she ever mention a singer named Johnny Favorite?"

The fat lady smiled. Somewhere under those acres of suet lurked a little girl with a brand-new party dress.

"Didn't he have a pair of golden tonsils?" She beamed and hummed a tune from long ago. "He was my favorite, all right. I read once in the scandal sheet that he consulted Zora, but when I asked her about it she clammed up. It's like a priest hearing confession, I guess."

"Is there anything more you can tell me, anything at all?"

"Sorry. We weren't that close. You know who might be able to help you out?"

"No! who?"

"Old Paul Boltz. He used to be her shill back then. He's still around."

"Where can I find him?"

"Over at Steeplechase. He's the watchdog there now." The fat lady fanned herself with a movie magazine. "Haggarty, can't you do something about the steam heat? It's like a boiler room in here. I'm about to melt!"

Haggarty laughed. "You'd make the world's biggest puddle if you did."

22

THE BOARDWALK AND BRIGHTON BEACH were deserted. Where summertime crowds lay sweating like wall-to-wall walruses a few determined scavengers probed the sand for discarded pop bottles. Beyond them, the Atlantic was the color of cast iron, surf surging against the breakwater in a leaden spray.

Steeplechase Park spanned twenty-five acres. The Parachute Jump, a hand-me-down from the '39 World's Fair, towered above the factory-size, glass-walled pavilion like the framework of a two-hundred-foot umbrella. A sign out front said THE FUNNY PLACE above the leering, painted face of founder George C. Tilyou. Steeplechase was as funny this time of year as a joke without a punchline, and I looked up at the grinning Mr. Tilyou and wondered what there was to laugh about.

I found a man-size hole in the chain-link fence and pounded on the salt-encrusted glass near the locked front entrance. The noise echoed through the empty amusement park like a dozen poltergeists on a ghostly spree. Wake up, old man! What if I was a gang of thieves out to boost the Parachute Jump?

I started on a circumnavigation of the vast structure, beating the glass with the flat of my hand. Turning a corner, I came face-to-face with the muzzle of a gun. It was a Colt's Police Positive .38 Special, but seen from my vantage point, it looked about the size of Big Bertha.

Holding the .38 without a tremor was an old party in a brown and tan uniform. A pair of pig-squint eyes sized me up above a nose shaped like a ball-peen hammer. "Freeze!" he said. His voice seemed to come from under water. I froze.

"You must be Mr. Boltz," I said. "Paul Boltz?"

"Never mind who I am. Who the fuck are you?"

"My name is Angel. I'm a private detective. I need to talk to you about a case I'm working on."

"Show me something to prove it."

When I started for my wallet Boltz jabbed his .38 emphatically at my belt buckle. "Left hand," he snarled.

I shifted the attaché case to my right hand and got out my wallet with my left.

"Drop it and take two steps back."

"Do not pass Go; do not collect two hundred dollars."

"What was that?" Boltz stooped and picked it up. His Police Positive stayed trained on my belly button.

"Nothing. Just talking to myself. Open the flap and you'll see my photostat right on top."

"This here honorary buzzer don't mean shit to me,'" he said. "I got a piece of tin at home just like it."

"I didn't claim it was valid; just look at the photostat."

The pig-eyed watchman flipped through the cardholders in my wallet without comment. I thought of rushing him then but let it rest. "Okay, so you're a private dick," he said. "What do you want with me?"

"You Paul Boltz?"

"What if I am?" He tossed my wallet onto the deck at my feet.

I picked it up with my left hand. "Look, it's been a hard day. Put the gun away. I need your help. Can't you tell when a guy is asking for a favor?"

He looked at the revolver for a moment, as if considering having it for supper. Then he shrugged and slipped it back into his holster, pointedly leaving the flap unbuttoned. "I'm Boltz," he admitted. "Let's hear your spiel."

"Is there someplace we can get out of all this wind?"

Boltz motioned his misshapen head, indicating I was to lead the way. He followed a half-pace behind, and we went down a short flight of steps to a door marked NO ENTRY. "In here," he said. "It's open."

Our footsteps boomed like cannon shots in the empty building. The place was large enough to contain a couple of airplane hangars with room left over for a half-dozen basketball courts. Most of the attractions remained from an earlier, unmechanized era. A large, undulating wooden slide gleamed in the distance like a mahogany waterfall. Another slide called the "Whirlpool" spiraled down from the ceiling, spilling out onto "The Human Pool Table," a series of polished, revolving disks built into the hardwood floor. It was easy to imagine Gibson girls in leg-o'-mutton sleeves and dapper gents tipping their straw boaters as the calliope played "Take Me Out to the Ball Game."

We paused in front of a row of "fun house" mirrors, the distorted images making freaks of us both. "Okay, shamus," Boltz said. "Give with your pitch."

I said: "I'm looking for a gypsy fortune-teller named Madame Zora. I understand you used to work for her back in the forties."

Boltz's phlegm-thickened laughter rose "to the lightbulb-studded girders overhead like the barking of a trained seal. "Bud," he chortled, "you ain't gonna get to first base the way you're headed."

"Why not?"

"Why not? I'll tell you why not. First off, she ain't, no gypsy, that's why not."

"I heard that, but I wasn't sure if it was on the level."

"Well, I'm sure. Didn't I know her racket inside and out?"

"You tell me."

"Okay, dick, I'll give it to you straight. She weren't no gypsy and her name wasn't Zora. I happen to know she was a Park Avenoo debutante."

A mule's kick would have seemed the kiss of an angel alongside that bombshell. It took a while to get my tongue back in gear. "Did you know her real name?"

"Whadya take me for, a gazoonie? I knew all about her. Her name was Maggie Krusemark. Her father owned more boats than the British navy."

My elongated reflection stretched like Plastic Man across the wavy surface of the trick mirror. "When did you see her last?" the rubber lips asked.

"Spring of forty-two. One day she pulled a fade. Left me holding the crystal ball, you might say."

"Did you ever see her with a singer named Johnny Favorite?"

"Sure, lots of times. She was stuck on him."

"Did she ever say anything about him that you can remember?"

"Power."

"What?"

"She said he had power."

"And that's all?"

"Look. I never paid much attention. To me it was just a carnie hustle. I didn't take it serious." Boltz cleared his throat and swallowed. "It was different with her. She was a believer."

"What about Favorite?" I asked.

"He was a believer, too. You could see it in his eyes."

"Have you ever seen him again?"

"Never. Maybe he flew off to the moon on his broomstick for all I care. Her, too."

"Did she ever mention a Negro piano player named Toots Sweet?"

"Nope."

"Can you think of anything else?"

Boltz spit on the floor between his feet. "Why should I? Them days are dead and buried."

There wasn't much else to talk about. Boltz walked me back outside and unlocked the gate. After a moment's hesitation, I gave him one of my Crossroads cards and asked him to call if anything came up. He didn't say he would, but he didn't tear up my card either.

I tried calling Millicent Krusemark from the first phone booth I came to but got no answer. Just as well. It had been a long day and even detectives are entitled to some time off. On my way back to Manhattan, I stopped in the Heights and gorged myself on seafood at Gage & Tanner's. After poached salmon and a bottle of chilled chablis, life no longer seemed like a glass-bottomed boat-ride through the city's sewer system.

23

TOOTS SWEET MADE PAGE 3 of the *Daily News.* No mention of the murder weapon in what was slugged SAVAGE VOODOO KILLING. There was a photo of the bloody drawings on the wall over the bed, and one of Toots playing the piano. The body had been discovered by the guitar player in the trio, who stopped by to pick up his boss before work. He was released I after questioning. There were no suspects, although it was widely known in Harlem that Toots was a long-standing member of a secret voodoo cult.

I read the morning paper on the uptown IRT, having left the Chevy in a parking lot around the corner from the Chelsea. My first stop was the Public Library where, after several misdirections, I asked the right question and came up with a current Paris telephone directory. There was a listing for an M. Krusemark on the Rue Notre Dames des Champs. I wrote it down in my notebook.

On my way to the office, I sat on a bench in Bryant Park long enough to chain-smoke three cigarettes and rehash recent events. I felt like a man chasing a shadow. Johnny Favorite had been mixed up in a weird underground world of voodoo and black magic. Offstage, he led a secret life, complete with skulls in his suitcase and fortune-telling fiancées. He was an, initiate, a hunsi-bosal. Toots Sweet got knocked off for talking. Somehow, Dr. Fowler was a part of it, too. Johnny Favorite cast a long, long shadow.

It was nearly noon by the time I unlocked the inner door to my office. I sorted the mail, finding a $500 check from the firm of McIntosh, Winesap, and Spy. All the rest was junk I filed in the wastebasket before phoning my answering service. There were no messages, although a woman who refused to leave a name or number called three times that morning.

Next, I tried to reach Margaret Krusemark in Paris, but the overseas operator could get no answer after twenty minutes of trying. I dialed Herman Winesap down on Wall Street and thanked him for the check. He asked how the case was getting along. I said just fine, mentioning I wanted to get in touch with Mr. Cyphre. Winesap said he was meeting him later in the afternoon on business matters and would see he got the message. I said fair enough, and we both chirped our goodbyes and hung up.

I was struggling back into my overcoat when the phone rang. I grabbed it on the third ring. It was Epiphany Proudfoot. She sounded out of breath. "I've got to see you right away," she said.

"What about?"

"I don't want to talk on the phone."

"Where are you now?"

"At the store."

I said: "Take your time. I'm going out for something to eat and will meet you back in my office at one-fifteen. You know how to find it?"

"I've got your card."

"Swell. See you in an hour."

She hung up without saying goodbye.

Before leaving, I locked Winesap's check in the office safe. I was kneeling there when I heard the doorstop's pneumatic wheeze in the outer room. Clients are always welcome, that's why COME IN is painted on the front door under the name of the firm. But clients usually knock on the inner door. When someone barges in without a word it's either a cop or trouble. Sometimes both in the same package.

This time it was a plainclothes dick wearing a wrinkled grey gabardine raincoat unbuttoned over a brown mohair pipe-rack special with cuffs sufficiently shy of his perforated brogans to provide a sneak preview of his white athletic socks.

"You Angel?" he barked.

"That's right."

"I'm Detective Lieutenant Sterne. This is my partner, Sergeant Deimos."

He nodded at the open-partition door where a barrel-chested man dressed like a longshoreman stood scowling. Deimos wore a knitted wool cap and a black-and-white plaid lumberjacket. He was clean-shaven, but his beard was so dark it looked like powder burn under the skin.

"What can I do for you, gentlemen?" I said.

"Answer a couple questions." Sterne was tall and lantern-jawed with a nose like the prow of an icebreaker. His face thrust forward aggressively above his stooped shoulders. When he spoke his lips scarcely moved.

"Be glad to. I was just heading for a bite to eat. Care to join me?"

"We can talk better here," Sterne said. His partner closed the door.

"Suits me." I walked around in back of the desk and got out a fifth of Canadian whisky and my Christmas cigars. "This is all the hospitality I can offer. Paper cups're over by the water cooler."

"Never drink on duty," Sterne said, helping himself to a handful of cigars.

"Well, don't mind me. This is my lunch hour." I carried the bottle over to the cooler, filled a cup halfway, and added a finger of water. "Cheers."

Sterne tucked the cigars in his breast pocket. "Where were you yesterday morning around eleven?"

"At home. Asleep."

"Sure is great being self-employed," Sterne cracked out of the side of his mouth to Deimos. The sergeant just grunted. "Why is it you're snoozing when the rest of the world is at work, Angel?"

"I was working late the night before."

"Where might that have been?"

"Up in Harlem. What's this all about, Lieutenant?"

Sterne got something out of his raincoat pocket and held it up for me to see. "Recognize this?"

I nodded. "One of my business cards."

"Maybe you'd like to explain how come it was found in the apartment of a murder victim."

"Toots Sweet?"

"Tell me about it." Sterne sat on the corner of my desk and tipped his grey hat back on his forehead.

"Not much to tell. Sweet was the reason I went up to Harlem. I needed to interview him regarding a job I'm working on. He turned out to be a cold lead, which I half-expected. I gave him the card in case anything came up."

"Not nearly good enough, Angel. Give it to me again."

"Okay. What I've got going is a missing persons' operation. The party in question took a walk more than a dozen years ago. One of my few leads was an old photo of the guy posing with Toots Sweet. I went uptown last night to ask Toots if he could help me out. He played cagey at first when I talked to him at the Red Rooster, so I tailed him down to the park after closing time. He went to some kind of voodoo ceremony over by the Meer. They shuffled around and killed a chicken. I felt like a tourist."

"Who-all is 'they'?" asked Sterne.

"About fifteen men and women, colored. I'd never seen any of them before except Toots."

"What did you do?"

"Nothing. Toots left the park alone. I tailed him home and got him to talk straight. He said he hadn't seen the guy I was looking for since the picture was taken. I gave him my card and said to call me if he thought of anything. Like it better this time?"

"Not much." Sterne looked at his thick fingernails with disinterest. "What did you use to get him to talk?"

"Psychology," I said.

Sterne raised his eyebrows and regarded me with the same disinterest he lavished on his fingernails. "So who is the famous party in question? The one that walked?"

"I can't give out that information without the consent of my client."

"Bullshit, Angel, You won't do your client any good downtown, and that's just where I'll take you if you clam up on me."

"Why be disagreeable, Lieutenant? I'm working for a lawyer named Winesap. That entitles me to the same right to privacy as him. If you pulled me in, I'd be out within the hour. Save the city carfare."

"What's this lawyer's number?"

I wrote it out on the desk pad along with his full name, tore the sheet loose, and handed it to Sterne. "I told you all I know. From what I read in the paper, it sounds like some of Toots' chicken-snuffing fellow parishioners put him away. If you make a pinch, I'll be happy to look him over in the lineup."

"That's white of you, Angel," Sterne sneered.

"What's this?" It was Sergeant Deimos asking. He'd been wandering around the office with his hands in his pockets, checking things out. He was asking about Ernie Cavalero's law degree from Yale. It was framed on the wall over the filing cabinet.

"That's a law degree," I said. "Used to belong to the guy that started the business. He's dead now."

"Sentimental?" Sterne muttered through his tight ventriloquist's lips.

"Adds a touch of class."

"What's it say?" Sergeant Deimos wanted to know.

"Beats me. I don't read Latin."

"So that's what it is. Latin."

"That's what it is."

"What difference would it make if it was Hebrew?" Sterne said. Deimos shrugged. "Any further questions, Lieutenant?" I asked.

Sterne turned his dead cop's gaze on me again. You could tell from his eyes that he never smiled. Not even during a third-degree session. He was just doing his job. "None. You and your 'right to privacy' can go eat lunch now. Maybe we'll call you, but I wouldn't hold your breath. Just another dead jigaboo. Nobody much gives a shit."

"Call if you need me."

"Sure thing. He's a real prince, right, Deimos?"

We all wedged into the tiny elevator together and rode down without saying a word.

24

GOUGH'S CHOP HOUSE WAS ACROSS 43rd Street from the Times Building. The place was packed when I got there, but I squeezed into a corner by the bar. I didn't have much time, so I ordered roast beef on rye and a bottle of ale. Service was fast in spite of the crowd, and I was laying the ale to rest when Walt Rigler spotted me on his way out and came over to jaw. "What brings you into this scribbler's den, Harry?" he shouted over the din of newspaper shoptalk. "I thought you ate at Downey's."

"I try not to be a creature of habit," I said.

"Sound philosophy. So what's up?"

"Very little. Thanks for letting me raid the morgue. I owe you one."

"Forget it. How goes your little mystery? Digging up any good dirt?"

"More than I can handle. Thought I had a strong lead yesterday. Went to see Krusemark's fortune-telling daughter, but I picked the wrong one."

"What do you mean, the wrong one?"

"There's the black witch and the white witch. One I want lives in Paris."

"I don't follow you, Harry."

"They're twins; Maggie and Millie, the supernatural Krusemark girls."

Walt rubbed the back of his neck and frowned. Someone's pulling your leg, pal. Margaret Krusemark's an only child."

I gagged on my ale. "You sure of that?"

"'Course I'm sure. I just checked it out for you yesterday. Had the family history on my desk all afternoon. Krusemark had a daughter by his wife. Just one, Harry. The *Times* doesn't make mistakes in the vital statistics department."

"What a sap I've been!"

"No argument on that score."

"I should have known she was playing me for a sucker. It was too pat."

"Slow down, pal, you're way ahead of me."

"Sorry, Walt. Just thinking out loud. My watch says five after one, is that right?"

"Close enough."

I stood up, leaving my change on the bar. "Got to run."

"Don't let me stop you." Walt Rigler grinned his lopsided grin.

Epiphany Proudfoot was waiting in the outer room of my office when I got there minutes later. She was wearing a tartan plaid kilt and a blue cashmere sweater and looked like a coed.

"Sorry I'm late," I said.

"Don't be. I was early." She tossed aside a well-thumbed back issue of *Sports Illustrated* and uncrossed her legs. On her, even the second-hand Naugahyde chair looked good.

I unlocked the door in the pebbled-glass partition and held it open. "Why did you want to see me?"

"This isn't much of an office." She picked her handbag and folded coat off the table holding up my collection of out-of-date magazines. "You must not be such a hot detective."

"I keep my overhead low," I said, ushering her inside. "You pay for getting the job done or you pay for interior decoration." I shut the door and hung my coat on the rack.

She stood by the window with the eight-inch gold letters, staring down at the street. "Who's paying you to look for Johnny Favorite?" she asked her reflection in the glass.

"I can't tell you that. One of the things my services include is discretion. Won't you sit down?"

I took her coat and hung it next to mine as she settled gracefully into the padded leather chair across from my desk. It was the only comfortable seat in the place. "You still haven't answered my question," I said, leaning back in my swivel chair. "Why are you here?"

"Edison Sweet has been murdered."

"Uh-huh. I read the papers. But you shouldn't be too surprised: you set him up."

She clenched her handbag on her lap. "You must be out of your mind."

"Maybe. But I'm not dumb. You were the only one who knew I was talking to Toots. You had to be the one who tipped off the boys that sent the gift-wrapped chicken foot."

"You've got it all wrong."

"Do I?"

"There was no one else. After you left the store, I called my nephew. He lives around the corner from the Red Rooster. It was him hid the claw in the piano. Toots was a blabbermouth. He needed reminding to keep his trap shut."

"You did a good job. It's shut for keeps now."

"Do you think I'd be coming to see you if I had anything to do with that?"

"I'd say you were a capable girl, Epiphany. Your performance in the park was quite convincing."

Epiphany bit her knuckle and frowned, squirming in the chair. She looked for all the world like a truant hauled onto the carpet by the school principal. If it was an act, it was a good one.

"You have no right to spy on me," Epiphany said, not meeting my gaze.

"The Parks Department and the Humane Society would disagree. Quite a gruesome little religion."

This time Epiphany looked me straight in the eye, her glance black with fury. "Obeah doesn't need to hang a man on the cross. There never was an Obeah Holy War, or an Obeah Inquisition!"

"Yeah, sure; you've got to kill the chicken to make the soup, right?" I lit a cigarette and blew a plume of smoke at the ceiling. "But it's not dead chickens that worry me; it's dead piano players."

"Don't you think I'm worried?" Epiphany leaned forward in the chair, the tips of her girlish breasts straining against the thin weave of her blue sweater. She was a tall drink of water, as they say uptown, and it was easy to imagine quenching my thirst on her tawny flesh.

"I don't know what to think," I said. "You call up saying you have to see me right away. Now that you're here, you act like you're doing me a favor."

"Maybe I am doing you a favor." She sat back and crossed her long legs, which wasn't hard to take either. "You come around looking for Johnny Favorite and the next day a man gets killed. That's not just a coincidence."

"What is it then?"

"Look: the newspapers are making a lot of noise about voodoo this and voodoo that, but I can tell you straight out that Toots Sweet's death didn't have anything to do with Obeah, not a single, blessed thing."

"How do you know that?"

"Did you see the pictures in the papers?"

I nodded.

"Then you know they're calling those bloody scribblings on the wall 'voodoo symbols'?"

Another silent nod.

"Well, the cops don't know any more about voodoo than they do about peas and rice! Those marks were supposed to look like vévé, but it just isn't so."

"What's vévé?"

"Magic signs. I can't explain their meaning to someone who's not an initiate, but all that bloody trash's got as much to do with the real thing as Santa Claus has to do with Jesus. I've been a mambo for years. I know what I'm talking about."

I stubbed out my butt in a Stork Club ashtray left over from a long-dead love affair. "I'm sure you do, Epiphany. You say the marks are phony?"

"Not phony so much as, well, wrong. I don't know how else to put it. Be like someone describing a baseball game and he kept calling a home run a touchdown. Get what I mean?"

I folded the copy of the *News* to page 3. Holding it so Epiphany could see, I pointed to the snakelike zigzags, spirals, and broken crosses in the photo. "Are you saying these look like voodoo drawings, 'vévé,' or whatever, but they're used incorrectly?"

"That's right. See that circle there, the one with the serpent swallowing its own tail? That's Damballah, sure enough vévé, a symbol of the geometric perfection of the universe. But no initiate would ever draw it right next to Babako like that."

"So, whoever drew those pictures at least knew enough about voodoo to know what Damballah or Babako looked like in the first place."

"That's what I've been trying to tell you all along," she said. "Did you know that Johnny Favorite was once upon a time mixed up with Obeah?"

"I know he was a hunsi-bosal."

"Toots really did have a big mouth. What else do you know?"

"Only that Johnny Favorite was running around with your mother at the time."

Epiphany made a face like tasting something sour. "It's true." She shook her head as if to deny it. "Johnny Favorite was my father."

I sat very still, gripping the arms of my chair as her revelation washed over me like a giant wave. "Who all knows about this?"

"No one, 'cept you and me and mama, and she's dead."

"What about Johnny Favorite?"

"Mama never told him. He was away in the army long before I was a year old. I told you the truth when I said we'd never met."

"How come you're opening up to me how?"

"I'm scared. There's something about Toots' death that has to do with me. I don't know how or why, but I can feel it deep down in my bones."

"And you think Johnny Favorite is mixed up in it somehow?"

"I don't know what to think. You're supposed to do the thinking. I figured you ought to know. Maybe it'll help some."

"Maybe. If you're holding out on me, now would be the time to tell."

Epiphany stared at her folded hands. "There's nothing more to tell." She stood up then, very brisk and efficient. "I must be going. I'm sure you have work to do."

"I'm doing it right now," I said, getting to my feet.

She collected her coat from the rack. "I trust you meant that stuff earlier, you know, about discretion."

"Everything you told me is strictly confidential."

"I hope so." She smiled then. It was a genuine smile and not designed to get results. "Somehow, against all my better judgment, I trust you."

"Thanks." I started around the desk when she opened the door.

"Don't bother," she said. "I can find my own way out."

"You have my number?"

She nodded. "I'll call you if I hear anything."

"Call me even if you don't."

She nodded a second time and was gone. I stood at the corner of my desk, not moving until I heard the door to the outer room close behind her. In three steps, I grabbed my attaché case, wrestled my coat off the rack, and locked the office.

I waited with my ear to the outer door, listening for the self-service elevator opening and closing before I left. The hallway was empty. The only sounds were Ira Kipnis adding up a late tax return and the electric drone of Madame Olga removing unwanted hair. I sprinted for the fire stairs and took the steps three at a time on my way down.

25

I BEAT THE ELEVATOR BY at least fifteen seconds and waited inside the stairwell with the fire door open just a crack. Epiphany walked past me out onto the street. I was right behind, following her around the corner and down into the subway.

She caught the uptown IRT local. I got on the next car in line and, as the train started to move, went outside and stood on the bucking metal platform above the coupling where I watched her through the glass in the door. She sat very primly with her knees tight together, staring up at the row of advertising above the windows. Two stops later, she got off at Columbus Circle.

She walked east along Central Park South, past the Maine Memorial topped with its seahorse-drawn chariot cast from the salvaged cannon of the sunken battleship. There were few pedestrians, and I stayed far enough back not to hear her heels tap on the hexagonal asphalt tiles bordering the park.

She turned downtown at Seventh Avenue. I watched her studying the entrance numbers as she hurried by the Athletic Club and the sculpture-encrusted Alwyn Court Apartments. At the corner of 57th Street she was stopped by an elderly lady lugging a heavy shopping bag, and I lingered in the entrance of a lingerie shop while she gave directions, pointing back toward the park without seeing me.

I almost lost her when she darted across the two-way traffic a moment before the light changed. I was marooned at the curb, but she slowed her pace to scrutinize the shop numbers located along the side of Carnegie Hall. Even before the WALK sign turned green, I saw her pause at the far end of the block and go inside the building. I already knew the address: 881 Seventh. It was where Margaret Krusemark lived.

In the lobby, I watched the brass arrow above the right-hand elevator come to rest at "11" as its sinistral twin descended. When the car door opened an entire string quartet got off, carrying their cased instruments. A delivery boy from Gristede's with a carton box of groceries on his shoulder was the only other passenger going up. The delivery boy got off at the fifth floor. I told the operator, "Nine, please."

I climbed the fire stairs to Margaret Krusemark's floor, leaving the frenzied rhythm of a tap-dancing class behind. The soprano was still yodeling in the distance as I walked along the deserted hallway to the door wearing the brand of Scorpio.

I unsnapped my attaché case on the threadbare carpet. A bunch of dummy forms and papers in the accordion file on top made it look official, but underneath a false bottom I kept the tools of the trade. A layer of polyurethane foam held everything in place. Nestled there were a set of case-hardened burglar's tools, a contact mike and miniaturized tape recorder, ten-power Lietz binoculars, a Minox camera with a stand for photographing documents, a collection of skeleton keys that cost me $500, nickel-steel handcuffs, and a loaded .38 Special Smith &Wesson Centennial with an Airweight alloy frame.

I got out the contact mike and plugged in the earphone. It was a nice piece of equipment. When I held the mike to the surface of the door, I heard everything that went on inside the apartment. If someone came along, I dropped the instrument in my shirt pocket, and the earphone looked like a hearing aid.

But no one came along. The soprano's warbling echo blended

with distant piano lessons in the empty hallway. Inside the apartment, I heard Margaret Krusemark say: "We were not the best of friends, but I had a great respect for your mother." Epiphany's mumbled reply was inaudible. The astrologer went on: "I saw quite a good deal of her before you were born. She was a woman of power."

Epiphany asked: "How long were you engaged to Johnny?"

"Two-and-a-half years. Cream or lemon, my dear?"

It was obviously teatime again. Epiphany chose lemon and said: "My mother was his mistress throughout your engagement."

"Dear child, don't you think I was aware of that? Johnny and I had no secrets from each other."

"Is that why you broke it off?"

"Our estrangement was strictly for the benefit of the press. We had our own private reasons for giving it out that we had broken up. In truth, we were never closer than during those final months before he went off to war. Our relationship was a peculiar one, I don't deny it. I should hope that you are sufficiently sophisticated not to be swayed by bourgeois convention. Your mother certainly never was."

"What could be more bourgeois than a *ménage à trois?*"

"It was not a *ménage à trois!* What do you think we were involved in, some hideous little sex club?"

"I'm sure I have not the faintest idea what you were involved in. Mama never mentioned you to me at all."

"Why should she? As far as she was concerned, Jonathan was dead and buried. He was all that linked us."

"But he's not dead."

"How do you know that?"

"I know it."

"Has someone been around asking questions about Jonathan? Child, answer me; all of our lives may depend upon it."

"How?"

"Never mind how. There has been someone asking about him, hasn't there?"

"Yes."

"What did he look like?"

"Just a man. Ordinary."

"Was he on the heavy side? Not fat exactly but overweight? Slovenly? By that I mean a sloppy dresser, wrinkled blue suit and shoes that need a shine. Full black mustache, closely cropped hair starting to go grey?"

Epiphany said: "Kind blue eyes. You notice them first."

"Did he say his name was Angel?" Margaret Krusemark's voice betrayed a strident urgency.

"Yes. Harry Angel."

"What did he want?"

"He's looking for Johnny Favorite."

"Why?"

"He didn't tell me why. He's a detective."

"A policeman?"

"No, a private detective. What is this all about?"

There was a faint clinking of china and then Margaret Krusemark said, "I'm not exactly sure. He was here. He didn't say he was a detective; he pretended to be a client. I know this is going to seem very rude, but I must ask you to leave now. I have to go out myself. It's urgent, I'm afraid."

"Do you think we're in danger?" Epiphany's voice broke on that final word.

"I don't know what to think. If Jonathan's come back, anything could happen."

"There was a man killed in Harlem yesterday," Epiphany blurted. "A friend of mine. He knew Mama and Johnny, too. Mr. Angel had been asking him questions."

A chair scraped against the parquet floor. "I've got to go now," Margaret Krusemark said. "Come, I'll get your coat, and we'll ride down together."

There was the sound of approaching footsteps. I pulled the contact mike from the door and yanked the earphone free, shoving the whole business into my coat pocket. With my attaché case tucked under my arm, I sprinted the length of the long hallway like Nashua on the home stretch. I hung onto the banister for balance and took the fire stairs four and five steps at a time.

It was too risky waiting for the elevator on the ninth floor, the odds of getting in the same car with the ladies too high, so I ran down the fire-stairs all the way to the empty lobby. Gasping, I paused long enough to check the indicators over the elevators. The one on the left was going up, its partner coming down. Either way, they would be here in a moment.

I ran out onto the sidewalk and stumbled across Seventh Avenue without paying heed to the traffic. Once on the other side, I loitered near the entrance of the Osborn Apartments, wheezing like an emphysema victim. A governess wheeling a perambulator clucked sympathetically as she passed.

26

EPIPHANY AND THE KRUSEMARK WOMAN came out of the building together and walked arm in arm uptown to 57th Street. I strolled along the other side of the avenue, keeping abreast of them. At the corner, Margaret Krusemark kissed Epiphany fondly on the cheek like a maiden aunt bidding farewell to her favorite niece.

When the light changed, Epiphany started across Seventh Avenue in my direction. Margaret Krusemark waved frantically at passing taxis. A new Checker cab approached with its rooflight on, and I flagged it down, climbing inside before Epiphany had me spotted.

"Where to, mister?" a round-faced driver asked as he dropped the flag.

"Like to make a deuce above what it says on the meter?"

"Whatcha got in mind?"

"Tail job. Pull over for a minute in front of the Russian Tea Room." He did as I asked and turned around in his seat to check me out. I gave him a glimpse of the honorary button pinned to my wallet and said: "See the dame in the tweed coat getting into the hack in front of Carnegie Hall? Don't lose her."

"A piece of cake."

The other cab made an abrupt U-turn on 57th. We pulled the same maneuver without being too obvious and stayed half a block behind as they turned downtown on Seventh. Round-face caught my glance in the rear-view mirror and grinned. "You promised a fin, right, mac?"

"A fin it is, if you don't get spotted."

"I'm too long in this game for that, mac."

We continued down Seventh to Times Square, passing in front of my office before the other cab took a left and started east on 42nd Street. Dodging artfully through traffic, we kept close but not conspicuous, and the driver gunned it a little to beat a red light at Fifth when it looked like we might get left behind.

There was a lot of congestion in the two blocks between Fifth and Grand Central and traffic slowed to a near-standstill. "You shoulda seen it here yesterday," Round-face said by way of explanation. "Saint Paddy's Day parade. It was a mess all afternoon."

Margaret Krusemark's cab turned uptown again at the corner of Lexington Avenue, and I saw it pull to a stop in front of the Chrysler Building. The roof light went on. She was getting out.

"Right here is fine," I said, and Round-face pulled over in front of the Chanin Building. It read a buck and a half on the meter. I gave him seven bills and told him to keep the change. He'd earned it even if he was a gouger.

I started across Lexington Avenue. The other cab was gone, and Margaret Krusemark was nowhere in sight. It didn't matter. I knew where she was heading. Passing through the revolving doors, I checked the directory in the angular marble-and-chromium lobby. Krusemark Maritime, Inc. was on the forty-fifth floor.

It wasn't until I stepped off the elevator that I changed my mind about confronting the Krusemarks. It was too early to tip my hand, not that I held anything worth betting on. The daughter found out I was looking for Johnny Favorite and ran straight to daddy. Whatever she had to tell him was too hot for the office switchboard or she'd have phoned. I was thinking how much I'd give to hear the small talk around the family conference table when I spotted a window washer on his way to work.

He was bald and middle-aged with the retread nose of a retired boxer. He ambled down the gleaming corridor whistling last summer's big hit, "Volare," a half-tone flat. He wore dirty green coveralls, and his safety harness dangled like a pair of unfastened suspenders.

"Got a minute, buddy," I called, and he paused mid-note and regarded me with lips still pursed, as if waiting for a kiss. "Bet you can't tell me whose picture is on a fifty-dollar bill."

"What is this? 'Candid Camera'?"

"Not a chancel I'm just betting you don't know whose face is on a fifty."

"Okay, wise guy; it's Thomas Jefferson."

"You're wrong."

"So? Big deal. What's this all about?"

I got out my wallet and removed the folded half-century note I carry for emergencies and occasional bribes and held it up so he could see the denomination. "I thought maybe you'd like to find out who the lucky president was."

The window washer cleared his throat and blinked. "Are you off your rocker or something?"

"How much do you get paid?" I asked. "Come on, you can tell me. It's not top-secret, is it?"

"Four-fifty an hour, thanks to the union."

"How'd you like to make ten times that? Thanks to me."

"Yeah? And just what do I gotta do for that much dough?"

"Rent me your outfit for an hour and take a walk. Go downstairs and buy yourself a beer."

He rubbed the top of his head although it needed no further polishing. "You are some kinda nut, aintcha?" There was a hint of real admiration in his voice.

"What difference does it make? All I want is to rent your rig, no questions asked. You make half a yard for sitting on your duff for an hour. How can you beat that?"

"Okay. You got a deal, buddy. Long as you're giving it away, I'm a guy who'll take it."

"Smart move."

The window washer jerked his head for me to follow and led me back down the corridor to a narrow door close by the fire exit. It was a custodial closet. "Leave all my gear in here when you're done with it," he said, unstrapping his safety harness and peeling off the dirty coveralls.

I hung my overcoat and suit jacket on top of a mop handle and pulled on the coveralls. They were stiff and smelled faintly of ammonia, like pajamas after an orgy.

"Better take off your tie," the window washer cautioned. "Unless you wanna look like you're running for office in the local."

I stuffed the necktie into my coat pocket and had the window washer show me how to use the safety harness. It seemed quite simple. "You ain't planning on going outside, are you?" he asked.

"You kidding? I just want to play a gag on a lady friend. She's a receptionist on this floor."

"Fine with me," the window washer said. "Just leave the stuff in the closet."

I tucked the folded fifty into his shirt pocket. "You and Ulysses Simpson Grant go have a party." His expression was blank as a poleaxed beef. I told him to look at the picture on the bill. He sauntered off whistling.

I removed my .38 before stashing the attaché case under the concrete sink. The Smith & Wesson Centennial is a handy piece. Its two-inch barrel fits conveniently in a pocket and, being hammerless, there's nothing to hang up in the fabric when you make your play. Once I had to cut loose with the gun still in my jacket pocket. Rough on my wardrobe, but a lot better than being fitted for one of those backless funeral home suits.

I slipped the little five-shot into my coveralls and transferred the contact mike to the other pocket. Bucket and brush in hand, I strolled down the corridor toward the impressive bronze and glass entrance of Krusemark Maritime, Inc.

27

THE RECEPTIONIST LOOKED RIGHT THROUGH me as I crossed the carpeted lobby between glass-cased tanker models and clipper ship prints. I winked at her, and she spun away on her swivel chair. The frosted doors to the inner sanctum had bronze fouled anchors mounted in place of handles, and I pushed through humming a sea chanty under my breath. "Yo ho, blow the man down . . . "

Beyond was a long hallway with offices opening off either side. I ambled along, swinging my bucket and reading the names on the doors. They were all the wrong names. At the end of the hall was a large room where a pair of Teletypes clattered like robot secretaries. A wooden ship wheel stood against one wall, and more clipper ships hung on the others. There were several comfortable chairs, a glass-topped table spread with magazines, and a pert blonde slicing envelopes with a letter opener behind an L-shaped desk. Off to one side was a polished mahogany door. At eye level, raised bronze letters

Said: ETHAN KRUSEMARK.

The blonde glanced up and smiled, spearing a letter like a lady D'Artagnan. The stack of mail beside her was a foot high. My hopes of being alone with the contact mike went right out the window, an image I would soon regret.

The blonde ignored me, busy with her simple task. Clipping

the bucket to my belt harness, I pulled open a window and closed my eyes. My teeth were chattering, but it wasn't from the rush of cold air.

"Hey! Please hurry up," the blonde called. "My papers are blowing all over the place."

Holding tight, I ducked under the bottom rail and sat backward on the sill, my legs still inside the security of the office. I reached up and hooked one strap of the safety harness to the outside casing. There was only the thickness of glass separating me from the blonde inside, but she might as well have been a million miles away. I switched hands and clipped in the other strap.

Standing up took everything I had in me. I tried remembering wartime buddies in the Airborne who walked away from hundreds of jumps without a scratch, but it wasn't any help. The thought of parachutes only made it worse.

There was barely room for my toes on the narrow ledge. I pushed down the window, and the comforting sound of the Teletypes inside was lost in the gusty wind. I told myself not to look down. That was the first place I looked.

The shadowed canyon of 42nd Street yawned beneath me, pedestrians and traffic reduced to ant specks and crawling metallic beetles. I looked east to the river, past the vertical brown-and-white stripes of the Daily News Building and the glistening, green slab of the United Nations Secretariat. A toylike tugboat steamed along, hauling a string of barges in its silver wake.

The strong, icy wind stung my face and hands and tore at my clothing, making the wide cuffs on my coveralls snap like battle flags. It wanted to tear me from the face of the building and send me sailing out over the rooftops, past the circling pigeons and billowing smokestacks. My legs trembled with cold and fear. If the wind didn't take me, I would soon vibrate free from my white-knuckled perch. Inside, the blonde sliced open the mail without a care in the world. As far as she was concerned, I was already gone.

Suddenly, it seemed very funny: Harry Angel, the Human Fly. I remembered a circus ringmaster's stentorian hoopla, " . . . where *angels* fear to tread," and laughed out loud. Easing back against the safety harness straps, I found to my joy that they supported me. It wasn't so bad. Window washers did it all day long.

I felt like a mountain climber on an incredible first ascent. Several floors above, radiator-cap gargoyles jutted from the corners of the skyscraper, and beyond them, the building's stainless steel spire tapered into the sunlight, shining like the ice-clad summit of an unconquered peak.

It was time to make my move. I unclipped the right-hand harness strap, bringing it over and attaching it to the same fastening which held the other. Then, inching along the sill, I unclipped the inner strap and reached across the void to the casing on the next window over. I blindly felt the brickwork until I found the fastener and clipped my strap to it.

Secured to both windows, I stepped across with my left foot. Unclip, clip, step over with the right foot: done. The entire traverse took no more than seconds, but it might have been a decade.

I looked into the office of Ethan Krusemark as I fastened the left-hand safety strap to the opposite casing of his window. It was a large corner room with two more windows on this wall and another three on the Lexington Avenue side. His desk was a vast, oval slab of Pentelic marble, completely bare except for an executive six-button telephone and a patinaed bronze statuette of Neptune waving his trident above the waves. A recessed bar near the door glittered with crystal. French impressionists hung on the walls. No clipper ships for the boss.

Krusemark and his daughter sat on a long beige couch set against the far wall. A pair of brandy snifters glistened in front of them on a low marble table. Krusemark looked much like his portrait: a ruddy-faced, aging pirate crowned with a mass of well-combed silver hair. To my way of thinking, the resemblance was more Daddy Warbucks than Clark Gable.

Margaret Krusemark had abandoned her solemn black outfit in favor of a peasant blouse and embroidered dirndl, but she still wore the upside-down gold pentacle. Occasionally, one of them looked straight across the room at me. I brushed soapy water on the glass in front of my face.

I got the contact mike out of my coveralls and plugged in the earphone. Wrapping the instrument in a large rag, I pressed it to the glass and pretended to wipe the window. Their voices sounded so clear and sharp, I could easily have been sitting next to them on the couch.

Krusemark was speaking: " . . . and he knew the date of Jonathan's birth?"

Margaret toyed nervously with the golden star. "He had it exactly," she said.

"It would be no trouble to look up. You're sure he's a detective?"

"Evangeline Proudfoot's daughter said he was. He knows enough about Jonathan to have gotten to her asking questions."

"What about the doctor in Poughkeepsie?"

"He's dead. Suicide. I called the clinic. It happened earlier this week."

"Then we'll never know if the detective spoke with him or not."

"I don't like it, Father. Not after all these years. Angel knows too much already."

"Angel?"

"The detective. Please pay attention to what I'm telling you."

"I'm digesting it all, Meg. Just give me time." Krusemark sipped his brandy.

"Why not get rid of Angel?"

"What good would it do? This town is crawling with two-bit private eyes. It's not Angel we need to worry about, but the man that hired him."

Margaret Krusemark gripped her father's hand in both of hers. "Angel will be back. For the horoscope."

"Draw it up for him."

"I already have. It was so much like Jonathan's, only the birthplace differed. I could have done it from memory."

"Good." Krusemark drained his brandy. "If he's any good at all, he'll have found out you have no sister by the time he comes back for the chart. Play him along. You're a clever girl. If you can't trick the information out of him, slip a drop of something in his tea. There are many ways to make a man talk. We must know the name of his client. We can't let Angel die until we find out who he's working for." Krusemark stood up. "I have several important meetings coming up this afternoon, Meg, so unless there's something else . . . "

"No, there's nothing else." Margaret Krusemark got to her feet and smoothed her skirt.

"Fine." He draped an arm around her shoulder. "Call me as soon as you hear from the detective. I picked up the art of persuasion in the Orient. We'll see if I've lost my touch."

"Thank you, Father."

"Come, I'll walk you out. What are your plans for the rest of the day?"

"Oh, I don't know. I thought I might go over to Saks and do some shopping. After that—" The rest of it was lost as the heavy mahogany door closed behind them.

I stuffed the rag-wrapped contact mike into my coveralls and tried the window. It was not latched and opened with a little effort. I undipped one side of the safety harness and swung my trembling legs inside. A moment later, I had the other strap undipped and was standing in the relative safety of Krusemark's office. The risk had paid off; playing window washer was a picnic compared with finding out about Krusemark's Oriental artistry first-hand.

I shut the window and glanced around. As much as I wanted

to do some snooping, I knew there wasn't time. Margaret Krusemark's brandy snifter sat barely touched on the marble table. No drop of something slipped in that. I breathed its fruity aroma and took a sip. The cognac slid like velvet fire across my tongue. I downed it in three quick swallows. It was old and expensive and deserved much better treatment, but I was in a hurry.

28

THE BLONDE SECRETARY MERELY GLANCED at me when I slammed the polished mahogany door. Perhaps she was accustomed to window washers having the run of her boss's office. I bumped into Ethan Krusemark himself striding back down the long corridor with his chest thrust forward like he had a row of invisible medals pinned to his grey flannel suit. He grunted in passing. I suppose he expected me to tug my forelock. Instead, I said, "Fuck you!" but it rolled off him like spit off a duck.

On my way out, I blew a loud kiss at the receptionist with the poker up her ass. The face she made suggested a mouthful of caterpillar guts, but two salesmen cooling their heels in matching Barcelona chairs thought it was real cute.

I did a quick-change number in the broom closet that would have made Superman envious. There wasn't time to repack the attaché case, so I stuffed my Smith & Wesson and the contact mike in my overcoat pockets and left the coveralls and safety harness crammed into the dented bucket. In the elevator, I remembered my necktie and made a clumsy, blind job of twisting a knot around my shirt collar.

There was no sign of Margaret Krusemark out on the street. She had mentioned going to Saks, and I figured she caught a cab. Deciding to give her time to change her mind, I cut across Lexington to Grand Central and went in through a side entrance.

I detoured down the ramp to the Oyster Bar and ordered a dozen bluepoints on the half-shell. They went fast. I sipped the juice from the empty shells and ordered another half-dozen, taking my time with them. Twenty minutes later I pushed my plate back and headed for a pay phone. I dialed Margaret Krusemark's number and let it ring ten times before hanging up. She was safe at Saks. Maybe she'd hit Bonwit's and Bergdorf's before heading home.

The shuttle train hauled my mollusk-stuffed carcass over to Times Square where I caught an uptown BMT local to 57th Street. I called Margaret Krusemark's apartment from the phone booth on the corner and again got no answer. Walking past the entrance to 881 Seventh, I spotted three people waiting for the elevator and continued on to the corner of 56th. I lit a cigarette and started back uptown. This time the lobby was empty. I went straight to the fire stairs. There was no percentage in being recognized by elevator operators.

Climbing eleven flights is all right if you're in training for the marathon, but no fun at all with eighteen oysters tumbling around inside. I took it easy, resting every couple of floors, surrounded by the cacophonous blend of a dozen disparate music lessons.

When I got to Margaret Krusemark's door I was breathing hard and my heart hammered like a metronome in presto. The hallway was deserted. I opened my attaché case and pulled on the rubber surgeon's gloves. The lock was a standard make. I rang the doorbell several times before sorting through my ring of expensive skeleton keys for the appropriate series.

The third key I tried did the trick. I picked up the attaché case, stepped inside, and closed the door behind me. The smell of ether was overpowering. It hung in the air, volatile and aromatic, bringing back memories of the ward. I got my .38 out of my overcoat and edged along the wall of the shadowed foyer. It didn't take a Sherlock to know something was very wrong.

Margaret Krusemark hadn't gone shopping after all. She was lying on her back in the sunlit living room, spread out across the low coffee table under all those potted palms. The couch we'd had tea on was pushed over against the wall so that she was all alone in the center of the rug like a figure on an altar.

Her peasant blouse was torn open, and her tiny breasts were pale and not at all unpleasant to look at except for the ragged incision that split her chest from a point below the diaphragm to midway up her sternum. The wound brimmed with blood and red rivulets ran down across her ribs and puddled on the tabletop. At least her eyes were closed; there was something to be said for that.

I put my gun away, and touched my fingertips to the side of her throat. Through the thin latex I could feel she was still warm. Her features were composed, almost as if she were only sleeping, and something very much like a smile lingered on her lips. At the far end of the room, a mantel clock chimed the hour. It was 5:00 P.M.

I found the murder weapon under the coffee table. An Aztec sacrificial knife from Margaret Krusemark's own collection, the bright obsidian blade dulled with drying blood. I didn't touch it. There was no sign of any struggle. The couch had been carefully moved. It was easy to reconstruct the crime.

Margaret Krusemark had changed her mind about shopping. She'd come straight home instead, and the murderer was waiting for her inside the apartment. He, or she, surprised her from behind and clamped an ether-soaked pad over her nose and mouth. She was unconscious before she had time to put up a fight.

A wrinkled prayer rug near the entrance showed where she'd been dragged into the living room. Carefully, almost lovingly, the killer had lifted her onto the table and moved the furniture back so there'd be lots of space to work in.

I had a long look around. Nothing seemed to be missing. Margaret Krusemark's collection of occult doodads appeared intact. Only the obsidian dagger was out of place, and I knew where to find that. No drawers were opened; no closets rifled. There was no attempt to simulate a burglary.

Over by the tall window, between a philodendron and a delphinium, I made one small discovery. Resting in the basin of a tall bronze Hellenic tripod was a glistening lump of blood-soaked muscle about the size of a misshapen tennis ball. It looked like something the dog might have dragged in, and I stared at it a long time before I knew what it was. Valentine's Day would no longer seem the same. It was Margaret Krusemark's heart.

Such a simple thing, the human heart. It goes on pumping day by day, year after year, until someone comes along and rips it out, and it ends up looking like so much dog food. I turned away from the Witch of Wellesley's ticker, feeling all eighteen oysters stampeding to get out.

After a bit of poking around, I found an ether-saturated rag in a woven wicker wastebasket in the foyer. I left it there for the homicide boys to play with. Let them take it downtown with the dead meat and run it through the lab. There'd be reports to file in triplicate. That was their job, not mine.

There was little of interest in the kitchen. It was just another kitchen: cookbooks, pots and pans, a spice rack, an icebox full of leftovers. A shopping bag from Bloomingdale's held the trash, but it was just trash: coffee grounds and chicken bones.

The bedroom looked more promising. The bed was unmade, rumpled sheets stained with sex. The witch was not without her warlocks. In a small adjoining bathroom I found the plastic case to her diaphragm. It was empty. If she got laid this morning, she must still be wearing it. The boys from downtown would find that, too.

Margaret Krusemark's medicine cabinet overflowed onto tall shelves framing either side of the mirror above the sink. Aspirin, tooth powder, milk of magnesia, and small vials of prescription drugs, competed for space with jars of foul-smelling powders marked by obscure alchemical symbols. A variety of aromatic herbs was sealed in matching metal canisters. Mint was the only one I recognized by smell.

A yellow skull grinned up at me from the top of a Kleenex box. There was a mortar and pestle on the counter next to the Tampax. A double-edged dagger, a copy of *Vogue,* a hairbrush, and four fat, black candles crowded the lid of the toilet tank.

Behind a jar of face cream I found a severed human hand. Dark and shriveled, it lay there like a discarded glove. When I picked it up it weighed so little I nearly dropped it. I didn't find any eye of newt but not because I didn't try.

There was a small alcove off the bedroom where she did her work. A filing cabinet crammed with customers' horoscopes meant nothing to me. I looked under the TV for Favorite and the *"L's"* for Liebling without success. There was a small row of reference texts and a globe. The books were propped against a sealed alabaster casket about the size of a cigar box. Carved on the lid was a three-headed snake.

I thumbed through the books hoping for some hidden scrap, but found nothing. Searching among the disordered papers on the desktop, a small printed card edged in black caught my attention. An inverted five-pointed star inscribed within a circle was printed at the top. Superimposed within the pentagram was the head of a horned goat. Below the talisman it said MISSA NIGER in ornate caps. The text was also in Latin. At the bottom were the numerals: III. XXII. MCMLIX. It was a date. Palm Sunday, four days away. There was a matching envelope addressed to Margaret Krusemark. I slipped the card back inside and stuck it in my attaché case.

Most of the other papers on the desk were sidereal calculations and horoscopes in progress. I glanced at them without interest and found one with my name written on the top. Wouldn't Lieutenant Sterne like to get his hands on that? I should have set fire to it, or flushed it down the toilet, but instead, like a dummy, I tucked it in my attaché case.

Finding the horoscope made me think to check Margaret

Krusemark's desk calendar. There I was on Monday the 16th: "H. Angel, 1:30 P.M." I ripped the page free and put it with the other stuff in my case. Today's page on the desk calendar showed an appointment for five-thirty. My watch was a few minutes fast, but twenty after was close enough.

On the way out, I left the apartment door slightly ajar. Someone else could find the body and call the police. I wanted no part of this mess. Fat chance! I was in it up to my neck.

29

THERE WAS NO RUSH GOING down the fire stairs. I'd had enough exercise for one day. When I hit the lobby I didn't make for the street, but cut through the narrow passage leading to the Carnegie Tavern. I always buy myself a drink after finding a body. It's an old family custom.

The bar was jammed with the Happy Hour crowd. I elbowed through the press and ordered a double Manhattan on the rocks. When it came, I took a long swallow and struggled back with it, stepping on toes all the way to the pay phone.

I dialed Epiphany Proudfoot's number and finished my drink while listening to the endless ringing. There was something ominous about not getting any answer. I hung up, thinking of Margaret Krusemark split like a Christmas goose eleven flights above. Hers was the last number that didn't answer. I left my empty glass on the shelf under the phone and shouldered through to the street.

A cab was letting someone out halfway down the block in front of the mosquelike City Center Theatre. I yelled and it waited with the door open, although I had to run to beat a determined woman who came charging across the street, brandishing a furled umbrella.

The cabby was a Negro who didn't bat an eyelash when I told him to take me to 123rd and Lenox. He probably figured it was my funeral and was happy to have the final tip. We drove uptown without any philosophy. A transistor radio on the front seat was loudly tuned to a scat-talking deejay on WOV: "the power-tower station, the nation's sensation . . ."

He dropped me in front of Proudfoot Pharmaceuticals twenty minutes later and sped off in a cadenza of rhythm-and-blues. The shop remained closed for business, the long green shade hanging behind the glass door like a flag lowered in defeat. I knocked and rattled the knob without success.

Epiphany had mentioned an apartment above the store, so I walked to the building's entrance further down Lenox and checked the names on the mailboxes in the lobby. Third from the left: PROUDFOOT, 2-D. The hall door was unlatched, and I went inside.

The narrow, tiled hallway smelled of urine and boiling pigs' feet. I climbed the age-scalloped marblesteps to the second floor and heard a toilet flush somewhere above. Apartment 2-D was at the far end of the landing. I rang the bell as a precaution, but there was no answer.

The lock was no problem. I had half a dozen keys to fit it. I pulled on my latex gloves and opened the door, sniffing instinctively for ether. The large, corner living room had windows facing both Lenox Avenue and 123rd Street. It was decorated with functional lay-away-plan furniture and African wood carvings.

The bed was carefully made in the bedroom. A pair of grimacing masks flanked a bird's-eye maple vanity table. I went through the dresser drawers and the closet without finding anything other than clothing and personal effects. Several silver-framed photographs stood on a bedside table, all of the same haughty, fine-featured woman. There was something of Epiphany in the lyric curve of her mouth, but the nose was flatter, and the eyes were wild and wide like a person possessed. I was looking at Evangeline Proudfoot.

She trained her daughter to be neat. The kitchen was clean and orderly, no dishes in the sink, or crumbs on the table. Fresh food in the refrigerator was the only sign of recent habitation.

It was dark as a cave in the last room. The light switch didn't work, so I used my penlight. I didn't want to trip over any bodies and checked the floor first. Once upon a time the room must have been an extra bedroom, but that was long ago. The window glass had been painted the same deep, midnight blue as the walls and ceiling. Over this swirled a neon rainbow of graffiti. Leaves and flowers entwined along one wall. Crudely drawn fish and mermaids cavorted across another. The ceiling was a panoply of stars and crescent moons.

The room was a voodoo temple. A brickwork altar stood against the far wall. Upon it, rows of covered earthenware jugs were ranked in tiers, like a stall in an outdoor market. Dozens of candle stubs rested in saucers beneath color lithographs of the Catholic saints pinned to the wall. A rusted sabre was stuck into the floorboards in front of the altar. Hanging to one side was a wooden crutch. An elaborate wrought-iron cross stood between the jugs supporting a battered silk top hat.

I saw several gourd rattles and a pair of iron clappers on a shelf. An assortment of colored bottles and jars clustered next to them. A childlike painting of a tramp steamer filled most of the wall above the altar.

I thought of Epiphany in her white dress, chanting and moaning, while drums throbbed and the gourds whispered like snakes moving in dry grass. I remembered the deft turn of her wrist and a bright fountaining of rooster blood in the night. On my way out of the humfo, I bumped my head on a pair of decorated wood-and-skin conga drums hanging from the ceiling.

I went through the hall closet without a score but got lucky in the kitchen and found a flight of narrow stairs leading to the store below. I went over the back room, searching among the inventory of dried roots, leaves, and powders without knowing what to look for.

The front was dim and empty. There was a pile of unopened mail on the glass countertop. I checked it with my flash: a phone bill, several letters from herbal supply houses, a printed message from Congressman Adam Clayton Powell, and an appeal from the March of Dimes. On the bottom was a cardboard poster. My heart turned a sudden cartwheel. The face on the poster was Louis Cyphre! He wore a white turban. His skin looked burnished by the desert wind. Across the top of the poster was printed: EL ÇIFR, MASTER OF THE UNKNOWN. The bottom bore this message: "The Illustrious and All-knowing el Çifr will address the congregation at the New Temple of Hope, 139 West 144th St., Saturday, March 21, 1959. 8:30 P.M. The public is cordially invited to attend, ADMISSION: FREE."

I slipped the poster inside my attaché case. Who can resist a free show?

30

AFTER LOCKING EPIPHANY PROUDFOOT'S APARTMENT, I walked up to 125th Street and caught a cab outside the Palm Cafe. The ride downtown on the West Side Highway gave me lots of time to think. I stared out at the Hudson, darker than the night sky, the brightly lighted stacks of luxury liners like floating carnivals between the pier sheds.

A carnival of death. Step right up and see the voodoo death ceremony! Hurry, hurry, hurry; don't miss the Aztec sacrifice! First time ever! The case was a sideshow. Witches and fortune-tellers; a client who dressed in blackface like the Sheik of Araby. I was the rube on this macabre midway, dazzled by the lights and sleight of hand. The shadow-play events screened manipulations I could barely discern.

I needed a bar close to home. The Silver Rail on 23rd and Seventh was within crawling distance. If I left on my hands and knees at closing time, it's' something I don't remember. How I found my bed at the Chelsea remains a mystery. Only the dreams seemed real.

I dreamt I was awakened from a deep sleep by the sounds of shouting on the street. I went to the window and parted the curtain. A mob seethed from curb to curb, howling and incoherent like a single, sinuous beast. Through this throng inched a two-wheeled cart, hauled by an ancient sway-backed nag. In the cart were a man and woman. I got my binoculars from the attaché case and had a closer look. The woman was Margaret Krusemark. The man was me.

In a moment of dream magic, I was suddenly in the cart, gripping the rough wooden rail while a faceless mob surged all around like an angry sea. Margaret Krusemark smiled seductively from the other side of the lurching cart. We were so close it was almost an embrace. Was she a witch on her way to burning? Was I the executioner?

The cart rolled on. Over the heads of the crowd I saw the guillotine's unmistakable silhouette rising above the steps of the McBurney Y.M.C.A. The Reign of Terror. Unjustly condemned! The cart jogged to a stop at the foot of the scaffold. Rude hands reached up and hauled Margaret Krusemark from her precarious perch. The crowd hushed, and she was permitted to mount the steps unassisted.

Among the front ranks of the spectators, one revolutionary caught my eye. He was dressed in black and carried a pike. It was Louis Cyphre. His Liberty cap hung at a rakish angle, crowned by a bold tri-colored badge. When he saw me, he waved his pike and gave a mock bow.

I missed the spectacle on the scaffold. Drums rolled, the blade crashed, and when I looked up, the executioner stood with his back to me, showing Margaret Krusemark's head to an adoring crowd. I heard my name called and stepped from the cart to make room for a coffin. Louis Cyphre smiled. He was having a swell time.

The scaffolding was slick with blood. I nearly slipped as I turned to face the taunting crowd. A soldier caught my arm and directed me almost gently toward the table. "You must lie down, my son," the priest said.

I knelt for a final prayer. The executioner stood beside me. A gust of wind lifted the black flap of his hood. I recognized the pomaded hair and mocking smile. The executioner was Johnny Favorite!

I woke up screaming louder than the ringing telephone. I lunged for the receiver like a drowning man after a life preserver.

"Hello . . . hello? Is this Angel? Harry Angel?" It was Herman Winesap, my favorite attorney.

"Angel speaking." My tongue felt several sizes too large for my mouth.

"Good God, man, where've you been? I've been calling your office for hours."

"I've been sleeping."

"Sleeping? It's practically eleven o'clock."

"I was working late," I said. "Detectives don't keep the same hours as Wall Street lawyers."

If his feathers were ruffled, he was sharp enough not to show it. "I appreciate that. You must do the job as you see fit."

"What's so important you couldn't leave a message?"

"You mentioned yesterday wanting to get together with Mr. Cyphre?"

"That's right."

"Well, he suggested lunch today."

"Same place as before?"

"No. Mr. Cyphre thought you might enjoy dining at Le Voisin. It's at 575 Park."

"What time?"

"One o'clock. You can still make it if you don't fall back to sleep."

"I'll be there."

Winesap hung up without his customary elaborate farewell. I dragged my aching self out of bed and limped to the shower. Twenty minutes of hot water and three cups of black coffee had me feeling almost human.

Wearing a pressed brown worsted suit, a white shirt crisp

from the laundry, and an unstained necktie, I was ready for the snootiest French restaurant. I drove uptown on Park, through the old railway tunnel under Murray Hill and over the auto viaduct that swept around either side of Grand Central like a divided mountain highway. Four blocks further, the New York Central Building's cupola top punctuated Park Avenue like a corbeled-Gothic exclamation point. The ramp inside spilled traffic onto upper Park, an avenue metamorphosing from a uniform canyon of brick and masonry to an antiseptic cordillera of glass-walled towers.

I found a parking spot near the Christian Science Church on the corner of 63rd and Park and walked east across the avenue. Le Voisin's awning boasted a Park Avenue address, but the entrance was on 63rd Street. I went in and checked my coat and attaché case. Everything about the place suggested the excellence of its customers' Dun & Bradstreet ratings.

The headwaiter greeted me with diplomatic reserve. I gave him Louis Cyphre's name, and he led me past the pastry tray to a table on the banquette. Cyphre stood up when he saw us coming. He was wearing grey flannel slacks, a navy blue yachting blazer, and a red-and-green silk foulard ascot. The embroidered insignia of the Racquet and Tennis Club adorned his breast pocket. Highlighting his lapel was a small gold star. It was upside down.

"Good to see you again, Angel," he said, gripping my hand.

We sat down and ordered drinks. I had a bottle of imported beer in deference to my hangover; Cyphre asked for Campari and soda. We made small talk while waiting. Cyphre told me of his plans for a trip abroad during Holy Week: Paris, Rome, the Vatican. He called Easter Sunday in Saint Peter's a truly splendid ceremony. An audience with the Pope was scheduled. I stared at him without expression and pictured his patrician face crowned by a turban. El Çifr, Master of the Unknown, meets his Holiness, the Supreme Pontiff.

We ordered lunch when the drinks arrived. Cyphre spoke to the waiter in French, and I couldn't follow what was said. I know enough of the language to stumble through a menu and ordered *tournedos Rossini* and an endive salad.

As soon as we were alone, Cyphre said: "And now, Mr. Angel, a full report to date, if you please." He smiled and sipped his ruby-red drink.

"There's a lot to tell. It's been a long week, and it's not over yet. Dr. Fowler is dead. Officially, it's suicide, but I wouldn't place any bets on it."

"Why not? The man was exposed, his career in jeopardy."

"There have been two other deaths, both murders, and both connected to this case."

"I take it that you haven't found Jonathan?"

"Not yet. I've found out a lot about him, none of it very endearing."

Cyphre twirled his swizzle-stick in his highball glass. "Do you think he's still alive?"

"So it would seem. I went up to Harlem Monday night to interview an old jazz piano player named Edison Sweet. I'd seen a photo taken of him with Favorite years ago, and it got me interested. I did some snooping and found that Sweet was a member of an uptown voodoo cult. This was the real thing: tom-toms, blood sacrifice, the whole bit. Back in the forties, Johnny Favorite was part of it, too. He was shacked up with a voodoo priestess named Evangeline Proudfoot and was heavy into the mumbo-jumbo. I learned all this from Sweet. The next day he was murdered. It was supposed to look like a voodoo killing, but whoever did it wasn't up on his vévé.

"Vévé?" Cyphre raised an eyebrow.

"Mystical voodoo symbols. They were smeared all over the walls in blood. An expert spotted them as phony. It was a red herring."

"You mentioned a second killing."

"I'll get to that; it was my other lead. I was curious about Favorite's society girlfriend and did some digging in that direction. It took me a while to find her even though she was under my nose the whole time. She was an astrologer named Margaret Krusemark."

Cyphre leaned forward like an eager back-fence gossip. "The shipbuilder's daughter?"

"The one and only."

"Tell me what happened."

"Well, I'm pretty sure she and her father were the pair who took Favorite out of the clinic in Poughkeepsie. I went to her pretending to be a client wanting a horoscope, and she managed to send me on a wild-goose chase for a time. When I finally got things straightened out, I went back to her apartment to see what I could find, and—"

"You broke in?"

"I used a twirl."

"A what?"

"A skeleton key."

"I see," Cyphre said. "Please continue."

"Okay. I let myself into her apartment, planning on going over the place with a fine-tooth comb, only it didn't work out that way. She was in the living room, dead as a side of beef. Someone cut her heart out. I found that, too."

"How revolting." Cyphre wiped his lips with his napkin. "There was no mention of any heart in the papers today."

"The homicide boys like to leave out certain details so they have some way to judge all the crackpot confessions that come in."

"Did you call the police? I saw no mention of you in what I read."

"No one knows I was there. I skipped. It wasn't the smartest thing to do, but the law already has me connected to the Sweet killing, and I didn't want to set them up with a double-header."

Cyphre frowned. "How exactly are you connected to the Sweet killing?"

"I gave him my business card. The cops found it at his place."

Cyphre didn't look happy. "And the Krusemark woman? Did you give her a card as well?"

"No. I'm clean on that score. I found my name on her desk calendar and a horoscope she'd drawn up, but I took them with me."

"Where are they now?"

"They're in a safe place. Don't worry."

"Why not destroy them?"

"That was my first thought. But the horoscope may lead somewhere. When Margaret Krusemark asked for my birthdate, I gave her Favorite's."

At this point the waiter arrived with our order. He uncovered the plates with a magician's flourish, and a wine steward materialized bearing a bottle of Bordeaux. Cyphre went through the ritual of cork sniffing and mulling a sample swallow before nodding his approval. Two glasses were poured, and the waiters withdrew as silently as pickpockets frisking a crowd.

"Château Margaux forty-seven," Cyphre said. "Excellent year for the Haut-Médoc. I took the liberty of ordering something I thought would go well with both our meals."

"Thanks," I said. "I'm not much up on wine."

"You'll like this." He lifted his glass. "To your continuing success. I trust you were able to keep my name out of things when the police contacted you?"

"When they tried to strong-arm me, I gave them Winesap's name and said I was working for him. That way I was entitled to the same right to silence as a lawyer."

"Quick thinking, Mr. Angel. And what are your conclusions?"

"Conclusions? I have no conclusions."

"Do you think Jonathan killed all those people?"

"Not a chance."

"Why not?" Cyphre speared a forkful of *pâté.* "Because the

whole deal seems made-to-order. I think Favorite is being set up as a fall guy."

"Interesting hypothesis."

I sipped a swallow of wine and met his glacial stare. "Trouble with it is, I don't know why. The answers are buried in the past."

"Uncover them. Spadework, man."

"My job would be a whole lot easier, Mr. Cyphre, if you'd stop holding out on me."

"I beg your pardon?"

"You haven't been much help at all. Everything I know about Johnny Favorite I had to find out on my own. You never gave me a clue. Yet you were mixed up with him. Had a deal going. You and this simple orphan kid who cuts pigeons apart and carries a skull in his suitcase. There's a lot you won't tumble to."

Cyphre crossed his silverware on his plate. "When I first met Jonathan he was working as a busboy. If there were skulls in his suitcase, I knew nothing of them. I'll be more than happy to tell you anything you care to ask."

"Okay. Why are you wearing an upside-down star?"

"This?" Cyphre glanced at his lapel. "Why, you're right, it's on crooked." He turned it carefully upright in his buttonhole. "It's the insignia of the Sons of the Republic. One of those zealous patriotic organizations. They made me an honorary member for assisting with a fund drive. It never hurts to appear patriotic." Cyphre leaned forward, his smile whiter than a toothpaste ad. "In France, I always wear the tricolor."

I stared at his dazzling smile, and he winked at me. An icy nightmare terror ran through my body like an electric current. I felt frozen, unable to move, mesmerized by Cyphre's immaculate smile. It was the smile at the foot of the scaffold. *In France, I always wear the tricolor.*

"Are you all right, Mr. Angel? You look a bit pale."

He was toying with me, grinning like the Cheshire cat. I folded my hands in my lap so he wouldn't see their shaking. "Something I swallowed," I said. "Got stuck in my throat."

"You must be more careful. A thing like that can choke a man."

"I'm fine. No need to worry. Nothing's going to stop me from getting to the truth."

Cyphre pushed his plate away, the elaborate *pâté* half-eaten. "The truth, Mr. Angel, is an elusive quarry."

31

WE SKIPPED DESSERT IN FAVOR of brandy and cigars. Cyphre's panatelas were as good as they smelled. No more was said about the case. I held up my end of the conversation as best I could, the feeling of dread gone hard in my gut like a cyst. Had I imagined that mocking wink? Mind reading is the world's oldest con, but knowing it didn't keep my fingers from trembling.

We left the restaurant together. A silver-grey Rolls waited at the curb. The uniformed chauffeur opened the rear door for Louis Cyphre. "We'll be in touch," he said, gripping my hand before climbing into the spacious car. The interior gleamed with polished wood and leather like an exclusive men's club. I stood on the sidewalk and watched them glide off around the corner.

The Chevy seemed a touch shabby as I turned on the ignition and started back downtown. It smelled like the interior of a 42nd Street movie house: stale tobacco and forgotten memories. I drove down Fifth, following the green stripe left over from the parade two days ago. On 45th Street I turned west. There was a parking spot mid-block between Sixth and Seventh, and I grabbed it.

In the outer room of my office, I found Epiphany Proudfoot asleep on the tan Naugahyde couch. She was wearing a plum-colored wool suit over a wide-collared grey satin blouse. Her dark blue coat was folded under her head as a pillow. An expensive leather overnight bag rested on the floor. Her body curved in a graceful Z-shape, legs folded beneath her and her arms cradling the blue coat. She looked as lovely as the figurehead of a sailing ship.

I gently touched her shoulder and her eyelashes fluttered.

"Epiphany?"

Her eyes opened wide, glowing like polished amber. She lifted her head. "What time is it?" she asked.

"Almost three."

"That late? I was so tired."

"How long have you been waiting here?"

"Since ten. You don't keep very regular hours."

"I had a meeting with my client. Where were you yesterday afternoon? I came to the store, but no one was there."

She sat up, easing her feet to the floor. "I was at a friend's. I've been afraid to stay at home."

"Why?"

Epiphany looked at me as if I was a stupid child. "Why do you think?" she said. "First Toots got killed. Then I heard on the news that the woman who was engaged to Johnny Favorite was murdered. For all I know, I'm next."

"Why do you call her the 'woman who was engaged to Johnny Favorite'? Don't you know her name?"

"Why should I know her name?"

"Don't get cute with me, Epiphany. I followed you to Margaret Krusemark's apartment when you left here yesterday. I overheard the two of you talking. You're playing me for a sap."

Her nostrils flared and her eyes caught the light and flashed like gemstones. "I'm trying to save my life!"'

"Playing both ends against the middle isn't the smartest way to go about it. What exactly did you have cooked up with Margaret Krusemark?"

"Nothing. Until yesterday I didn't even know who she was."

"You can do better than that, Epiphany."

"How? By making it up?" Epiphany came around the low table. "After I phoned you yesterday, I got a call from this woman, Margaret Krusemark. She told me she was a friend of my mother's from long ago. She wanted to come up and see me, but I said I had to go downtown, so she invited me to drop by her place when I had the time. There was no mention of Johnny Favorite until I got there, and that's the truth."

"All right," I said, "I'll take your word for it. There's no one to contradict you. Where did you spend last night?"

"The Plaza. I figured some swank hotel'd be the last place anyone would think to look for a black girl from Harlem."

"Still staying there?"

Epiphany shook her head. "Can't afford it. Besides, I didn't really feel safe. I couldn't sleep a wink."

"You must feel safe here," I said. "You were out like a light when I came in."

She reached up a delicate hand and smoothed the lapel of my overcoat. "I feel a whole lot safer now that you've come."

"Me big brave detective?"

"Don't put yourself down." Epiphany took hold of both my lapels and stood very close. Her hair smelled clean and crisp, like sun-dried linen. "You've got to help me," she said.

I lifted her chin until our eyes met and traced my fingertips across her cheek. "You can stay at my place. It's more comfortable than sleeping in the office."

She said thank you, very solemnly, as if I were a music teacher and had just praised her for a successful lesson.

"I'll take you there now," I said.

32

I PARKED THE CHEVY CLOSE to the corner of Eighth Avenue and 23rd Street, in front of the old Grand Opera House, once the headquarters of the Erie Railroad. A citadel where "Jubilee" Jim Fisk barricaded himself from his irate stockholders and where his body lay in state after Ned Stokes gunned him down on the back, stairs of the Grand Central Hotel, it was presently the home of a neighborhood R.K.O.

"Where's the Grand Central Hotel?" Epiphany asked as I locked the car.

"Down on lower Broadway above Bleecker Street. It's called the Broadway Central now. Once upon a time, it was the La Farge House."

"You sure know a lot about the city," she said, taking my arm as we crossed the avenue.

"Detectives are like cab drivers; they pick up the geography on the job." I subjected Epiphany to a running line of tour-bus patter all the way downtown. She seemed to enjoy playing the part of a sightseer and encouraged my pendantry with occasional questions.

The cast-iron façade of an old commercial building on 23rd Street caught her fancy. "I don't think I've ever been in this part of town before."

We passed Cavanaugh's Restaurant. "Diamond Jim Brady used to court Lillian Russell in there. Back in the nineties the district was very fashionable. Madison Square was the center of town, and over on Sixth were all the swank department stores, Stern Brothers, Altman's, Siegel-Cooper, Hugh O'Neill's. The old buildings are used as lofts now, but they still look the same. Here's where I live."

Epiphany craned her neck and stared up at the red-brick Victorian extravagance of the Chelsea. Her smile told me she was charmed by the delicate iron balconies embellishing every floor. "Which one is yours?"

I pointed. "Sixth floor. Under the arch."

"Let's go in," she said.

Aside from the fireplace with its carved black griffins, the lobby was unprepossessing. Epiphany paid no more attention to it than she had to the bronze plaques outside. She did manage a double-take when a white-haired woman walking a leashed leopard strode off the self-service elevator.

I had two rooms and a kitchenette with a small balcony overlooking the street. Not very grand by New York standards, but it might have been J. P. Morgan's mansion from the look on Epiphany's face when I unlocked the door.

"I love high ceilings," she said, draping her coat over the back of the couch. "They make you feel important."

I took her coat and hung it with mine in the closet. "These higher than the Plaza?"

"About the same. Your rooms are bigger."

"But no Palm Court downstairs. Can I get you a drink?"

She thought that would be nice, so I went back to the kitchenette and mixed us both a highball. When I returned, carrying the glasses, she was leaning against the door jamb, staring in at the double bed in the other room.

"Those are the accommodations," I said, handing her a drink. "We'll work out some kind of arrangement."

"I'm sure we will," she said, her voice husky with innuendo.

She took a sip, proclaimed it just right, and sat down on the couch by the fireplace. "Does this work?"

"It does when I remember to buy wood."

"I'll remind you. It's a sin not to use it."

I opened my attaché case and showed her the el Çifr poster. "Know anything about this character?"

"El Çifr? He's some kind of swami. Been around Harlem for years, since I was a little girl anyway. He has his own small sect but preaches anywhere he's invited, for Daddy Grace, Father Divine, the Muslims, you name it. Even from the pulpit of the Abyssinian Baptist once. I get his posters in the mail a couple times a year and stick them in the window of the shop same as I do for the Red Cross and Sister Kenny. You know, public service."

"Have you ever seen him in person?"

"Never. What do you want to know about Çifr for? He have something to do with Johnny Favorite?"

"Maybe. I can't say for sure."

"Meaning you don't want to."

I said: "Let's get something settled right at the start. Don't pump me for information."

"Sorry. Just curious. I figure I've got a stake in this, too."

"You're in over your head. That's why certain things you're better off not knowing."

"Afraid I'll tell someone else?"

"No," I said. "I'm afraid someone else will think you've got something to tell."

The ice rattled against the sides of Epiphany's empty glass. I made her a fresh drink and another for myself and sat next to her on the couch. "Cheers," she said as we clinked glasses.

"I'll be honest with you, Epiphany," I said. "I'm no closer to finding Johnny Favorite than I was the first night we met. He was your father. Your mother must have talked about him. Try and remember anything she might have told you, however insignificant it may seem."

"She hardly mentioned him."

"She must have told you something."

Epiphany toyed with an earring, a small cameo edged in gold. "Mama said he was a person of strength and power. She called him a magician. Obeah was only one of many avenues he explored. Mama said he taught her a lot about the black arts, more than she wanted to know."

"What do you mean?"

"Play with fire and you're liable to get burned."

"Your mother wasn't interested in black magic?"

"Mama was a good woman; her spirit was pure. She once told me that Johnny Favorite was as close to true evil as she ever wanted to come."

"That must have been his attraction," I said.

"Maybe. It's usually some badass makes a young girl's heart beat faster."

Is yours beating faster now, I wondered. "Can you think of anything else your mother told you?" Epiphany smiled, her gaze as unwavering as a cat's.

"Well, there is one thing more. She said he was a fabulous lover."

I cleared my throat. She leaned back against the couch cushions, waiting for me to make my move.

I excused myself and went into the bathroom. The maid had left her mop and bucket leaning against the full-length mirror, saving herself a trip to the utility closet at quitting time. Her limp grey smock hung over the mop handle like a misplaced shadow. Zipping my trousers, I stared at my reflection in the mirror. I told myself I was a fool to be messing around with a suspect. Unwise and unethical, also dangerous. Tend to business and sleep on the couch. My reflection leered back in a totally brainless manner.

Epiphany smiled when I returned to the room. She had removed her shoes and suit jacket. Her slender neck flowed into the open collar of her blouse with a grace that reminded me of hawks in flight. "Care for a refill?" I reached for her empty glass.

"Why not?"

I made them stiff, killing the bottle, and when I handed one to Epiphany I noticed the top two buttons on her blouse were undone. I hung my jacket over the back of a chair and loosened my necktie. Epiphany's topaz eyes followed every move. Silence enclosed us like a bell jar.

My pulse hammered at my temples as I dropped to one knee on the couch beside her. I took her unfinished drink and placed it next to mine on the coffee table. Epiphany's lips parted slightly. I heard a sharp intake of breath when I reached behind the nape of her neck and drew her to me.

33

THE FIRST TIME ON THE couch was a frenzied tangle of clothing and limbs. Three celibate weeks did little to enhance my lovemaking skills. I promised a better performance if given a second chance.

"Has nothing to do with chance." Epiphany slipped her unbuttoned blouse off her shoulders. "Sex is how we speak to the gods."

"Let's continue the conversation in the bedroom?" I kicked free of my tangled trousers and shorts.

"I'm serious." She spoke in a whisper as she removed my necktie and slowly unbuttoned my shirt. "There is a story older than Adam and Eve. That the world began with the copulation of the gods. Us being together is like a mirror of Creation."

"Don't get too serious."

"It's not serious, it's joyful." She dropped her brassiere to the floor and unzippered her wrinkled skirt. "The female is the rainbow; the male, lightning and thunder. Here. Like this."

Wearing only nylons and her garter belt, Epiphany arched into a supple backbend with the ease of a yoga master. Her body was lithe and strong. Delicate muscles rippled beneath her fawn-colored flesh. She was fluid as a flight of birds.

Or a rainbow, for that matter; her hands touched the floor behind her, back bent in a perfect arc. Her slow, easy movement was like all natural wonders, a glimpse at perfection. She lowered herself until she was supported only by her shoulders, elbows and the soles of her feet. It was the most carnal position I had ever seen a woman assume. "I am the rainbow," she murmured.

"Lightning strikes twice." I knelt before her, a fervent acolyte, and gripped the altar of her open thighs, but the mood was broken when she closed the distance like a limbo dancer and swallowed me up. The rainbow turned into a tigress. Her taut belly throbbed against me. "Don't move," she whispered, contracting hidden muscles with a rhythmic pulse. It was hard to keep from yelling when I came.

Epiphany settled against my chest. I brushed my lips across her damp forehead. "It's better with drums," she said.

"You do this in public?"

"There are times when spirits possess you. Banda or at a bambouché, times when you can dance and drink all night, yes, and fuck till dawn."

"What's banda and bambouché?"

Epiphany smiled and toyed with my nipples. "Banda's a dance in honor of Guédé. Very savage and wild and sacred, and always done in the hounfort of the société. What you would call the voodoo temple."

"Toots said 'humfo.'"

"Different dialect; same word."

"And bambouché?"

"Bambouché's just a party. Habitants of the société letting off a little steam."

"Something like a church social?"

"Uh-huh, but a whole lot more fun."

We spent the afternoon like naked children, laughing, taking showers, raiding the icebox, conversing with the gods. Epiphany found a Puerto Rican station on the radio, and we danced until our bodies ran with sweat. When I suggested going out for dinner, my giggling mambo led me to the kitchenette and lathered our privates with whipped cream. It was a sweeter feast than Cavanaugh's ever served Diamond Jim and his buxom Lil.

And as it grew dark, we picked our clothes off the floor and retired to the bedroom, lighting several plumber's candles discovered in the utility drawer. In the pale light her body glowed like tree-ripened fruit. You wanted to taste her all over.

Between tastes, we talked. I asked Epiphany where she was born.

"The Woman's Hospital on 110th Street. But I was raised by my grandmother until I was six in Bridgetown, Barbados. What about you?"

"A little place in Wisconsin you've never heard of. Just outside Madison. By now it's probably part of the city."

"Doesn't sound like you go back much."

"I haven't been back since I went in the army. That was the week after Pearl Harbor."

"Why not? Can't be that bad."

"There was nothing there for me anymore. My parents were both killed when I was in an army hospital. I might have gone home for the funeral but was in no condition to travel. After my discharge it was just a bunch of fading memories."

"Were you the only child?"

I nodded. "Adopted. But that made them love me all the more." I said this like a Boy Scout pledging allegiance. Belief in their love was what I had in place of patriotism. It endured the years that have eroded even their features. Try as I might, I remembered only blurred snapshots from the past.

"Wisconsin," Epiphany said. "No wonder you know about church socials."

"Also square dancing, hotrods, bake sales, Four-H, and keggers."

"Keggers?"

"Kind of a high school bambouché."

She fell asleep in my arms, and I lay awake for a long time

afterward watching her. Her teacup breasts rose and fell with the gentle movement of her breathing, nipples like chocolate candy kisses in the candlelight. Her eyelids fluttered as dream shadows passed behind them. She looked like a little girl. Her innocent expression bore no resemblance to the ecstatic grimace masking her features when she arched howling beneath me like a tigress.

It was madness to have gotten involved with her. Those slender fingers knew how to grip a knife. She sacrificed animals without a qualm. If she killed Toots and Margaret Krusemark, I was in big trouble.

I can't remember falling asleep. I drifted off trying to contain my feelings of tenderness for a girl whom I had every reason to believe was extremely dangerous. Just like it said on the "Wanted" circulars.

My dreams were a succession of nightmares. Violent, distorted images alternated with scenes of utter desolation. I was lost in a city whose name I did not know. The streets were empty, and when I came to an intersection, the sign-posts were all blank. None of the buildings seemed familiar. They were windowless and very tall.

I saw a figure in the distance posting a billboard against a blank wall. As he glued the random strips, an image began to form. I walked closer. The face of Louis Cyphre leered down from the billboard, his joker's smile three yards wide like the grinning Mr. Tilyou at Steeplechase Park. I called to the workman and he turned, gripping his long-handled brush. It was Cyphre. He was laughing.

The billboard parted and opened like a theater curtain, revealing an unending expanse of rolling wooded hills. Cyphre dropped his brush and gluepot and ran inside. I was close behind, dodging through the underbrush like a panther. Somehow, I lost him and with that came the revelation that I was lost as well.

The game trail I followed meandered past parks and meadows. I stopped to drink from a brook and found a heelprint in the moss along the bank. Moments later, a shrill cry pierced the tranquility.

I heard it a second time and hurried in that direction. A third scream brought me to the edge of a small clearing. At the far side a bear mauled a woman. I ran toward them. The huge carnivore shook his limp victim like a rag doll. I saw the girl's bleeding face. It was Epiphany.

I hurled myself at the bear without thinking. The beast reared and swatted me head over heels. There was no mistaking those ursine features. In spite of fangs and dripping muzzle, the bear looked exactly like Cyphre.

When I looked again, sprawled yards away, it was Cyphre. He was naked in the tall grass and instead of mauling Epiphany he was making love to her. I lunged forward and caught him by the throat, pulling him off the moaning girl. We wrestled beside her in the grass. Although he was stronger, I had him by the throat. I squeezed until his face darkened with blood. Epiphany screamed behind me. Her screams woke me up.

I was sitting in bed, sheets wound about me like a shroud. My legs straddled Epiphany's waist. Her eyes were wide with terror and pain. I had her around the throat, my hands locked in a death grip. She was no longer screaming.

"Oh, my God! Are you all right?"

Epiphany gasped for breath, scuttling to a safe corner of the bed when I took my weight off her. "You must be crazy," she coughed.

"Sometimes I'm afraid I am."

"What got into you?" Epiphany rubbed her neck where the dark imprints of my fingers marred her flawless complexion.

"I don't know. Would you like some water?"

"Yes, please."

I went out to the kitchenette and returned with a cold glass of ice water. "Thanks." She smiled as I handed it to her. "You treat all your girlfriends like that?"

"Not as a rule. I was having a dream."

"What kind of dream?"

"Someone was hurting you."

"Someone you know?"

"Yes. I've been dreaming about him every night. Crazy, violent dreams. Nightmares. And the same man keeps turning up, mocking me. Causing pain. Tonight I dreamt he was hurting you."

Epiphany put down the glass and took my hand. "Sounds like some boko's put a powerful wanga on you."

"Speak English, doll."

Epiphany laughed. "I better educate you fast. A boko is a hungan who is evil. Who deals only in black magic."

"A hungan?"

"A priest of Obeah. Same as a mambo, like me, only a man. Wanga's what you'd call an evil curse or charm. You know, a hex, a spell. What you say about your dreams makes me think some sorcerer's got you in his power."

I felt my heart beat faster. "Someone's working magic on me?"

"That's how it looks."

"Would the man in my dreams be the one?"

"Most likely. You know him?"

"Sort of. Let's say I've gotten involved with him recently."

"Is it Johnny Favorite?"

"No, but you're getting warm."

Epiphany gripped my arm. "That's the sort of bad business my father was into. He was a devil worshiper."

"Aren't you?" I stroked her hair.

Epiphany pulled away, offended. "Is that what you think?"

"I know you're a voodoo mambo."

"I am a high-type mambo. I work for good, but that doesn't mean I don't know about evil. When your adversary is potent, it's best to stay on guard."

I put my arm around her. "Think you could make a charm that would protect me in my dreams?"

"If you were a believer, I could."

"I'm gaining faith by the minute. Sorry if I hurt you."

"That's all right." She kissed my ear. "I know a way to make all the pain go away."

And she did.

34

I OPENED MY EYES TO dust motes dancing in a narrow slice of early-morning sunlight. Epiphany lay beside me, the covers thrown back over her slender arm and cinnamon shoulder. I sat up and reached for a cigarette, settling against my pillow. The line of sunlight bisected the bed, traveling the topography of our bodies like a thin, golden highway.

I leaned and kissed Epiphany's eyelids when the pounding started on the front door. Only a cop announced himself with such a knock. "Come on! Open up in there, Angel!" It was Sterne.

Epiphany's eyes widened in terror. I held my finger to my lips. "Who is it?" I made my voice sound thick with sleep.

"Lieutenant Sterne. Come on, Angel, we ain't got all day."

"Be right there."

Epiphany sat up, wild-eyed, pleading in silent panic for some explanation. "It's the law," I whispered. "I don't know what they want. Probably just talk. You could stay in here."

"Hurry it up, Angel!" Sterne bellowed.

Epiphany shook her head, bounding from the room with long-legged strides. I heard the bathroom door close quietly as I stood and kicked most of her scattered clothing under the bed. The pounding continued without a break. I carried her open suitcase over to the closet and shoved it on the top shelf under my own empty luggage.

"I'm coming, I'm coming," I called, pulling on a wrinkled bathrobe. "You don't have to kick it down."

In the living room, I found one of Epiphany's stockings draped over the back of the couch. I tied it around my waist under the robe and unlocked the front door.

"About time," Sterne snorted, shouldering past. Sergeant Deimos was right behind, wearing a drip-dry olive-green suit and a straw hat with a madras band. Sterne had on the same mohair outfit as before, but without the grey raincoat.

"You boys are the breath of springtime," I said.

"Sleeping late as usual, Angel?" Sterne pushed his sweat-stained hat back on his head and surveyed the disordered room. "Whaddja have, a rumble in here?"

"I ran into an old war buddy, and I guess we tied one on last night."

"A great life, ain't it, Deimos?" Sterne said. "Party all night, drinking at the office, sleep in any time you feel like it. We sure were dumb to join the force. What was the name of this war buddy of yours?"

"Pound," I improvised. "Ezra Pound."

"Ezra? Sounds like a farmer."

"Nope. Runs an auto body shop in Hailey, Idaho. He caught an early morning flight out of Idlewild. Went straight from here to the airport at five A.M."

"Is that a fact?"

"Would I lie to you, Lieutenant? Look, I'm in bad need of coffee. You fellows mind if I put on a pot?"

Sterne sat on the arm of the couch. "Go ahead. We don't like it, we'll dump it in the toilet."

As if on cue, a loud bumping noise came from the bathroom. "Someone in there?" Sergeant Deimos jerked his thumb at the closed door.

The bathroom door opened and Epiphany appeared, carrying the bucket and mop. She was wearing the maid's grey smock, her hair tied up under a bit of dirty rag, and she shuffled into the room, slouching like an ancient crone.

"I'ze all done wid de bat'room for today, Mistuh Angel," she whined, her nasal accent pure Amos and Andy. "I sees you got company, so I be back later to finish up, if dat's okay wid you."

"That'll be fine, Ethel." I swallowed a smile as she shambled past. "I should be going out soon, so just let yourself in when you've a mind."

"Dat I will. Dat I surely will." She smacked her lips as if her dentures were slipping and headed for the door. "Mo'nin', gentermans. Hopes I din' disturb y'all too much."

Sterne stared at her with his mouth open. Deimos just stood there scratching the back of his head. I wondered if they noticed she was barefoot and held my breath until the front door closed.

"Jungle bunnies," Sterne muttered. "They should of never let 'em out of the watermelon patch."

"Oh, Ethel's all right," I said, filling the coffee pot in the kitchenette alcove. "She's a little dimwitted but keeps the place nice and clean."

Sergeant Deimos chuckled. "Yeah, Lootenant, somebody's gotta swab out the john."

Sterne regarded his partner with weary disgust, as if cleaning toilets might be a task for which the sergeant was best qualified. I adjusted the flame on my two-burner stove. "What was it you fellows wanted to see me about?" I dropped a slice of bread into the toaster.

Sterne got up from the couch and walked into the foyer, leaning against the alcove wall next to the refrigerator. "Does the name Margaret Krusemark mean anything to you?"

"Not a whole lot."

"What do you know about her?"

"Only what I read in the papers."

"Which is?"

"That she was a millionaire's daughter and got herself murdered the other day."

"Anything else?"

I said: "I can't keep up with every murder in town. I've got my own work to look after."

Sterne shifted his weight and looked at a spot on the ceiling above my head. "When do you do that, when you're sober?"

"What's this?" Sergeant Deimos called from the other room. I looked down the hallway at him. He was standing by my open attaché case and held up the printed card I found on Margaret Krusemark's desk.

I smiled. "That? My nephew's confirmation announcement."

Deimos looked at the card. "Why is it in a foreign language?"

"It's Latin," I said.

"With him everything is Latin," Sterne said, tight-lipped.

"What's this gizmo mean up at the top?" Deimos pointed to the inverted pentagram.

"I can tell you guys aren't Catholic," I said. "That's the emblem of the Order of Saint Anthony. My nephew's an altar boy."

"Looks like the same gizmo the Krusemark dame was wearing."

My toast popped up, and I plastered it with butter. "Maybe she was Catholic, too."

"She was no Cat'lic," Sterne said. "Heathen is more like it."

I munched my toast. "What's all this got to do with the price of salami? I thought you were investigating the death of Toots Sweet?"

Sterne's dead eyes met my gaze. "That's right, Angel. It just so happens the M.O. in both killings is very similar."

"You think they're connected?"

"Maybe I should ask you that."

The coffee started perking, and I lowered the flame. "What good would that do? You might as well ask the guy at the desk downstairs."

"Don't get smart, Angel. The nigger piano player was mixed up in voodoo. This Krusemark broad was a stargazer, and from the looks of things dabbled in a little black magic on the side. They both get bumped off the same week, one day apart, under extremely similar circumstances, by a person or persons unknown."

"In what way were the circumstances similar?"

"That comes under the heading of police business."

"So how can I help if I don't know what you want?" I got three mugs out of the cupboard and lined them on the counter.

"You're holding out on us, Angel?"

"Why shouldn't I hold out on you?" I turned off the flame and poured the coffee. "I don't work for the city."

"Lissen, wise ass: I called your fancy mouthpiece downtown. It looks like you've got us over a barrel. You can clam up, and we gotta keep hands off. But if I find out you've broken so much as a parking regulation, I'm gonna come down on you like a pile-driver. You won't be able to get a license to sell peanuts in this town."

I sipped my coffee, breathing the fragrant, steam. "I always obey the law, Lieutenant," I said.

"Bullshit! Guys like you play jumprope with the law. Someday real soon you're gonna slip, and I'll be there waiting with open arms."

"Your coffee's getting cold."

"Fuck the coffee!" Sterne snarled. His lip curled over his crooked, yellow teeth, and he backhanded the mugs off the counter. They crashed against the opposite wall and bounced along the floor. Sterne regarded the splattered brown stain thoughtfully, like a 57th Street gallery-goer studying an action painting. "Looks like I made a mess," he said. "No problem. The nigger can mop up when I'm gone."

"And when might that be?" I asked.

"When I damn well please."

"Suits me." I carried my cup back into the living room and sat on the couch. Sterne stared at me as if I was something unpleasant he'd just stepped in. Deimos looked at the ceiling.

I held the cup in both hands and ignored them. Deimos started to whistle but quit after four, tuneless notes. I always keep a couple pet cops around the place was what I'd say when friends came over. They're better company than parakeets and no trouble if housebroken.

"Awright. Let's breeze," Sterne barked. Deimos sauntered past as if it was his idea.

"Hurry back," I said.

Sterne pulled his hat brim down. "I'll be waiting for you to step outta line, ass-wipe." He slammed the door hard enough to dislodge a Currier & Ives lithograph from the foyer wall.

35

THE GLASS WAS CRACKED IN the frame, a frozen lightning bolt zigzagging between the bare-knuckled fists of the Great John L. and Jake Kilrain. I hung it back on the wall and heard a soft tapping at the front door. "Come on in, Ethel. It's open."

Epiphany peered inside, still wearing her rag bandanna. "Are they gone for good?"

"Probably not. But they won't bother us any more today."

She carried the bucket and mop into the foyer and closed the door. Leaning back, she started to giggle. There was an edge of hysteria in her laughter, and when I took her in my arms, I felt her body tremble under the thin cotton smock. "You were terrific," I told her.

"Wait'll you see how clean I got the toilet."

"Where'd you go?"

"I hid on the fire stairs until I heard them leave."

"Hungry? There's a pot of coffee made and eggs in the fridge."

We fixed breakfast, a meal I usually skip, and carried our plates into the living room. Epiphany dipped her toast in egg yolk. "Did they find anything of mine?"

"They weren't looking, really. One of them poked around my attaché case. He found something I took from the Krusemark apartment but didn't know what it was. Hell, I don't even know what it is."

"Can I see?"

"Why not?" I got up and showed her the card.

"MISSA NIGER," she read. *"Invito te venire ad clandestinum ritum . . . "*

She held the card like it was the ace of spades. "This is an announcement of a Black Mass."

"A what?"

"Black Mass. It's some kind of magical ceremony, devil worship. I don't know too much about it."

"How do you know for sure, then?"

"Because that's what it says. *Missa niger* is the Latin for black mass."

"You read Latin?"

Epiphany grinned with pleasure. "What else do you learn after ten years in parochial school."

"Parochial school?"

"Sure. I want to Sacred Heart. My mama didn't think much of the public school system. She believed in discipline. 'Those nuns sure will whip some sense in your thick head,' she used to say."

I laughed. "The voodoo princess at Sacred Heart. I'd love to see your yearbook pictures."

"I'll show you sometime. I was class president."

"I'll bet you were. Can you translate the whole thing?"

"Easy," Epiphany smiled. "It says: 'You are invited to attend a secret ceremony to the glory of Lord Satan and his power.' That's all. Then there's the date, March 22nd, and the time, 9:00 P.M. And down here it says, 'Eastside Interborough Rapid Transit, 18th Street Station.'"

"What about the letterhead? That upside-down star with the goat head? Have any idea what it means?"

"Stars are an important symbol in every religion I know anything about, the Islamic star, the star of Bethlehem, star of David. The talisman of Agove Royo has stars in it."

"Agove Royo?"

"Obeah."

"That invitation have anything to do with voodoo?"

"No, no. This is devil worship." Epiphany was pained by my ignorance. "The ram is a sign of the devil. An inverted star means bad luck. Probably also a satanic symbol."

I grabbed Epiphany and wrapped her in my arms. "You are worth your weight in gold, babe. Does Obeah have a devil?"

"Many devils."

She smiled at me, and I patted her bottom. Nice bottom. "It's time to brush up on my black magic. We'll get dressed and go to the library. You can help me with my homework."

It was a beautiful morning, warm enough to go without a coat. Bright sunshine dazzled on the mica specks in the sidewalk. Spring was officially one day off, but we might not see weather this good again until May. Epiphany wore her plaid skirt and sweater and looked invitingly like a schoolgirl. Driving up Fifth, I asked how old she was.

"Seventeen, last January sixth."

"Christ, you're not old enough to buy a drink."

"Not true. When I'm dressed up I get served without any problems. They never asked for my I.D. at the Plaza."

I believed her. In her plum-colored suit she looked five years older. "Aren't you a little young to be running the store?"

Epiphany's amused look contained a trace of scorn. "I've been in charge of accounting and inventory since my mama took ill," she said. "I only tend the counter at night. In the daytime I have a staff of two."

"And what do you do in the daytime?"

"Study mostly. Go to class. I'm a freshman at City."

"Good. You should be an old hand in the library. I'll leave the research to you."

I waited in the main reading room while Epiphany sorted through the file cards. Scholars of all ages sat in silent rows between the long wooden tables where precisely arranged lampshades wore numbers like convicts on parade. The room had ceilings as high as a train station with huge chandeliers like inverted wedding cakes hanging in the Beaux Arts vastness. Only occasional muffled coughing disturbed the cathedral hush.

I found a vacant seat at the far end of a reading table. The number on the lampshade corresponded to the number engraved on a brass oval countersunk into the tabletop in front of me: 666. I remembered the snotty maître d' at the Top of the Six's and changed my seat; 724 felt a lot more comfortable.

"Wait'll you see what I've found." Epiphany dropped an armload of books with a dusty thump. Heads turned halfway down the table. "Some of it is trash, but there's an edition of the *Grimoire of Pope Honorius* privately printed in Paris in 1754."

"I don't read French."

"It's in Latin. I'll translate. Here's a new one that's mostly pictures."

I reached for the oversized coffee-table volume and opened it at random to a full-page medieval painting of a horned monster with lizard scales and talons in place of feet. Flames issued from his ears and between the stalactite rows of tusks accentuating his gaping mouth. It bore the caption: SATAN, PRINCE OF HELL.

I thumbed several pages. An Elizabethan woodcut showed a woman in a farthingale kneeling behind a naked devil with the build of a lifeguard. He had wings, a goat's head, and fingernails like Slovenly Peter. The woman hugged his legs, her nose nestled directly beneath his uplifted tail. She was smiling.

"The abominable kiss," Epiphany said, looking over my shoulder. "That's how a witch traditionally sealed her allegiance to the devil."

"I guess they didn't have notary publics in those days." I turned a few more pages, flipping through a succession of demons and familiars. There were many inverted five-pointed stars in the section on talismans. I came across one with the figure 666 printed at the center and pointed it out to Epiphany. "My least favorite number."

"It's from the Book of Revelations."

"The what?"

"The Bible: 'Let him that hath understanding count the number of the beast; for it is the number of a man; and his number is six hundred threescore and six.'"

"Is that a fact?"

Epiphany frowned at me over the tops of her reading glasses. "Don't you know anything?"

"Not a whole lot, but I'm learning fast. Here's a woman named for the restaurant where I ate yesterday." I showed Epiphany the engraving of a plump matron wearing a peasant's cowled hood.

"*Voisin* is French for "neighbor,'" she said.

"Those nuns did drum some book learning into you at that. Here, read the caption."

Epiphany took the book and read the small print beneath the engraving in a whisper: "Catherine Deshayes, called La Voisin, a society fortune-teller and sorceress. Arranged Black Masses for the Marquise de Montespan, mistress of King Louis XIV, as well as for other notables. Arrested, tortured, tried and executed in 1680."

"Just the book we need."

"It's entertaining, but the meat and potatoes are in these: *Malleus Maleftcarum*, and Reginald Scott's *The Discoverie of Witchcraft*, and Aleister Crowley's *Magick*, and the *Secrets of Albertus Magnus*, and—"

"Okay, check them out. I want you to go on home and curl up on the couch with a good book. Mark any passages you think I should read, especially stuff dealing with the Black Mass."

"This is a research library," Epiphany said. "No books go out. We can run uptown to the library on campus."

"I've got work. You'll do okay. Here's the key to my place." I got out my wallet and slipped her a twenty. "That's for cab fare."

"I've got money of my own."

"Hang on to it. I might want to borrow some."

"I don't want to be alone."

"Keep the chain on the door. You'll be fine."

I put Epiphany in a cab out front. She was afraid, and it made her look like a little girl. Our searing, snake-tongued kiss earned a contemptuous stare from two passing businessmen and much applause and whistling from a hookey-playing urchin bootblack sitting on the base of the uptown lion.

36

I DROPPED THE CHEVY OFF at the garage and walked back to Broadway on the sunny side of 44th. I was taking my time, enjoying the weather, when I spotted Louis Cyphre coming out of the main entrance to the Astor. He wore a tan beret, tweed Norfolk coat, twill breeches, and tall, polished riding boots. In a gloved hand he carried a scuffed leather travel bag.

I watched him wave off a doorman's offer of a cab. He started downtown past the Paramount Building at a brisk pace. I considered catching up with him but figured he was heading for the Crossroads office and decided to save my breath. I didn't think of it as tailing him; I was much too close. But when he reached the entrance to my building and continued on without a pause, I instinctively fell back and lingered by a shop window, curiosity at full throttle. He crossed 42nd Street and turned west. I watched from the corner, then kept pace with him, following along the opposite side of the street.

Cyphre stood out in the crowd. Not hard to do among the pimps, hustlers, drug addicts, and runaways crowding 42nd Street when you're dressed as if you were going to the Horse Show at the Garden. I guessed his eventual destination to be Port Authority: He surprised me mid-block and ducked into Hubert's Museum and Flea Circus.

I dodged four lanes of two-way traffic like "Crazy Legs" Hirsch evading defensive linemen only to be brought up short by a signboard at the entrance. Glitter-edged letters announced: THE AMAZING DR. CIPHER. Eight-by-ten glossies showed my client wearing a top hat and tails like Mandrake the Magician. LIMITED ENGAGEMENT, it said.

The main floor of Hubert's was a penny arcade; the stage was downstairs. I went in, bought a ticket and found a place in the dark along the chest-high plywood barrier that discouraged audience participation. On the small, brightly lit stage, a buxom belly dancer gyrated to a quavering Arabic lament. I counted five other shadowy spectators besides myself.

What the hell was the elegant Louis Cyphre doing in a low-rent place like this? Flea circus card tricks don't keep a man in limousines and Wall Street lawyers. Maybe he got his kicks performing in public. Or else it was a setup. An act meant for me to catch.

When the scratchy record came to an end, someone backstage picked up the needle and started it over again. The belly dancer looked bored. She stared at the ceiling. Her mind was on other things. Eight bars into the third replay the machine was switched off, and she made a beeline for the wings. No one applauded.

The six of us stared at an empty stage without complaint until an old geezer wearing a red vest and sleeve garters appeared. "Ladies and Gentlemen," he wheezed, "it is with great awe and trepitude that I present to you the amazing, mysterious, unforgettable: Dr. Cipher. Let's give him a nice welcome." The old man was the only one clapping as he shuffled off.

The lights dimmed to blackness. A muffled bumping and whispering backstage as in amateur theatricals was followed by a blinding, phosphorescent flash. The lights came immediately back on, but my eyes took a few moments to refocus. A blurred, blue-green retinal afterimage hovered about the figure on stage, obscuring his features.

"Which one of us knows how our days shall end? Who can

say if tomorrow will come?" Louis Cyphre stood alone, center stage, surrounded by wispy tendrils of smoke and the smell of burnt magnesium. He wore a black Edwardian soup-and-fish with long swallow-tails and a two-button vest. A hinged black case the size of a breadbox stood on a table to one side. "The future is an unwritten text, and he who dares read those blank pages does so at his own peril."

Cyphre removed his white gloves and with a trickster's midair fingersnap, they were gone. He picked a carved ebony wand off the table and gestured toward the wings. The belly dancer made a subdued entrance, her ample body draped in a floor-length velvet cloak.

"Time paints a portrait no man can ignore." Cyphre waved his hand in a small circle above the dancer's head. At this command she began to pirouette. "Which of us would peek at the finished work? It is a different thing to observe the mirror day by day; there the nuance of change goes unnoticed."

The dancer's back turned toward the spectators. The luster of her flowing black hair surged in the spotlight. Cyphre thrust the ebony wand like a sword at his audience of six. "Those who would behold the future, look on me with terror!"

The belly dancer came about full-face: a toothless, haggard crone. Lank strands of ashen hair framed her ruined features. One blind eye caught the light like glazed pottery. I hadn't seen her slip on the mask, and the effect of her transformation was staggering. The drunk beside me gasped himself sober in the dark.

"Flesh is mortal, my friends," Dr. Cipher intoned. "And lust sputters and dies like a candle in the winter wind. Gentlemen, I offer you the pleasures your hot blood so recently imagined."

He gestured with his wand and the belly dancer opened the folds of her heavy cloak. She still wore the tasseled costume, but her wrinkled breasts sagged, deflated behind sequined pasties. A once-sumptuous belly hung slack between angular, skeletal hips.

It was another woman entirely. There was no way to fake those swollen arthritic knees and emaciated thighs.

"To what uses shall we come?" Dr. Cipher smiled like a G.P. making a house call. "Thank you, my dear; most enlightening." He dismissed the ancient woman with a wand stroke, and she hobbled offstage. There was a smattering of applause.

Dr. Cipher held up his hand. "Thank you, my friends." He nodded graciously. "The tomb lies at the end of every path. Only the soul is immortal. Guard this treasure well. Your decaying husk is but a temporary vessel on an endless voyage.

"Let me tell you a story: when I was a young man and just beginning my travels, I struck up a conversation with a retired seaman in a waterfront bar in Tangier. My nautical companion was a German, born in Silesia, but spending his last days in the Moroccan sun, wintering in Marrakech and drinking the summers away at whatever seaport suited his fancy.

"I remarked that he had found a comfortable berth.

"'It has been smooth sailing five-and-forty years now,' he replied.

"'You are a lucky man,' I said, 'not to have weathered any of life's storms.'

"'Luck?' the old seafarer laughed, 'luck, you call it? Count yourself lucky, then. This year I must pass it to another.'

"I asked him to explain. He told me the story much as I tell it to you. When he was my age and first shipping out, he encountered an old beachcomber in Samoa who gave him a bottle containing the soul of a Spanish quartermaster who once sailed with King Philip's armada. Any illness or misfortune which might befall him was instead suffered by this tormented prisoner. How the Spaniard's soul came to inhabit the bottle, he knew not, but at the age of seventy, he must give it away to the first young man who would accept it or suffer the consequences of taking the unfortunate conquistador's place within.

"Here the old German looked at me sadly. He had but a month

to go before his seventy-first birthday. 'Time,' he said, 'to learn what life is all about.'

"He gave me the bottle. A handblown rum bottle, amber in color, and easily hundreds of years old. It was stoppered with a gold plug."

Dr. Cipher reached behind the black case on the table and produced the bottle. "Behold." He sat it on top of the case. His description had been exact, omitting only the frenzied scuttling shadow inside.

"I have had a long and happy life; but listen—" All six of us craned forward to hear. "Listen . . . " Cyphre's voice trailed away to a whisper. Out of the ensuing silence came a tiny, bell-chime complaint, like a chain of paperclips dragged across a crystal goblet. I strained to make out the fragile sound. It seemed to be coming from within the amber bottle.

"Ay-you-da-may . . . ay-you-da-may . . . " Over and over, the same haunted, melodic phrase.

I tried to spot Louis Cyphre's lips moving. His smile reached out beyond the footlights. He was gloating with raw, unconcealed pleasure.

"Mysterious fate," he said. "Why should I spend a life free from pain while another human soul is doomed to eternal anguish within a rum bottle?" He withdrew a black velvet sack from his pocket and stuffed the bottle inside. Pulling the drawstrings tight, he placed it on top of his case. His smile reflected the footlights. Without a sound, he spun gracefully and struck the sack a sabre-stroke with the ebony wand. There was no sound of breaking glass. An empty sack was flipped into the air and deftly caught. Louis Cyphre crumpled it into a ball and shoved it into his pocket, acknowledging the applause with a curt nod.

"I want to show you something else," he said. "But before I do, I must emphasize that I am not an animal trainer, merely a collector of exotics."

He tapped the black case with his wand. "I bought the contents of this box in Zurich from an Egyptian merchant I had known years before in Alexandria. He claimed what you are about to see were souls originally enchanted at the court of Pope Leo X. An amusement for his Medici imagination. This seems an impossible claim, does it not?"

Dr. Cipher unsnapped the metal fasteners securing the case and opened it to form a triptych. A miniature theatre unfolded, with scenery and background tableaux painted in the meticulous perspective of the Italian Renaissance. The stage was peopled with white mice, all costumed in tiny silks and brocade as characters from *commedia dell'arte.* There was Punchinello and Columbine, Scaramouche and Harlequin. Each walked on its hind legs in an elaborate pantomime. The silvery tinkle of a music box accompanied the elaborate acrobatics.

"The Egyptian claimed they would never die," Cyphre said. "An extravagant boast, perhaps. I can only say that I have not lost any in six years' time."

The diminutive performers walked on tightropes and brightly colored balls, brandished matchstick swords and parasols, tumbled and took pratfalls with clockwork precision.

"Presumably, enchanted subjects should require no sustenance." Dr. Cipher leaned over the top of the case and observed the performance with delight. "I provide them with food and water daily. They have incredible appetites, I might add."

"Toys," the man next to me muttered in the dark. "They gotta be toys."

As if on cue, Cyphre reached down and Harlequin scampered up his coat sleeve and perched, sniffing the air, on his shoulder. The spell was broken. It was only a rodent wearing a tiny diamond-patterned outfit. Cyphre pinched the pink tail and lowered a splay-legged Harlequin back to the stage, where it paraded around on its front paws in a totally unmouselike manner.

"As you see, I have no need for television." Dr. Cipher folded the sides of the miniature stage closed and secured the fasteners.

There was a handle on top, and he lifted it off the table like a suitcase. "Whenever the box is opened, they perform. Even show business has its Purgatory."

Cyphre tucked the wand under his arm and dropped something on the table. There was a flash of white light, and I was blind in its momentary brilliance. I blinked and rubbed my eyes. The stage was bare. A plain wooden table stood alone and naked in the spotlight.

Cyphre's amplified, disembodied voice issued from an unseen speaker: *"Zero, the point intermediate between positive and negative, is a portal through which every man must eventually pass."*

The old party in sleeve garters shuffled out and carried the table into the wings as a worn recording of "Night Train" bleated from the hidden loudspeaker. The belly dancer reappeared, plump and pink, and began a bump-and-grind as mechanical as the piston-driven music. I groped my way up the sagging stairs. The prickling dread I felt in the French restaurant had returned. My client was toying with me, playing tricks with my mind like a three-card monte dealer fleecing the suckers.

37

OUT FRONT, A FAT YOUNG man wearing a pink shirt, khaki pants, and dirty white bucks removed the glossy photos from the glass-covered signboard. A nervous pill-popper in an army fatigue jacket and tennis shoes looked on.

"Great show," I said to the fat kid. "That Dr. Cipher is a marvel."

"Weird," he said.

"This the last performance?"

"I guess so."

"I'd like to congratulate him. Is there some way to get backstage?"

"You just missed him." He freed a picture of my client from the signboard and slipped it in a manila envelope. "He doesn't like to stick around after a show."

"Missed him? That's impossible."

"He uses a tape recorder at the end of the act. Gives him a head start. Doesn't take off his costume or anything."

"Was he carrying a leather bag?"

"Yeah, and his big black case."

"Where does he live?"

"How should I know?" The fat young man blinked at me. "Are you a cop or something?"

"Me? No, nothing like that. Just wanted to tell him he's made a new fan."

"Tell his agent." He handed me an 8 by 10 photo. Louis Cyphre's perfect smile shone brighter than the glossy surface. I flipped the photo over and read what was rubber-stamped on the back:

WARREN WAGNER ASSOCIATES
WY 9-3500

The jittery pill-popper turned his attentions to a pinball machine inside the entrance. I gave the fat young man back his picture. "Thanks," I said, and melted into the crowd.

I caught an uptown cab which dropped me off on Broadway in front of the Rivoli Theatre, across from the Brill Building. The tramp in the army coat was off duty. I took the elevator to the eighth floor. The peroxided receptionist had silver fingernails today. She didn't remember me. I showed her my card. "Mr. Wagner in his office?"

"He's busy right now."

"Thanks." I stepped around her desk and jerked open the door marked PRIVATE.

"Hey!" She was right behind me, clawing like a harpy. "You can't go in the—"

I closed the door in her face.

". . . three percent of the gross is an insult," piped a midget wearing a red turtleneck sweater. He sat on the ratty couch, his little feet sticking straight out like a doll's.

Warren Wagner, Jr. glowered at me from behind his burn-branded desk. "What the hell do you mean barging in like this?"

I said: "I need you to answer two questions and don't have the time to wait."

"Do you know this man?" asked the midget in his whisky falsetto. I recognized him from the Saturday matinees of my childhood. He was in all the "Hell's Kitchen Kid" comedies, and his ancient, wrinkled features were the same when he was young, but the spiky black crewcut was now as white as a detergent commercial.

"Never saw him before in my life," Warren Jr. snarled. "Take a powder, creep, before I call a cop."

"You saw me on Monday," I said, keeping the edge out of my voice. "I was working undercover." I got out my wallet and let him look at the photostat.

"So, you're a shamus. Big deal. That doesn't give you the right to come crashing into a private meeting.

"Why not save the adrenaline and tell me what I need to know. I'll be out of your hair in thirty seconds."

"Johnny Favorite means less than nothing to me," he said. "I was only a kid then."

"Forget about Johnny Favorite. Tell me about a client of yours who calls himself Dr. Cipher."

"What about him? I just signed him last week."

"What's his real name?"

"Louie Seafur. You'll have to get my secretary to spell it for you."

"Where does he live?"

"Janice can tell you that," he said. *"Janice!"*

Silver-nails opened the door and peeked timidly in. "Yes, Mr. Wagner?" she squeaked.

"Give Mr. Angel here the information he requires, please."

"Yes, sir."

"Thanks a lot," I said.

"Next time, knock." Silver-nailed Janice didn't give me the benefit of her jiggling, gum-chewer's smile, but she did look up Louis Cyphre's address in her circular file. She even wrote it out. "You belong in a zoo yourself," she said as she handed me the memo. She'd been saving that one all week.

The 1-2-3 Hotel was on 46th between Broadway and Sixth, name and address all in the same package: 123 West 46th. Elaborate finials, gables, and dormers crowned an otherwise unpretentious brick building. I went in and gave the desk clerk my business card, wrapped in a ten-spot. "I want the room number of a man named Louis Cyphre," I said, spelling it for him. "And you don't need to say anything to the house dick."

"I remember him. Had a white beard and black hair."

"That's the party."

"Checked out over a week ago."

"Any forwarding address?"

"Not a one."

"What about his room? Rented it yet?"

"Wouldn't do you any good; been cleaned top to bottom."

I stepped back into the sunshine and headed toward Broadway. It was a beautiful day for walking. A Salvation Army trio, tuba, accordion, and tambourine, serenaded a chestnut vendor under the Loew's State marquee where new "Lounger Seats" were promised for the grand reopening Easter Sunday. I savored the sounds and smells, trying to remember the real world of a week ago when there was no such thing as magic.

I used a different approach with the desk clerk in the Astor. "Excuse me, I wonder if you might help me out. I was supposed to meet my uncle in the coffee shop twenty minutes ago. I'd like to phone him, but I don't know the room number."

"What's your uncle's name, sir?"

"Cyphre. Louis Cyphre."

"I'm terribly sorry. Mr. Cyphre checked out this morning."

"What? Back to France?"

"He left no forwarding address."

I should have chucked the whole thing right there and taken Epiphany for a Circle Line cruise around the island. Instead I phoned Herman Winesap downtown and demanded to know what was going on. "What the hell is Louis Cyphre doing at Hubert's Flea Circus?"

"What business is it of yours? You were not hired to follow Mr. Cyphre. I suggest you stick to the job you're getting paid for."

"Did you know he was a magician?"

"No."

"Doesn't that fact intrigue you, Winesap?"

"I have known Mr. Cyphre for many years and fully appreciate his sophistication. He is a man with a wide range of interests. It wouldn't surprise me in the least that prestidigitation was among them."

"In a penny arcade flea circus?"

"Perhaps it is a hobby, a form of relaxation."

"Doesn't make sense."

"Mr. Angel, for fifty dollars per diem, my client, yours too, I might add, for that price he can always find someone else to work for him."

I told Winesap I got the message and hung up.

After a trip to the cigar stand for additional dimes, I made three more calls. The first, to my answering service, yielded a message from a lady in Valley Stream with a missing pearl necklace. Someone in her bridge club was suspected. I didn't write down the number.

Next, I called Krusemark Maritime, Inc., and learned that the President and Chairman of the Board was in mourning and not available. I tried his home number and got some flunky who took my name. I didn't have to wait long.

"What do you know about it, Angel?" the old brigand barked.

"Some. Why don't we save it. I need to talk to you. Soon as I can get there'd be as good a time as any."

"All right. I'll call downstairs and tell them to expect you."

38

NUMBER TWO, SUTTON PLACE WAS the building where Marilyn Monroe lived. A private driveway curved off 57th Street, and my cab let me out under a pink limestone vault. Across the way, a row of four-story brick townhouses was marked for doom. Stark whitewash crosses were crudely brushed on every window like a child's painting of a graveyard.

A doorman festooned with more gilt braid than an admiral hurried to assist me. I gave my name and asked for the Krusemark residence.

"Yes, sir," he said. "Elevator on the left."

I got off on the fifteenth floor, stepping into a spartan walnut-paneled foyer. Tall gilt-framed mirrors on either side provided an infinity of foyers. There was only one other door. I rang the bell twice and waited.

A dark-haired man with a mole on his upper lip opened the door. "Mr. Angel, please come in. Mr. Krusemark is waiting for you." He wore a grey suit with tiny maroon pinstripes and seemed more like a bank teller than a butler. "Right this way, please."

He led me through large, luxuriously furnished rooms with views of the East River and the Sunshine Biscuit Company over in Queens. Precisely arranged antiques suggested those period display rooms at the Metropolitan. These were rooms for signing treaties with quill pens.

We came to a closed door and my grey-suited guide knocked once and said: "Mr. Angel is here, sir."

"Bring him in where I can see him." Even through the door's thickness, Krusemark's husky growl reverberated with authority.

I was ushered into a small, windowless gym. The walls were mirror-covered, and the multiple reflections of stainless steel body-building machinery gleamed endlessly in every direction. Ethan Krusemark, wearing boxer shorts and a skivvy, lay on his back under one of these shining contraptions, doing leg presses. For a man his age, he was pumping a lot of iron.

At the sound of the door closing, he sat up and looked me over. "We're burying her tomorrow," he said. "Toss me that towel."

I flipped it to him, and he wiped the sweat from his face and shoulders. He was powerfully built. Knotted muscles bunched beneath his varicose veins. This was one old man you didn't want to fool with.

"Who killed her?" he growled at me. "Johnny Favorite?"

"When I find him, I'll ask."

"That danceband gigolo. I should have deep-sixed the bastard when I had the chance." He smoothed his long silver hair carefully back into place.

"When was that? When you and your daughter snatched him from the clinic upstate?"

His eyes locked on mine. "You're way out of line, Angel."

"I don't think so. Fifteen years ago, you paid Dr. Albert Fowler twenty-five thousand dollars for one of his patients. You gave your name as Edward Kelley. Fowler was supposed to make it look like Favorite was still a vegetable in some forgotten ward. Up until a week ago he did a pretty good job for you."

"Who's paying you to dig into this?"

I got out a cigarette and rolled it between my fingers. "You know I won't tell you that."

"I could make it worth your while."

"I'm sure you could," I said, "but it's still no dice. Mind if I smoke?"

"Go right ahead."

I lit up, exhaled, and said: "Look. You want the man who killed your daughter. I want Johnny Favorite. Perhaps we're both interested in the same guy. We won't know unless we find him."

Krusemark's thick fingers curled into a fist. It was a big fist. He punched the flat of his other hand and a noise like a board snapping echoed in the gleaming room. "Okay," he said. "I was Edward Kelley. It was me paid Fowler the twenty-five Gs."

"Why did you use the name Kelley?"

"You think I'd use my own name? The Kelley business was Meg's idea, don't ask me why."

"Where did you take Favorite?"

"Times Square. It was New Year's Eve 1943. We dropped him off in the crowd, and he walked out of our lives. So we thought."

"Let's take that one again," I said. "You expect me to buy that after paying twenty-five grand for Favorite you lost him in a crowd?"

"That's the way it happened. I did it for my daughter. I always gave her what she wanted."

"And she wanted Favorite to disappear?"

Krusemark pulled on a terrycloth robe. "I think it's something they cooked up together before he went overseas. Some kind of hocus-pocus they were fooling around with at the time."

"You mean black magic?"

"Black, white, what difference does it make? Meg was always a funny kid. She played with tarot cards before she could read."

"What got her started?"

"I don't know. A superstitious governess; one of our European cooks. You never know what, really goes on inside people's heads when you hire them."

"Did you know your daughter once ran a fortune-telling parlor at Coney Island?"

"Yes, I set her up in that, too. She was all I had, so I spoiled her."

"I found a mummified human hand in her apartment. Know about that?"

"The Hand of Glory. It's a charm supposed to open any lock. The right hand of a convicted murderer, cut off while his neck is still in the noose. Meg's has a pedigree. Came from some Welsh highwayman named Captain Silverheels condemned in 1786. She bought it in a Paris junk shop years ago."

"Just a souvenir of the Grand Tour, like the skull Favorite kept in his suitcase. They seem to have had similar tastes."

"Yeah. Favorite gave that skull to Meg the night before he shipped out. Everybody else gave their girl a class ring or a varsity sweater or something like that. He picks a skull."

"I thought Favorite and your daughter had broken things off by then."

"Officially, yes. Must have been some game they were playing."

"Why do you say that?" I flicked an inch-long ash onto the floor.

"Because nothing changed in their relationship."

Krusemark pressed a button next to the door. "Like a drink?"

"A little whisky would taste good."

"Scotch?"

"Bourbon, if you've got it. On the rocks. Did your daughter ever mention a woman named Evangeline Proudfoot?"

"Proudfoot? Can't place it. She might have."

"What about voodoo? Did she talk about voodoo?"

There was a single knock and the door swung open. "Yes, sir?" asked the man in grey.

"Mr. Angel will have a glass of bourbon, ice only. Some brandy for me. Oh, and Benson?"

"Yes, sir?"

"Bring Mr. Angel an ashtray."

Benson nodded and closed the door behind him.

"He the butler?" I asked.

"Benson is my private secretary. That's a butler with brains." Krusemark mounted a mechanical bicycle and began methodically pedaling imaginary miles. "What were you saying about voodoo?"

"Johnny Favorite was mixed up in Harlem voodoo back in his skull-giving days. I wonder if your daughter ever mentioned it."

"Voodoo was one she missed," he said.

"Dr. Fowler told me Favorite was suffering from amnesia when you took him from the hospital. Did he recognize your daughter?"

"No, he didn't. He acted like a sleepwalker. Didn't say much. Just stared out the car window into the night."

"In other words, he treated you like strangers?"

Krusemark pedaled for all he was worth. "Meg wanted it that way. She insisted that we not call him Johnny and that nothing be said about their past relationship."

"Didn't that strike you as odd?"

"Everything Meg did was odd."

I heard the faint chiming of crystal outside the door an instant before Benson knocked. The butler with brains wheeled in a portable bar. He poured me a drink and a snifter of brandy for the boss and asked if there would be anything else.

"This is fine," Krusemark said, holding the tulip-shaped glass under his nose like a blossom. "Thank you very much, Benson."

Benson left. I spotted an ashtray next to the ice bucket and stubbed out my smoke.

"I once heard you tell your daughter to slip me a mickey. Said you picked up the art of persuasion in the Orient."

Krusemark gave me an odd look. "It's clean," he said.

"Persuade me." I handed him my glass. "Drink it yourself."

He took several healthy swallows and handed me back the drink. "It's too late for playing games. I need your help, Angel."

"Then play straight with me. Did your daughter ever see Favorite again after that New Year's Eve?"

"Never."

"You sure of that?"

"Of course I'm sure. Do you have reason to doubt it?"

"My business is doubting what other people tell me. How do you know she never saw him again?"

"We had no secrets. She wouldn't hide a thing like that."

"You don't seem to know women as well as you do the shipping business," I said.

"I know my own daughter. If she ever saw Favorite again, it was on the day he killed her."

I sipped my drink. "Nice and neat," I said. "A guy with total amnesia, doesn't even know his own name, wanders off into a New Year's mob fifteen years ago, vanishes without a trace, and then suddenly shows up out of the blue and starts killing people."

"Who else did he kill? Fowler?"

I smiled. "Dr. Fowler was a suicide."

"That's easy enough to arrange," he snorted.

"Is it? How would you go about arranging it, Mr. Krusemark?"

Krusemark fixed me with a steely buccaneer's stare. "Don't go putting words into my mouth, Angel. If I wanted Fowler knocked off, I would have had it done years ago."

"That I doubt. As long as he kept the lid on the Favorite business he was worth much more to you alive."

"It was Favorite I should have had put away, not Fowler," he growled. "Whose murder are you investigating anyway?"

"I'm not investigating anybody's murder," I said. "I'm looking for a man with amnesia."

"I hope to hell you find him."

"Did you tell the police about Johnny Favorite?"

Krusemark rubbed his blunt chin. "That was a tough one. I wanted to point them in the right direction without implicating myself."

"I'm sure you came up with a good story."

"I came up with a dandy. They asked if I knew what sort of

characters Meg was romantically involved with. I gave them the names of a couple fellows I remembered hearing her mention, but I said the only really big romance in her life had been with Johnny Favorite. Naturally, they wanted to hear more about Johnny Favorite."

"Naturally," I said.

"So, I told them about their engagement and how weird he was and all that stuff. Stuff that never got into the papers back when he was a headliner."

"I'll bet you laid it on good and heavy."

"They were looking to buy; selling it was a snap."

"Where did you tell them they could find Favorite?"

"I didn't. I said I hadn't seen him since the war. Said the last thing I'd heard was he'd been wounded. If they can't trace it from there, they ought to look for other work!"

"They'll trace it to Fowler," I said. "That's when their problems will start."

"Forget their problems. What about your problems? Where do you go from New Year's 1943?"

"No place." I finished my drink and set the glass on the bar. "I can't find him in the past. If he's here in the city, he'll surface again soon. Next time, I'll be waiting."

"Think I'm a target?" Krusemark slid off his Exercycle.

"What do you think?"

"I'm not going to lose any sleep over it."

"Might be a good idea if we kept in touch," I said. "My number's in the book if you need me." I wasn't about to hand my business card over to another potential corpse.

Krusemark clapped me on the shoulder and flashed his million-dollar smile. "You got more on the ball than New York's Finest, Angel." He walked me to the front door, exuding charm like a pig sweating blood. "You'll be hearing from me; you can count on that."

39

KRUSEMARK'S DYNAMIC-TENSION HANDSHAKE STAYED WITH me all the way to the street. "Cab, sir?" the doorman asked, touching his braid-crusted cap.

"No, thanks. I'll walk a few blocks." I needed to think, not discuss philosophy or the mayor or baseball with some cabbie.

Two men were waiting on the corner as I came out of the building. The short, stocky one wearing a blue rayon windbreaker and black chinos looked like a high school football coach. His companion was a kid in his twenties with a d.a. haircut and the wet, imploring eyes of a greeting-card Jesus. His two-button green sharkskin suit, had pointed lapels and padded shoulders and seemed several sizes too large.

"Hey, buddy, got a minute?" the coach called, ambling toward me with his hands in his jacket pockets. "I got something to show you."

"Some other time," I said.

"Right now." The blunt muzzle of an automatic pointed up at me from out of the V in the coach's half-zippered windbreaker. Only the front sight was exposed. It was .22-caliber, which meant the guy was good, or thought he was.

"You're making a mistake," I said.

"No mistake. You're Harry Angel, right?" The automatic slid back out of sight into the wind-breaker.

"Why ask if you already know?"

"There's a park across the street. Let's you and me take a walk over there where we can talk nice and private."

"What about him?" I nodded at the kid in the sharkskin suit nervously watching us with his liquid eyes.

"He comes too."

The kid fell in behind us, and we crossed Sutton Place and started down the steps to a narrow park fronting on the East River. "Cute trick," I said, "cutting the pockets out of your jacket."

"Works nice, don't it?"

A promenade runs along the river's edge, the water ten feet below an iron railing. At the far end of the little park a white-haired man in a cardigan sweater walked a Yorkshire terrier on a leash. He was coming toward us but kept to the dog's mincing pace. "Wait here till that bozo makes himself scarce," the coach said. "Enjoy the view."

The kid with the stigmata eyes leaned his elbows against the railing and stared at a barge breasting the current in the channel off Welfare Island. The coach stood behind me, balanced on the balls of his feet like a prizefighter. Further along, the Yorkshire terrier lifted his leg on a litter basket. We waited.

I looked up at the ornate latticework of the Queensborough Bridge and the cloudless blue sky caught in its girdered intricacies. Enjoy the view. Such a beautiful day. You couldn't ask to die on a nicer day, so enjoy the view and don't make a fuss. Just stare at the sky quietly until the only witness is out of the way and try not to think of the iridescent undulance of the oily river beneath your feet until they drop you over the railing with a bullet in your eye.

I tightened my grip on the attaché case. My snub-nosed Smith & Wesson might as well have been at home in a drawer. The man with the dog was less than twenty feet away. I shifted my weight and glanced at the coach, waiting for him to make a mistake. The quick flicker of his eyes as he checked the dog walker's progress was all I needed.

I swung the attaché case full strength, driving it up between the spread of his legs. He screamed with true sincerity and bent double, a stray shot burning through his windbreaker and splattering off the pavement. It made no more noise than a sneeze.

The Yorkshire terrier strained at his leash, barking shrilly. I gripped the attaché case with both hands and slammed it against the coach's head. He grunted and went down. I kicked his elbow and a pearl-handled Colt Woodsman spiraled across the concrete.

"Get a cop!" I yelled at the open-mouthed gentleman in the cardigan sweater as the Christ-eyed kid closed on me with a short, leather-covered sap in his bony fist. "These guys want to kill me!"

I used the attaché case like a shield and caught the kid's first swing on its expensive calfskin surface. I kicked at him, and he danced back away from me. The long-barreled Colt lay tantalizingly close. I couldn't risk stooping for it. The kid saw it too and tried to cut me off, but he wasn't fast enough. I kicked the automatic under the railing into the river.

That left me wide open. The kid caught the side of my neck with his weighted sap. Now it was my turn to scream. The pain brought tears to my eyes as I hacked for breath. I shielded my head as best I could, but the kid was in the driver's seat. He struck a glancing blow off my shoulder, and then I felt my left ear explode. As I went down, I saw the man in the cardigan swoop his yapping terrier in his arms and run hollering up the park steps.

I watched his departure on my hands and knees through a pink haze of pain. My head roared like an express train on fire. The kid sapped me again, and the train went into a tunnel.

Pinpoints of light dazzled in the blackness. The rough concrete under my cheek felt slick and sticky. I might have been out as long as Rip van Winkle, but when I opened the eye that still worked I saw the kid helping the fallen coach to his feet.

It had been a rough day for the coach. He cupped his groin with both hands. The kid tugged at his sleeve, urging him to hurry, but he took his time and hobbled over to where I was lying and kicked me square in the face. "That's for you, prick," I heard him say before he kicked me a second time. After that, I was no longer listening.

I was under water. Drowning. Only it wasn't water, it was blood. A torrent of blood swept me along, tumbling me over and over. I was drowning in it, unable to breathe. I gasped for air and swallowed sweet mouthfuls of blood.

The bloody tide deposited me on a distant shore. I heard the roaring surf and crawled to keep from being pulled back under. My hands touched something cold, and metallic. It was the curved leg of a park bench.

Voices approached out of the fog. "There he is, officer. That's the man. Oh my God! Look what they've done to him."

"Take it easy, fella," another voice said. "Everything's okay now." Strong arms lifted me from the gory tidepool. "Just lean back, fella. You're gonna be okay. Can you hear what I'm saying?"

When I tried to answer I made a noise like gargling. I clung to the park bench, a life raft in a stormy sea. The swirling red mists parted, and I saw an earnest, square face surrounded by blue. A double row of gold buttons shone like rising suns. I focused on the badge until I could almost read the numbers. When I tried to say thanks, I made the gargling noise again.

"You just relax, fella," the square-faced patrolman said. "We'll get some help here in a minute."

I closed my eyes and heard the other voice say, "It was simply awful. They tried to shoot him."

The patrolman said: "Stay with him. I'm gonna find a call box and send for an ambulance."

The sun felt warm on my battered face. Each separate injury pulsed and throbbed as if a miniature heart worked within it. I reached up and explored my features. Nothing felt familiar. It was a stranger's face.

The sound of voices brought the realization that I'd been unconscious again. The patrolman thanked the man with the dog, calling him Mr. Groton. He said to come by the precinct house at his convenience to make a statement. Mr. Groton said he'd be there this afternoon. I gargled my gratitude, and the patrolman told me to take it easy. "Help is on its way, fella."

The ambulance crew seemed to arrive that very moment, but I knew there'd been another lapse. "Easy does it," one of the attendants said. "Take his legs, Eddie."

I said I could walk, but my knees buckled when I tried to stand. I was lowered to a stretcher, lifted and carried. There didn't seem much point in paying attention to what was going on. The inside of the ambulance smelled like vomit. Above the mounting wail of the siren, I could hear the driver and his partner laughing.

40

THE WORLD CAME BACK INTO focus in the Bellevue emergency room. An intense young intern cleaned and stitched my lacerated scalp and said he'd do the best he knew how with what was left of my ear. Demerol made it all seem okay. I treated the nurse to a broken-toothed smile.

A precinct detective showed up just as they were taking me out for X rays. He walked alongside the wheelchair and asked if I knew the men who tried to rob me. I did nothing to discourage his holdup assumptions, and he left after I described the coach and the kid.

As soon as they finished taking pictures of the inside of my head, the doc said he thought it was a good idea if I got some rest. That was okay with me, and I was put to bed in the accident ward and given another needle under the nightshirt. The next thing I remember was the nurse waking me for dinner.

Halfway through the strained carrots, I found out they were holding me overnight for observation. The X rays revealed no fractures, but concussion was still a possibility. I felt too shitty to make much of a fuss, and after the baby-food meal, the nurse walked me to a pay phone in the corridor, and I called Epiphany to say I wasn't coming home.

She sounded worried at first, but I joked with her and said I'd be fine after a night's sleep. She pretended to believe me. "Know what I did with the twenty you gave me?" she asked.

"Nope."

"Bought a load of firewood."

I told her I had plenty of matches. She laughed, and we said goodbye. I was falling for her. Bad luck for me. The nurse led me back to a waiting needle.

My sleep was nearly dreamless, yet the spectre of Louis Cyphre parted the heavy curtain of drugs and mocked me. Most, of it was lost on waking, but one image remained: an Aztec temple rising abruptly above a crowded plaza, the steep steps slick with blood. At the top, looking down in his flea circus soup-and-fish on the feathered nobles below, Cyphre laughed and hurled the dripping heart of his victim high into the air. The victim was me.

Next morning, I was finishing my Cream of Wheat when Lieutenant Sterne paid a surprise visit to the ward. He was wearing the same brown mohair suit, but his blue flannel shirt and no necktie told me he was off-duty. His face was still all cop.

"Looks like someone did a pretty good job on you," he said.

I showed him my smile. "Don't you wish it'd been you?"

"If it was me, you wouldn't be getting out for a week."

"You forgot the flowers," I said.

"I'm saving 'em for your grave, asshole." Sterne sat on the white chair next to the bed and stared at me like a vulture eyeing a squashed possum on the highway. "I tried to reach you yesterday evening at home, and your answering service told me you were in the hospital. This is the first they'd let me speak to you."

"What's on your mind, Lieutenant?"

"I thought you might be interested in something we found in the Krusemark apartment, seeing as how you never knew the lady."

"I'm holding my breath."

"That's what they do in the gas chamber," Sterne said. "Hold their breath. It don't do no good."

"What is it that they do up in Sing Sing?"

"What I do is I hold my nose. Because they shit their pants the second the juice hits 'em, and it smells like a wienie roast in the toilet."

With a nose like yours, I thought, you'd need both hands! I said: "Tell me what you found in the Krusemark apartment."

"It's what I didn't find. What I didn't find was the page for March 16th on her desk calendar. It was the only page missing. You get so you notice things like that. I sent the page underneath to the lab, and they checked it for impressions. Guess what they found?"

I said I had no idea.

"The initial *H,* followed by the letters *A-n-g."*

"Spells *hang."*

"We're gonna hang your ass, Angel. You know damn well what it spells."

"Coincidence and proof are two different things, Lieutenant."

"Where were you Wednesday afternoon around half past three?"

"Grand Central Terminal."

"Waiting for a train?"

"Eating oysters."

Sterne shook his big head. "No good at all."

"The counterman will remember. I was there a long time. Ate a lot. We joked about it. He said oysters looked like gobs of spit. I said they were good for your sex life. You can check it."

"You bet your ass I'll check it." Sterne got to his feet. "I'll check it five ways from Sunday, and you know what? I'll be there holding my nose when they strap you in the hot-seat."

Sterne reached out a blunt hand. He picked an untouched paper cup of canned grapefruit juice off my tray, downed it in a swallow, and walked out the door.

It was nearly noon before the paperwork was done, and I was able to follow.

41

OUTSIDE BELLEVUE, FIRST AVENUE WAS all torn up, but no one was working on a Saturday. Wooden saw-horse barricades emblazoned DIG WE MUST surrounded the project, corralling dirt piles and stacked cobblestones. Only a thin skin of tar covered the old paving in this part of town. Random patches of cobbled surface remained from a century ago. Cast iron shepherd's-crook lampposts and occasional slabs of bluestone sidewalk were other survivors of a forgotten past.

I expected a tail but spotted none as I walked to a cab stand outside the airline terminal building on 38th Street. The weather was still warm but had clouded over. The weight of my .38 bumped against me in my jacket pocket at every step.

My first stop was the dentist. I called him from the hospital, and he agreed to open his office in the Graybar Building long enough to fit me with temporary caps. We talked about fishing. He said it was a shame he wasn't out dunking bloodworms into Sheepshead Bay.

Numb with painkiller, I hurried to make a one o'clock appointment in the lobby of the Chrysler Building. I was ten minutes late, but Howard Nussbaum patiently waited for me at the Lexington Avenue entrance.

"This is blackmail, Harry, pure and simple," he said as he shook my hand. He was a small, worried-looking man in a brown suit.

"I don't deny it, Howard. Be thankful I'm not after your money."

"The wife and I planned an early start for Connecticut. She's got relatives in New Canaan. So what's a few hours, I said. Soon as I got your call I told Isobel we'd have to be a little late."

Howard Nussbaum was in charge of key control for a company that handled security in a number of big midtown office buildings. He owed his job to me, or rather to the fact that I omitted his name from a report I once filed for his firm tracing a grand master that had turned up in the purse of a teenage prostitute. "Did you bring it?" I asked.

"Would I come and not bring it?" He reached inside his jacket and handed me a small unsealed brown envelope. I slid a brand-new key out onto the palm of my hand. It looked exactly like any other key.

"This a master?"

"I should trust you with a master key to the Chrysler Building?" Howard Nussbaum's frown deepened. "It's a submaster for the forty-fifth floor. There's not a lock on the floor it won't fit. Mind telling me who you're going after?"

"Ask me no questions, Howard. That way you're not an accessory."

"I'm an accessory all right," he said. "I've been an accessory all my life."

"Have fun in Connecticut."

I rode up in the elevator, studying the little brown envelope and picking my nose so that the operator looked away. The envelope was stamped and pre-addressed. Howard's instructions were to seal the key inside when I was done and drop it in the nearest mailbox. There was an off-chance that somewhere among my half-G set of twirls I had one that would work the same trick. But skeleton keys require locks with mechanisms worn through the use of duplicates, and Howard Nussbaum's firm will replace a lock rather than save money on third-generation keys.

The lights were dim behind the frosted doors of Krusemark

Maritime, Inc. At the other end of the corridor a distant typewriter tapped erratically. I pulled on my surgeon's gloves and slipped the sub-master into the first of many locks. It was a door-opening charm on a par with Margaret Krusemark's mummified Hand of Glory.

I checked out the entire office, moving through rooms of shrouded typewriters and silent telephones. No overambitious junior executives giving up their golf games this Saturday. Even the Teletype machines had the weekend off.

I set up the Minox and the copying easel on the L-shaped desk and turned on the fluorescent lights. My penknife and a bent paperclip were all it took to pop the locked filing cabinets and desk drawers. I didn't know what I was looking for, but Krusemark had something he wanted to hide bad enough to send the goon squad after me.

The afternoon dragged on. I thumbed through hundreds of files, photographing anything that looked promising. Several altered manifests and one letter referring to a congressman open to bribery were the best I could do in the way of criminal activity. That didn't mean it wasn't there. There's always a little crime under the corporate rug if you know where to look.

I shot fifteen rolls of film. Every major deal Krusemark Maritime had a finger in passed under my copying easel. Somewhere, lurking behind all the statistics, was enough crime to keep the D.A.'s office hopping for months.

When I finished the filing cabinets, I let myself into Krusemark's private office with the submaster and bought myself a drink at the mirrored bar. I carried the crystal balloon snifter with me as I went over the wall paneling and looked behind all the paintings. There was no sign of a safe or any tricky carpentry.

Other than the couch, the bar, and the marble-slab desk, the room was bare; no files, no drawers or shelves. I sat my empty glass on the center of the gleaming desk. No papers or letters, not even a pen-and-pencil set disfigured the polished surface. The bronze statuette of Neptune stood far at the other end, poised above his perfect reflection.

I looked under the marble slab. You couldn't see it from above, but a shallow recessed steel drawer was cleverly concealed underneath. It wasn't locked. A small lever alongside released a catch and hidden springs sent it gliding open like a drawer in a cash register. Inside were several expensive fountain-pens, a photograph of Margaret Krusemark in an oval silver frame, an eight-inch dirk with a gold-mounted ivory grip, and a scattering of letters.

I picked up a familiar envelope and removed the card. An inverted pentagram was embossed at the top. The Latin words were no longer a problem. Ethan Krusemark had his own invitation to the Black Mass.

42

I PUT EVERYTHING BACK THE way I found it and packed my camera away. Before leaving, I rinsed the snifter in the executive washroom and set it carefully in line on a glass shelf above the bar. I had planned on leaving it on Krusemark's desk so he'd have something to think about Monday morning, but it no longer seemed like such a cute idea.

When I hit the street it was raining. The temperature had dropped fifteen degrees. I turned up my jacket collar and dodged across Lexington Avenue to Grand Central, calling Epiphany from the first empty phone booth. I asked how long it would take her to get ready. She said she'd been ready for hours.

"Sounds inviting, sweetheart," I said, "but I'm talking about business. Take a cab. Meet me at my office in half an hour. We'll have dinner and then go uptown to hear a lecture."

"What lecture?"

"Maybe it's a sermon."

"Sermon?"

"Bring my raincoat in the front closet and don't be late."

Before heading for the subway, I found a newsstand with a key cutter and had a copy made of Howard Nussbaum's submaster. The original I sealed in the little preaddressed envelope and dropped in a mailbox by a row of pay lockers.

I took the shuttle over to Times Square. It was still raining when I left the subway, and the reflections of neon signs and traffic lights writhed on the wet pavement like fire snakes. I dodged from doorway to doorway trying to keep dry. The pimps and pushers and teenage hookers huddled in the juice bars and penny arcades, forlorn as rain-soaked cats. I bought a pocketful of cigars at the store on the corner and glanced up, through the drizzle at the headlines moving across Times Tower . . . TIBETANS BATTLE CHINESE IN LHASA . . .

When I got to my office at ten past six, Epiphany was waiting in the Naugahyde chair. She was all dressed up in her plum-colored suit and looked fantastic. She felt and tasted even better.

"Missed you," she whispered. Her fingers lightly traced the bandage covering my left ear and hovered over the spot where my scalp was shaved. "Oh, Harry, are you all right?"

"I'm fine. Maybe not so pretty anymore."

"The way the side of your head is stitched makes you look like Frankenstein."

"I've been avoiding mirrors."

"And your poor, poor mouth."

"How's the nose?"

"About the same, only a little more so."

We ate at Lindy's. I told Epiphany if anyone stared at us, the other customers would think we were celebrities. No one stared.

"Did that Lieutenant come and see you?" She dunked a shrimp into a bowl of cocktail sauce packed in crushed ice.

"He brightened my breakfast hour. Smart of you to say you were the answering service."

"I'm a smart girl."

"You're a good actress," I said. "You fooled Sterne twice the same day."

"I am not one woman, but many. Just as you are more than one man."

"Is that voodoo?"

"That's common sense."

By eight o'clock we were driving uptown through the park. As we passed the Meer, I asked Epiphany why she and her group were out sacrificing under the stars that night, instead of at home in the humfo. She said something about tree loa.

"Loa?"

"Spirits. Manifestations of God. Many, many loa. Rada loa, petro loa: good and evil. Damballa is a loa. Badé is the loa of the wind; Sogbo, the lightning loa; Baron Samedi, the keeper of the cemetery, lord of sex and passion; Papa Legba watches over homes and meeting places, gates and fences. Maître Carrefour is the guardian of all crossroads."

"He must be my patron loa," I said.

"He is the protector of sorcerers."

The New Temple of Hope on 144th Street had at one time been a movie house. The old marquee hung out over the sidewalk with EL ÇIFR in foot-high letters on all three sides. I parked further down the block and took Epiphány's arm as we walked back toward the bright lights.

"What're you interested in Çifr for?" she asked.

"He's the magician in my dreams."

"Çifr?"

"The good Doctor Cipher himself."

"What do you mean?"

"This swami business is just one of several roles I've seen him play. He's like a chameleon."

Epiphany's grip tightened on my arm. "Be careful, Harry, please."

"I try to be," I said.

"Don't joke. If this man is what you say, he must have plenty power. He is no one to fool with."

"Let's go inside."

A life-sized cardboard cutout of Louis Cyphre in his sheik's outfit stood by the empty ticket booth, beckoning the faithful with an outstretched arm. The lobby was a gilded plaster pagoda, a movie-palace pleasure dome. In place of popcorn and candy, the refreshment stand carried a complete line of inspirational literature.

We found seats off the side aisle. An organ murmured behind the closed red-and-gold curtains. The orchestra and balcony filled to capacity. No one but me seemed to notice that I was the only Caucasian in sight.

"What denomination is this?" I whispered.

"Basic Baptist, with frills." Epiphany folded her gloved hands in her lap. "This is the Reverend Love's church! Don't tell me you haven't ever heard him?"

I confessed my ignorance.

"Well, his car is about five times bigger than your office," she said.

The houselights dimmed, the organ music swelled, and the curtain parted to reveal a one-hundred-voice choir grouped in the shape of a cross. The congregation rose to their feet, singing "Jesus Was a Fisherman." I joined in the hand clapping and bestowed my smile upon Epiphany who surveyed the proceedings with the stern detachment of a true believer among the barbarians.

As the music reached a crescendo, a small brown man dressed in white satin appeared on stage. Diamonds flashed on both hands. The choir broke ranks as he stood there, marching with drill-team precision, and formed around him in white-robed rows, like rays of light reflecting from the risen moon.

I caught Epiphany's eye and mouthed the question, "Reverend Love?"

She nodded.

"Please be seated, brothers and sisters," Reverend Love spoke from center stage. His voice was comically high and shrill. He sounded like the emcee at Birdland.

"Brothers and sisters, I welcome you with love to the New Temple of Hope. I rejoice in the happy sound you make. Tonight, as you know, is not one of our regular meetings. We are honored to have with us this evening a very holy man, the illustrious el Çifr. Although not of our faith, this is a man I respect, a man of great wisdom with much to teach. It will profit us all to listen closely to the words of our esteemed guest, el Çifr."

Reverend Love turned and held out his open arms toward the wings. The choir broke into a chorus of "A New Day Is Dawning." The congregation clapped their hands as Louis Cyphre swirled onto the stage like a sultan.

I rummaged in my attaché case for the ten-power Trinovids. Wrapped in his embroidered robes and crowned by a turban, el Çifr might well have been another man, but when I brought his features into focus through the binoculars, it was unmistakably my client in blackface. "It is the Moor, I know his trumpet," I whispered to Epiphany.

"What?"

"Shakespeare."

"?"

El Çifr greeted his audience with a fancy salaam. "May prosperity smile upon you all," he said, bowing low. "Is it not written that Paradise is open to those who dare but enter?"

A smattering of "Amens" rippled through the congregation.

"The world belongs to the strong, not the meek. Is this not so? The lion devours the fold; the falcon feasts on the blood of the sparrow. Who denies this denies the order of the universe."

"That's true, that's true," an impassioned voice called from the balcony.

"Sounds like the flip side of the Sermon on the Mount," Epiphany quipped out of the side of her mouth.

El Çifr paced the apron of the stage. He held his palms together like a supplicant, but his eyes were ablaze with raw fury. "It is the hand holding the whip that drives the wagon. The rider's flesh does not feel the sting of the spurs. To be strong in this life requires an act of will. Choose to be a wolf, not a gazelle."

The congregation responded to his every suggestion, clapping and shouting agreement. His words were chorused like Scripture. "Be a wolf . . . be a wolf . . . " they called.

"Look about you here on these crowded streets. Do not the strong rule?"

"They do. They do."

"And the meek suffer in silence!"

"Amen. They surely suffer."

"It is a wilderness out there, and only the strong shall survive."

"Only the strong . . . "

"Be like the lion and the wolf, not the lamb. Let other throats be cut. Do not obey the herd-instinct of cowardice. Steep your hearts in bold deeds. If there can be but one winner, let it be you!"

"One winner . . . bold deeds . . . be a lion . . . "

He had them eating out of his hand. He whirled on the stage like a dervish, robes billowing, his melodic voice exhorting the faithful: "Be strong. Be bold. Know the urge to attack as well as the wisdom of retreat. When opportunity comes, seize it, as a lion seizes the fawn. Tear success out of defeat; rip it free; devour it. You are the most dangerous beast on the planet. What is there to be afraid of?"

He danced and chanted, ranting of power and strength. The congregation howled a frenzied litany. Even members of the choir shouted angry responses and shook their fists in the air.

I found myself daydreaming, not paying attention to the rhetoric, when suddenly my client said something out of left field that brought me up short.

"If thine eye offend thee, pluck it out," el Çifr said, looking, or so it seemed, straight at me. "That is a fine quotation, but I say also, if anyone's eye offend you, rip it out. Claw it out! Shoot it out! An eye for an eye!"

His words shot through me like a spasm of pain. I sat forward in my seat, alert as I could be.

"Why turn the other cheek?" he continued. "Why be hit at

all? If hearts are steeped against you, cut them out. Don't wait to be the victim. Strike first at your enemies. If their eyes offend you, blow them out. If their hearts offend you, rip them out. If any member offends you, cut it off and shove it down their throats."

El Çifr was shrieking above the roars of his audience. I felt numb, transfixed. Was I imagining it all or had Louis Cyphre just described three murders?

At last, el Çifr thrust both hands above his head in a victory salute. "Be strong," he yelled. "Promise me to be strong!"

The audience was frantic. "We will . . . we promise," they screamed. El Çifr disappeared into the wings as the choir regrouped onstage and burst into a lusty arrangement of "The Strong Arm of the Lord."

I grabbed Epiphany's hand and pulled her with me into the aisle. There were others ahead of us, and I hauled her along, shouldering past with a murmured "Excuse me, please." We hurried on through the lobby and out onto the street.

The silver-grey Rolls waited at the curb. I recognized the uniformed chauffeur lounging against the front fender. He jumped to attention as a door marked FIRE EXIT opened and a rectangular carpet of light reached across the pavement. Two Negroes in three-button suits and dark glasses stepped out and surveyed the situation. They looked as solid as the Great Wall of China.

El Çifr joined them on the sidewalk, and they started for the car, flanked by another pair of heavyweights. "Just a minute," I called, and made my move. I was immediately strong-armed by the lead bodyguard.

"Don't go be doin' nothin' you're likely to regret," he said, blocking my path.

I didn't argue. A return trip to the hospital was not on the agenda. As the chauffeur opened the rear door, I caught the eye of the man in the turban. Louis Cyphre stared at me without expression. He lifted the hem of his robes and climbed into the Rolls. The chauffeur closed the door.

I watched them drive off from around the bodyguard's bulk. He stood there, impassive as an Easter Island statue, waiting for me to try something. Epiphany came up from behind and linked her arm through mine. "Let's go home and build a fire," she said.

43

PALM SUNDAY WAS SLUMBEROUS AND sensual, the novelty of waking up beside Epiphany compounded by finding myself on the floor, nestled among couch cushions and tangled blanketed Only a single charred fragment remained in the fireplace. I started a pot of coffee and brought the Sunday papers in off the doormat. Epiphany was awake before I finished the comics.

"Sleep well?" she whispered, curling in my lap. "No bad dreams?"

"No dreams at all." I ran my hand over her smooth brown flank.

"That's good."

"Maybe the spell is broken?"

"Maybe." Her warm breath fanned my neck. "It was me dreamed about him last night."

"Who? Cipher?"

"Cipher, Çifr, whatever you want to call him. I dreamed I was at the circus and he was the ringmaster. You were one of the clowns."

"What happened?"

"Nothing much. It was a nice dream." She sat up straight. "Harry? What has he got to do with Johnny Favorite?"

"I'm not sure. I seem to be mixed up in some sort of struggle between two magicians."

"Is Çifr the man who wants you to find my father?"

"Yes."

"Harry, be careful. Don't trust him."

Can I trust you, I thought, hugging her slender shoulders. "I'll be all right."

"I love you. I don't want anything bad to happen now."

I choked back the urge to echo her words, to say I love you over and over again. "It's just a schoolgirl crush," I said, heart racing.

"I'm not a child." She stared deep into my eyes. "I gave my virginity at twelve as an offering to Baka."

"Baka?"

"An evil loa; very dangerous and bad."

"Your mother let this happen?"

"It was an honor. The most powerful houngan in Harlem performed the rite. And he was older than you by twenty years, so don't tell me I'm too young."

"I like your eyes when you get mad," I said. "They glow like embers."

"How'm I supposed to get mad at someone sweet as you?" She kissed me. I kissed her back, and we made love sitting in the overstuffed armchair surrounded by the Sunday funnies.

Later, after breakfast, I carried the stack of library books into the bedroom and stretched out with my homework. Epiphany kneeled beside me on the bed, wearing my bathrobe and her reading glasses. "Don't waste time looking at pictures," she said, taking the book from my hands and closing it. "Here." She handed me another, not much heavier than a dictionary. "The chapter I marked is all about the Black Mass. The liturgy is described in detail, everything from the backwards Latin to the virgin deflowered on the altar."

"Sounds like what happened to you."

"Yes. There are similarities. Sacrifice. The dancing. Violent passions are aroused, same as Obeah. The difference is between appeasing the force of evil and encouraging it."

"Do you really believe there's such a thing as the force of evil?"

Epiphany smiled. "Sometimes I think you're the child. Can't you feel it in your sleep at night, when Çifr haunts your dreams?"

"I'd rather feel you," I said, reaching for her supple waist.

"Be serious, Harry, these aren't just another bunch of crooks. They are men of power, demonic power. If you can't defend yourself, you're lost."

"You hinting it's time to tackle the books?"

"It's nice to know what you're up against." Epiphany tapped the open page with her forefinger. "Read this chapter and the next one on invocations. Then in Crowley's book I've marked some interesting spots. The Reginald Scott you might as well skip." She stacked the books in order of importance, a hierarchy of hell, and left me to my studies.

I read until it grew dark, a do-it-yourself course in the satanic sciences. Epiphany built a fire and declined an invitation to dine at Cavanaugh's, magically reincarnating a bouillabaisse she made while I was in the hospital. We ate by firelight, shadows shifting like imps on the walls around us. There wasn't much talk; her eyes said it all. They were the most beautiful eyes I had ever seen.

Even the nicest times have to end. About seven-thirty, I started getting ready for work. I dressed in jeans, a navy blue turtleneck, and a stout pair of lace-top, rubber-soled hiking boots. I loaded my black-bodied Leica with Tri-X and got the .38 out of my raincoat pocket. Epiphany, tousle-headed, watched in silence, wrapped in a blanket before the fire.

I laid everything out on the dining table: camera, two extra rolls of film, revolver, the handcuffs from my attaché case, and my indispensable twirls. I added Howard Nussbaum's submaster to the key ring. In the bedroom I found a box of cartridges under my shirts and tied five extra shells in the corner of a handkerchief. I hung the Leica around my neck and pulled on a leather aviator's jacket I'd had since the war. All the service patches were removed. Nothing flashy to catch the light. It was lined with shearling and just the thing to wear on cold winter stakeouts. The Smith & Wesson went into the right-hand pocket with the extra rounds; the cuffs, film, and keys went into the left.

"You forgot your invitation," Epiphany said as I reached under the blanket and pulled her close one last time.

"Don't need one. I'm crashing this party."

"What about your wallet? Think you'll need that?"

She was right. I'd felt it in my jacket from the night before. We started laughing and kissing at the same time, but she broke away with a shiver and hugged the blanket tight. "Go away," she said. "Sooner you go, sooner you'll be back."

"Try not to worry," I said.

She smiled to show me everything was okay, but her eyes were large and wet. "Take care of yourself."

"That's my motto."

"I'll be waiting for you."

"Keep the chain on the door." I got my wallet and a knitted navy watch cap. "Time to go."

Epiphany ran down the hall, shedding the blanket like an emerging nymph. She kissed me long and deeply at the door. "Here," she said, pressing a small object into my hand. "Keep this with you always." It was a leather disk with a crudely drawn tree flanked by zigzag lightning bolts inked on the suede side.

"What's this?"

"A hand, a trick, a mojo; people call it different things. A charm. The talisman is the symbol of Gran Bois, a loa of great power. He overcomes all bad luck."

"You once said I needed all the help I can get."

"You still do."

I pocketed the charm, and we kissed again, somewhat chastely. Nothing more was said. I heard the chain slide into place as I started for the elevator. Why didn't I tell her I loved her when I had the chance?

I took the Eighth Avenue IND downtown to 14th Street where

I caught the BMT over to Union Square and hurried down the iron stairs to the IRT platform, just missing an uptown local. I had time to eat a penny's worth of peanuts before the next train. The car was nearly empty, but I didn't take a seat. I leaned against the closed double doors watching the dirty white tiles slide by as we left the station.

The lights blinked off and on when the train rounded a bend after entering the tunnel. The metal wheels screamed like wounded eagles against the rails. I gripped a pole for balance and stared out into blackness. We gathered speed and a moment later it was there.

You had to look close to see it. Only the lights of our passing train reflecting on the soot-covered tiles revealed the ghostly presence of the abandoned 18th Street station. Most passengers, making this same trip twice every working day of their lives, probably never noticed it. According to the official subway map, it didn't exist.

I could make out the mosaic numerals decorating each tile column and saw a shadowy stack of trash cans against the wall. Then, we were back in the tunnel, and it was gone, like a dream you no longer remember.

I got off at the next stop, 23rd Street. I climbed the stairs, crossed the avenue, descended, and shelled out fifteen cents for another token. There were several people on the platform waiting for the downtown train, so I stood around admiring the new Miss Rheingold who had a ballpoint mustache and SUPPORT MENTAL HEALTH penciled across her forehead.

A train marked "Brooklyn Bridge" pulled in, and everyone got on except me and an old woman loitering at the end of the platform. I strolled along in her direction looking at wall posters, pretending to be interested in the smiling man who got his job through the *New York Times* and the cute Chinese kid munching a slice of rye bread.

The old woman ignored me. She wore a shabby black overcoat

with several buttons missing and carried a shopping bag. Out of the corner of my eye, I watched her climb up on the wooden bench, reach above her head to open the wire cage around the light, and quickly unscrew the bulb.

She was off the bench and had the lightbulb in her shopping bag by the time I strolled up. I smiled at her. "Save your strength," I said. "Those bulbs won't do you any good. They've all got a left-hand thread."

"Don't know what you're talking about," she said.

"The Transit Department uses a special lightbulb with a left-handed thread. To discourage theft. They won't fit an ordinary socket."

"I got no idea what you're talking about." She hurried away from me down the platform, not once looking back. I waited until she was safely in the ladies restroom.

An uptown express roared through as I started down the narrow metal ladder at the end of the platform. A pathway alongside the tracks led away into darkness. At distant intervals along the tunnel wall the feeble glow of low-wattage bulbs marked the way through the gloom. Between trains it was very quiet, and I surprised several rats scuttling among the cinders on the track bed beside me.

The subway tunnel was like an endless cave. Water dripped from the ceiling, and the dirty walls were slick with slime. Once, a downtown local sped past and I pressed back against the clammy wall and stared up at lighted cars flashing only inches from my face. A little boy kneeling on the seat spotted me, his bland expression expanding with astonishment. His car was gone even as he started to point.

It seemed as if I had walked many more than five city blocks. There were occasional alcove openings with conduits and metal ladders leading up. I hurried along, my hands in my pockets. The checkered grip of the .38 felt rough and comforting.

I didn't see the abandoned station until I was ten feet from the ladder. The soot-covered tiles gleamed like a ruined temple in the moonlight. I stood very still and caught my breath, my heart bumping against the Leica hanging under my jacket. In the distance, I heard a baby cry.

44

THE SOUND ECHOED IN THE darkness. I listened for a long time before deciding it came from the opposite platform. Crossing four sets of tracks didn't look like fun, and I debated the risks of using my penlight before remembering I'd left it at home.

Distant lights from the tunnel gleamed along twin ribbons of track. Although it was dark, I could make out rows of iron girders like shadowed tree trunks in a midnight forest. What I couldn't see were my own feet, and I felt the lurking menace of the third rail, lethal as a hidden rattlesnake in the gloom.

I heard a train approaching and looked back down the tunnel. Nothing in sight on my track bed. It was an uptown local, and when it passed through the abandoned station, I took advantage of the cover to step between the girders over two sets of third rails. I followed the trackbed of the downtown express, measuring my pace to the spacing of the ties.

The sounds of another train alerted me. I checked my rear and felt an adrenaline surge. The train was highballing down the tunnel. I stepped between the girders separating the express tracks and wondered if the motorman had me spotted. The train roared through like an angry dragon, spitting sparks from its clattering wheels.

I made a final third-rail crossing, and the deafening noise covered any sounds of my climbing onto the opposite platform. As the four red lights on the rear car flickered out of sight, I was flat against the cold tiles of the station wall.

The baby was no longer crying. At least not loud enough to be heard over the drone of chanting. It sounded like gobbledygook, but I knew from my afternoon's research that it was Latin in reverse. I was late for church.

I got the .38 out of my pocket and eased along the wall. A faint, ephemeral curtain of light hung in the air ahead. Soon, I could discern grotesque silhouettes swaying in what was once the entrance alcove of the station. The turnstiles and gates had been removed long ago. From the corner I saw the candles: fat, black candles arranged along the inner wall. If this was by the book, they were made from human fat, like the ones in Maggie Krusemark's bathroom.

The congregation wore robes and animal masks. Goats, tigers, wolves, horned creatures of every variety; all chanting a backwards litany. I slipped my pistol into my pocket and took out the Leica. The candles surrounded a low altar draped in black cloth. A cross hung upside down on the tile wall above it.

The presiding priest was plump and pink. He wore a black chasuble embroidered with cabalistic symbols in a riot of gold thread. It was open down the front. Underneath he was naked, his erection trembling in the candlelight. Two young acolytes, naked under their thin cotton surplices, stood on either side of the altar swinging censers. The smoke had the acrid sweetness of burning opium.

I took a couple of pictures of the priest and his pretty young punks. There wasn't enough light to do much more. The priest recited the looking-glass prayers, and the congregation responded with howls and grunts. An uptown express came rattling through, and I counted the crowd in the flickering light. Seventeen including the priest and the altar boys.

From what I could tell, the congregation were all naked beneath their swirling capes. I thought I spotted Krusemark's hard old-man's body. He was wearing the mask of a lion. I saw the flash of his silver hair as he shuffled and howled. I took four more shots before the train was gone.

The priest beckoned, and from out of the shadows came a lovely adolescent girl. Her waist-length blonde hair fell across her mourner's cape like sunlight dispelling night. She stood absolutely still as the priest undid the fastenings. The cape slid in silence to the ground, revealing slender shoulders and budding breasts, a patch of pubic floss like spun gold in the candlelight.

I snapped more pictures as the priest escorted her to the altar. Her dull and languorous movements suggested heavy sedation. She was lowered onto the black cloth and lay on her back, legs dangling and arms spread. In each upturned palm the priest placed a squat black candle.

"Accept the unblemished purity of this virgin," the priest intoned. "O Lucifer, we implore thee." He dropped to his knees and kissed the girl between her legs, leaving tangled pearls of spittle shining there. "May this chaste flesh honor your divine name."

He rose and one of the altar boys handed him an open silver box. He withdrew a sacramental wafer, then turned the box over, scattering the translucent disks at the feet of the congregation. There was more reverse-gear Latin as the worshipers stamped on the wafers. Several urinated noisily against the pavement.

One acolyte handed the priest a tall silver chalice; the other stooped and gathered bits of broken wafer off the floor, placing them inside. The congregation snuffled and grunted like rutting swine as he balanced the chalice on the perfect belly of the teen-age girl. "O Astaroth, Asmodeus, princes of friendship and love, I beg you to accept this blood which is shed for thee."

A baby's lusty howls pierced the bestial grunting. The altar boy stepped out of the shadows carrying a squirming infant. The priest grasped it by a leg and held it high in the air, kicking and screaming. "O Baalbarith, O Beelzebub," he cried, "this child is offered in thy name."

It happened very quickly. The priest gave the baby to an acolyte and was handed the knife in return. The bright blade caught the candlelight as they cut the infant's throat. The tiny creature bucked for life, his cries a muffled gargle. "I sacrifice you to Divine Lucifer. May the peace of Satan always be with you." The priest held the chalice under the spouting blood. I finished the roll as the baby died.

The congregation's throaty moaning grew louder than the accelerating rumble of an oncoming train. I slumped against the wall and reloaded the camera. No one was paying any attention to me. The acolyte shook the limp child to catch the final precious drops. A vivid splattering glistened on the dirty walls and across the pale flesh of the girl on the altar. I wished every frame I'd shot had been a bullet and other blood darkened the forgotten tiles.

A train came crashing through, casting its bold light on the proceedings. The priest drank from the chalice and hurled what was left out over the crowd. The masqueraders howled with delight. The dead baby was discarded. The acolytes stood jerking each other off, heads back and laughing.

Tossing his chasuble aside, the plump, pink priest kneeled above the blood-splattered virgin, entering her with short, doglike thrusts. The girl made no response. The candles remained upright in her outstretched hands. Her wide-open eyes stared sightlessly into the darkness.

The congregation went wild. Casting off cloaks and masks, they coupled frantically on the pavement. Men and women in every possible combination, including a quartet. The stark light of the passing train cast their frenzied shadows against the subway wall. Their howls and moans carried above the violent clatter of the wheels.

I saw Ethan Krusemark cornholing a hairy little man with a potbelly. They were standing in the men's room entrance and looked like a silent stag movie in the flickering light. I shot a whole roll of the shipping tycoon in action.

The party went on for at most half an hour. It was early in the season for subway orgies, and the cold, clammy air eventually sapped the enthusiasm of even the most ardent devil worshiper. Soon, they were all hunting for lost clothing, grumbling over hard-to-find shoes in the dark. I kept my eye on Krusemark.

He packed his costume in a valise and gave some of the others a hand cleaning up. The black altar cloth and inverted cross were removed, the blood wiped away with rags. At length, the candles were extinguished, and the group began dispersing in singles and pairs. Some, headed uptown, others down. Several with flashlights started across the tracks to the other side. One carried a heavy, dripping sack.

Krusemark was among the last to go. He stood whispering to the priest for several minutes. The blonde girl slouched like a zombie behind them. They said goodbye and shook hands like Presbyterians at the close of service. Krusemark passed within an arm's length as he walked uptown along the deserted platform.

45

KRUSEMARK ENTERED THE TUNNEL, WALKING rapidly along the narrow pathway. This wasn't the first time he'd taken a stroll in the subway. I let him get as far as the first naked lightbulb before following. I matched his pace, step for step, soundless as a shadow on my rubber-soled boots. If he chanced to look back, the game was up. Tailing a man in a tunnel was like staking out a divorce case by hiding under the hotel room bed.

The approach of a downtown train gave me the opening I needed. As the rumbling thunder of the oncoming express built to an iron crescendo, I started running for all I was worth. The train's roar drowned the slap of footfalls. The .38 was in my hand. Krusemark never heard a thing.

As the last car shot past, Krusemark disappeared. He was less then ten yards away, and then he was gone. How could I have lost him in a tunnel? Another five strides and I saw the open doorway. It was a service exit of some kind, and Krusemark was starting up a metal ladder fastened to the back wall.

"Freeze!" I held the Smith & Wesson at arm's length in a two-handed grip.

Krusemark turned, blinking in the half-light. "Angel?"

"Turn around and face the ladder. Place both hands on a rung above your head."

"Be reasonable, Angel. We can talk this over."

"Move it!" I lowered my aim. "The first one goes through your kneecap. You'll use a cane for the rest of your life."

Krusemark did as he was told, dropping his leather satchel to the floor. I stepped behind him and frisked him down. He was clean. I got my bracelets out of my jacket pocket and clipped one cuff to his right wrist and the other to the rung he gripped. He faced me, and I backhanded him full strength across the mouth with my left.

"You filthy scum!" I jammed the muzzle of the .38 under his chin, forcing his head back. His eyes were wide as a trapped stallion's. "I'd like to spray your brains all over the wall, cocksucker."

"Have you gone m-mad?" he stammered.

"Mad? Goddamned right I'm mad. I've been mad ever since you set your goons on me."

"You're making a mistake."

"Bullshit! Everything you say is a crock of shit. Maybe if I rearrange some teeth, it'll help you remember." I grinned at him, exposing my temporary dental work. "Like your torpedoes did to me."

"I don't know what you're talking about."

"Sure you do. You set me up and now you're trying to save your ass. You've been lying since the first minute I met you. Edward Kelley is the name of an Elizabethan magician. That's why you used it as an alias, not because your daughter thought it was cute."

"You seem to know all about it."

"I've been doing some homework. I brushed up on my black magic. So save the crap about how the maid slipped your daughter the tarot cards when she was in knee socks. It was you all the time. You're the devil worshiper."

"I'd be a fool if I wasn't. The Prince of Darkness protects the powerful. You should pray to Him yourself, Angel. You'd be surprised at the good things that would happen."

"Like what? Slitting babies' throats? Where'd you snatch the kid from, Krusemark?"

He sneered at me. "There was no snatching involved. We paid hard cash for the little bastard. One less welfare mouth for the taxpayers to feed. You are a taxpayer, aren't you, Angel?"

I spit in his face. I'd never done that to anyone before. "A cockroach is the chosen of God alongside you. I don't feel a thing when I step on a roach, so stepping on you should be a pleasure. Let's start at the beginning. I want to know all about Johnny Favorite. The works. Everything you've ever seen or heard."

"Why should I? You won't kill me. You're too weak." He wiped the saliva off his cheek.

"I don't need to kill you. I can walk out of here and leave you hanging. How long do you think it would be before someone found you? Two days? A week? Two weeks? You can pass the time counting the trains go by."

Krusemark looked a little ashen, but he kept on bluffing. "What good would it do you?" The rest of it was lost in the roar of a passing train.

"It might give me a few laughs," I said after it passed. "And when these pictures are developed, I'll have something in my scrapbook to remember you by." I held up a yellow roll of film so he could get a good look. "My favorite is the one of you screwing the little fat man. I might even get an enlargement of that."

"You're bluffing."

"Am I?" I showed him my Leica. "I shot two rolls of thirty-six. It's all in black-and-white, as they say."

"There's not enough light to take, pictures down here."

"There is for Tri-X. Photography must not be one of your hobbies. I'll hang some of the juicier blowups on your office bulletin board. The newspapers might get a kick out of them, too. Not to mention the police." I turned to leave. "See you around. Why don't you try praying to the devil? Maybe he'll come and set you free."

Krusemark's disdainful smirk melted into a frown of deep concern. "Angel, wait. Let's talk this over."

"That's just what I had in mind, big shot. You talk, I'll do the listening."

Krusemark held out his free hand. "Give me the film. I'll tell you everything I know."

That made me laugh. "No deal. First you sing. If I like the tune, then you get the film."

Krusemark rubbed the bridge of his nose and stared at the dirty floor. "All right." His eyes flickered like yo-yos as he watched me toss and catch the film. "I first met Johnny in the winter of '39. It was Candlemas eve. There was a celebration at the home of, well, her name doesn't matter; she's been dead ten years now. She owned a townhouse on Fifth near where they're building that ugly Frank Lloyd Wright museum. In the old days the place was famous for society balls; Mrs. Astor, the Four Hundred, that sort of thing. But the big ballroom was used only for Old Faith ceremonies and Sabbats when I knew it."

"Black Masses?"

"Sometimes. I never went to one there, but I had friends who did. Anyway, it was the night I met Johnny. I was impressed with him right at the start. He couldn't have been more than nineteen or twenty, but he had something special. You could feel the power running out of him like an electric current. His eyes were more alive than any I'd seen before in my life, and I've been around some.

"I introduced him to my daughter, and they hit it off right away. She was already more versed in the dark arts than me, and she recognized that special something in Johnny. His career was only getting started, and he was hungry for fame and wealth. Power was something he already had in spades. I watched him conjure up Lucifuge Rofocale, right in my own living room. That's a very complicated procedure."

"You expect me to swallow this?" I asked.

Krusemark leaned back against the ladder, resting one foot on the bottom rung. "Swallow it, spit it out; I don't give a damn. It's the truth. Johnny was in a lot deeper than I had the nerve to go. The things he did would have driven an ordinary man nuts. He always wanted more. He wanted it all. That's why he made a pact with Satan."

"What kind of pact?"

"The usual arrangement. He sold his soul for stardom."

"Crap!"

"It's true."

"It's bullshit, and you know it. What'd he do, sign a contract in blood?"

"I don't know the details." Krusemark's haughty glance was impatient and scornful. "Johnny was alone at midnight in Trinity Churchyard for the invocation. You shouldn't take what I say so lightly, Angel, not when playing with forces beyond your control."

"Okay, let's say I buy it: Johnny Favorite made—a deal with the devil."

"Lord Satan Himself rose from the depths of Hell. It must have been magnificent."

"Sounds pretty risky, selling your soul. Eternity's a long time."

Krusemark smiled. On him it was more of a leer. "Pride," he said. "Johnny's sin was pride. He thought he could outwit the Prince of Darkness Himself."

"How?"

"You must understand I'm not a scholar, only a believer. I attended the ritual as a witness, but I can't tell you anything about the magic nature of the invocations or what went on during the week-long preparations preceding it."

"Get to the point."

Before he could get started, he was interrupted by a downtown express. I watched his eyes, and he met my gaze. Not an eyelid flicker betrayed him as he shuffled and reshuffled his story until the last car roared past.

"With Satan's help, Johnny made it big in a hurry. Real big. Overnight, he was a headliner; within a couple years he was rich as Fort Knox. I guess it went to his head. He started thinking it was him that was the source of the power and not the Dark One. It wasn't long before he was boasting he found a way to duck out of his end of the bargain."

"Did he?"

"He tried. He had quite a library, and he came across an obscure rite in a manuscript by some Renaissance alchemist. It involved the transmutation of souls. Johnny had the idea that he could switch psychic-identities with someone else. Actually become the essence of the other person."

"Go on."

"Well, he had to have a victim. Someone his own age, born under the same sign. Johnny found a young soldier just back from North Africa. One of our first casualties. He had a brand-new medical discharge and was out celebrating New Year's Eve. Johnny picked him up in the crowd at Times Square. He drugged him in a bar and took him back to his place. That's where the ceremony took place."

"What kind of ceremony?"

"The transmutation rite. Meg assisted him. I was the witness. Johnny had an apartment at the Waldorf where he kept one room empty at all times for ceremonial use. The maids were told he practiced singing there.

"Dark velour curtains covered the windows. The soldier was bound naked on his back on a rubber mat. Johnny branded a pentacle on his chest. There was an incense brazier smoking in each corner, but the smell of burning flesh was much stronger.

"Meg unsheathed a virgin dagger, one never used before. Johnny blessed it in Hebrew and Greek. The prayers were new to me; I couldn't understand a word. When he finished, he bathed the blade in the altar flame and cut the soldier deeply across each tit. He dipped the dagger into the kid's blood and traced a circle with it on the floor around the body.

"There were more chants and incantations then. I didn't follow any of it. What I remember are the smells and the dancing shadows. Meg sprinkled handfuls of chemicals into the fire, and the flames changed color, green and blue, violet, pink. It was hypnotic."

"Sounds like the floorshow at the Copa. What happened to the soldier?"

"Johnny ate his heart. He cut it out so fast it was still beating when he wolfed it down. That was the end of the ceremony. Maybe he did gain possession of the guy's soul; he still looked like Johnny to me."

"What good did killing the soldier do him?"

"His plan was to drop out of sight when he had the chance and resurface as the soldier. He'd been stashing money in secret hiding places for some time. Lord Satan presumably would never know the difference. Trouble was, he didn't cover all the bases. He got shipped overseas before he could pull the switch and what came back couldn't remember its own name let alone a Hebrew incantation."

"And that's when your daughter entered the picture."

"Right. A year had gone by. Meg insisted we help him. I put up the cash to bribe the doctor, and we dropped Johnny off at Times Square on New Year's Eve. Meg made sure of that. It was the starting point, the last place the soldier remembered before Johnny drugged him."

"What happened to the body?"

"They dismembered it and fed the pieces to the hunting dogs in my kennel upstate."

"What else do you remember?"

"Nothing really. Maybe Johnny laughing after it was over. He joked about the victim. Said the poor bastard had no luck at all. They sent him overseas to the invasion at Oran and who ends up shooting at him: the fucking French! Johnny thought that was really funny."

"I was at Oran!" I grabbed Krusemark by his shirt and slammed him back against the ladder. "What was the soldier's name?"

"I don't know."

"You were there in the room."

"I didn't know anything about it until just before it happened. I was only the witness."

"Your daughter must have told you."

"No, she didn't. She didn't know herself. It was part of the magic. Only Johnny could know his victim's true name. Someone he trusted had to guard the secret for him. He sealed the soldier's dogtags in an ancient Egyptian Canopic urn and gave it to Meg."

"What did this urn look like?" I was close to choking him. "Did you ever see it?"

"Many times. Meg kept it on her desk. It was alabaster, white alabaster, and had a three-headed snake carved on the lid."

46

I WAS IN A HURRY. Keeping the .38 tight against Krusemark's ribs, I unlocked the handcuffs and stuffed them in my jacket pocket. "Don't make a move," I said, backing toward the open entrance, my gun aimed at his midsection. "Don't even breathe."

Krusemark rubbed his wrist. "What about the film? You promised me the film."

"Sorry. I was lying about that. I pick up bad habits hanging around guys like you."

"I must have that film."

"Yeah, I know. A blackmailer's dream come true."

"If it's money you want, Angel . . . "

"You can wipe your ass with your stinking money."

"Angel!"

"See you around, hotshot." I stepped out onto the pathway as an uptown, local thundered by. I didn't care if the motorman saw me or not. My only mistake was shoving the Smith & Wesson back into my pocket. We all do dumb things sometimes.

I didn't hear Krusemark coming until he had me around the throat. I figured him all wrong. He was like a wild animal, dangerous and strong. Incredibly strong for a man his age. His breath came in short, angry snorts. He was the only one of us that was breathing.

Even with both hands I couldn't break his choke-hold. Shifting my weight, I got one of my feet hooked between his legs and pulled us off balance. We fell together against the side of the moving train, and the impact spun us apart like rag dolls, flinging me back against the subway wall.

Krusemark managed to stay on his feet. I wasn't so lucky. Sprawled like a drunk on the dusty path, I watched the iron wheels rush by, inches from my face. The train sped past. Krusemark aimed a kick at my head. I caught his foot and yanked him down. I'd been kicked enough for one week.

There wasn't time to grab the .38. Krusemark sat facing me on the path, and I sprang at him, driving my fist into the side of his neck. He made the sort of grunt you'd expect from a toad if you stepped on one. I hit him again, hard, and felt his nose collapse like rotten fruit. He grabbed my hair, yanking my head against his chest, and we grappled on the narrow pathway, gouging and kicking.

There was nothing fair about the fight. The Marquis of Queensberry would not have approved. Krusemark got me down and had his hard hands around my throat. When I couldn't part his weightlifter's grip, I pushed my right palm under his chin and levered his head back. It didn't work, so I jabbed my thumb into his eye.

That did the trick. I heard Krusemark scream even as a local train roared on down the tunnel. His grasp relaxed, and I twisted free, sucking in air. I parried his groping hands, and we wrestled, rolling together onto the tracks. I ended up on top and heard Krusemark's head thud against a wooden tie. I kneed him in the groin for good measure. There wasn't much fight left in the old man.

I stood up and felt my pocket for the Smith & Wesson. The gun was gone, lost in the struggle. A crunch of cinders alerted me as Krusemark's shadowy form staggered upright. He lurched and threw a wild roundhouse right. Stepping inside, I pounded him twice in the midsection. He was hard and solid, but I knew I hurt him.

I took a left on the shoulder where it did no harm and poked my right fist into his face, connecting with the ridge of bone above his eye. It felt like hitting a stone wall. My hand went numb with pain.

That punch didn't slow Krusemark down at all. He lumbered on, throwing hard, skillful jabs as he came. I couldn't block them all, and he stung me a few times as I groped in my jacket for the handcuffs. I used the bracelets like a flail, backhanding him across the face. The crack of steel on bone was music to my ears. I hit him again, above the ear, and he went down backward with a grunt.

Kruaemark's sudden scream echoed and died in the dripping tunnel like the sound of someone falling from a great height. A metallic, beetle-wing hum of electricity crackled in the darkness. The third rail.

I didn't want to touch the body. It was too dark to see him clearly, and I stepped back onto the safety of the path. In the light of a distant bulb, I could make out his obscure form, sprawled across the tracks.

I went back into the exit alcove and poked around inside the leather valise at the foot of the ladder. The papier-mâché lion mask snarled up at me. Under the tangled black cape, I found a small plastic flashlight. That was all. I stepped out into the tunnel and switched it on. Krusemark lay crumpled like a pile of old clothing, his face frozen in his final agony. The sightless eyes stared down the tracks above an open mouth arrested in a soundless scream. A curling tendril of acrid smoke rose above his scorched flesh.

I wiped my prints off the handle and threw his valise down beside him. The mask fell out on the cinders. Flashing the beam up and down the pathway, I spotted my .38 lying against the wall a few feet away. I picked it up and put it in my pocket. The knuckles on my right hand throbbed painfully. The fingers wiggled, so I knew they weren't broken. I couldn't say the same for the Leica. A spiderweb of tiny cracks was frozen deep in the lens.

I checked my pockets. Everything was there except Epiphany's leather good-luck charm. It was lost in the fight. I had a quick look around but didn't spot it. There were more important things to do. I kept Krusemark's flash and hurried up the path, leaving the shipping millionaire lying on the tracks to be dismembered by the next train through. The rats would feast tonight.

I left the subway at the 23rd Street station and caught an uptown cab at the corner of Park Avenue South. I gave the driver Margaret Krusemark's address and ten minutes later he dropped me in front of Carnegie Hall. An old man in shabby clothes stood near the corner, cranking out Bach on a violin held together with masking tape.

I took the elevator to the eleventh floor, not caring if the wizened operator remembered me or not. It was too late for such niceties. The door to Margaret Krusemark's apartment had been sealed by the police. A strip of gummed paper was plastered across the lock. I tore it free, found the right twirl, and let myself in, wiping the knob with my sleeve.

Switching on daddy's flashlight, I probed the beam into the living room. The coffee table on which the body sprawled had been removed, along with the couch and the Persian carpet. In their place remained exact adhesive-tape outlines. The tracing of Margaret Krusemark's arms and legs protruding at either end of the, table's rectangular shape looked like a cartoon of a man wearing a barrel.

There was nothing that interested me in the living room, and I continued down the hallway to the witch's bedchamber. The drawers on her desk and filing cabinets all wore a Police Department seal. I flashed my light across the desktop. The calendar and scattered papers were gone, but the row of research books stood intact. At one end, the alabaster Canopic urn gleamed like polished bone.

My hands trembled as I picked it up. I fumbled for several minutes, but the lid with the carved three-headed snake remained stuck tight. In desperation, I hurled the jar to the floor. It shattered like glass.

I spotted a metallic shine among the shards and grabbed the flashlight off the desk. A set of army dogtags gleamed in the coils of a beaded chain. I picked it up, holding the small, oblong tag under the light. An involuntary chill spread through my body. I ran my icy fingers across the raised letters. Along with the serial number and blood type was a machine-stamped name: ANGEL, HAROLD R.

47

THE DOGTAGS CLINKED IN MY pocket on the way down. I stared at the elevator operator's shoes and ran my thumb over the indented metal letters like a blind man reading a text in Braille. My knees felt weak, but my mind raced along trying to put it all together. Nothing quite fit. It had to be a setup, the dogtags a plant. The Krusemarks, one or both, were in on it; Cyphre was the brains. But why? What was it all about?

Out on the street, the chill night air stung me from my trance. I dropped Krusemark's plastic flashlight in a litter basket and hailed a passing cab. Before anything else, I knew I had to destroy the evidence locked in my safe. "Forty-second and Seventh," I told the driver, settling back with my feet up on the jumpseat as we headed straight down the avenue, catching each green light in sequence.

Steam clouds curled from under the manhole covers like the last act of *Faust*. Johnny Favorite sold his soul to Mephistopheles, then tried to get out of it by sacrificing a soldier with my name. I thought of Louis Cyphre's elegant smile. What did he hope to gain by this charade? I remembered New Year's 1943 on Times Square as clearly as if it were the first night of my life. I was stone-cold sober in a sea of drunks, my dogtags securely in the coin pocket of my wallet when it got lifted. Sixteen years later they turn up in a dead woman's apartment. What in hell was going on?

Times Square blazed like a neon purgatory. I fingered my improbable nose and tried to remember the past. Most of it was gone, wiped out by a French artillery round at Oran. Bits and pieces remained. Smells often bring them back. Damn it, I knew who I was. I know who I am.

The lights were on in my office when we pulled to a stop in front of the novelty shop. The meter said seventy-five cents. I thrust a dollar at the driver and mumbled, "Keep the change." I hoped there was still time.

I took the fire stairs to the third floor so the noise of the elevator wouldn't give me away. The hallway was dark, ditto my waiting room, but the light from the inner office shone on the pebbled glass in the front door. I pulled my gun and eased inside. The door to the inner office stood wide open, spilling light across my threadbare carpet. I waited a moment but didn't hear a thing.

The office was a mess; my desk ransacked, drawers upended, the contents scattered on the linoleum. The dented green filing cabinet was lying on its side, glossy photographs of runaway kids curled like autumn leaves in the corner. When I righted my overturned swivel chair I saw the steel door to the office safe hanging open.

Then the lights went out. Not in the office, inside my head. Someone got the drop on me with what felt like a baseball bat. I heard the sharp crack it made connecting even as I fell forward into blackness.

Cold water splashing on my face brought me around. I sat up, sputtering and blinking. My head throbbed like an aspirin jingle. Louis Cyphre stood above me, dressed in a tuxedo, pouring water from a paper cup. In his other hand he held my Smith & Wesson.

"Find what you were looking for?" I asked.

Cyphre smiled. "Yes, thank you." He crumpled the paper cup and added it to the mess on the floor. "A man in your profession shouldn't house his secrets in tin cans like that one." He pulled the horoscope Margaret Krusemark did of me from his inside jacket pocket. "I imagine the police will be happy to have this."

"You'll never get away with it."

"But, Mr. Angel, I already have."

"Why did you come back? You had the chart."

"I never left. I was in the other room. You walked right past me."

"A trap?"

"Indeed, and a good one, too. You fell into it most eagerly." Cyphre slipped the horoscope back into his pocket. "Sorry about that nasty tap, but I needed some of your things."

"Such as?"

"Your revolver. I have use for it." He reached into his pocket and slowly removed the dogtags, dangling them in front of me by the beaded chain. "And for these."

"That was clever," I said. "Planting those in Margaret Krusemark's apartment. How'd you get her father to cooperate?"

Cyphre's smile widened. "How is Mr. Krusemark, by the way?"

"Dead."

"Pity."

"I can see you're all broken up about it."

"The loss of one of the faithful is always regrettable." Cyphre toyed with the dogtags, winding the chain between tapered fingers. Fowler's engraved golden ring flashed on his manicured hand.

"Cut the crap! Having a gag name doesn't make you the real thing."

"Would you prefer cloven hooves and a tail?"

"I didn't figure it out until tonight. You were toying with me. Lunch at Voisin. I should have guessed when I learned that 666 was the number of the Beast in the Book of Revelation. I'm not as quick as I used to be."

"You disappoint me, Mr. Angel. I should have thought you would have had very little difficulty deciphering my name." He chuckled out loud at his own lame joke.

"Framing me for your killings is pretty smart," I said. "There's just one hitch."

"And what might that be?"

"Herman Winesap. No cop'd believe a story about a client pretending to be Lucifer—only a crackpot would come up with something like that. But I have Winesap to corroborate me."

Cyphre hung the dogtags around his neck with a lupine grin. "Attorney Winesap was lost in a boating accident at Sag Harbor yesterday. Most unfortunate. The body has not yet been recovered."

"Thought of everything, haven't you?"

"I try to be thorough," he said. "You must excuse me now, Mr. Angel. As enjoyable as this conversation is, I'm afraid I have business to attend to. It would be indeed unwise for you to try and stop me. Should you show yourself before I'm gone, I shall be forced to shoot." Cyphre paused in the doorway like a showman milking his exit line. "As much as I'm eager to collect my collateral, it would be a real pity to be killed by your own gun."

"Kiss my ass!" I said.

"No need for that, Johnny," Cyphre smiled. "You've already kissed mine."

He closed the outer office door quietly behind him. I scrambled on my hands and knees across the litter-strewn floor to the open safe. In an empty cigar box on the bottom shelf I kept an extra gun. I felt my heart tom-tomming inside my chest as I swept aside a concealing sheaf of documents. It was still there. I flipped up the lid and removed a .45-caliber Colt Commander. The big automatic felt like a dream come true in my hand.

I jammed the extra clip in my pocket and hurried to the outer door. With my ear to the glass, I listened for the sounds of the elevator closing. The moment I heard it, I slid the pistol's receiver, cocking the piece and introducing a round into the chamber. I saw the top of the elevator car slide past the circular glass window in the door as I ran for the fire stairs.

I took the stairs four at a time, clinging to the railing for balance, and set a new elevator-racing record. Gasping in the stairwell, I held the fire door open with my foot, the automatic braced against the jamb with both hands. My percussive heartbeat crashed in my ears.

I prayed that Cyphre would still have my gun in his hand when the door slid open. That would make it self-defense. Let's see how good his magic was against Colonel Colt's. I imagined the heavy slugs slamming into him, lifting him off his feet, his dark blood staining the lace-front evening shirt. Posing as the devil might con voodoo piano players and middle-aged lady astrologers, but it didn't wash with me. He picked the wrong man to play the patsy.

The circular window in the outer door filled with light as the elevator clanked to a stop. I steadied my aim and held my breath. Louis Cyphre's satanic charade had come to an end. The red metal door slid open. The car was empty.

I staggered forward like a sleepwalker, not believing what I saw. He couldn't be gone. There was no way. I had watched the indicator above the door and seen the numbers light up as the car descended without stopping. He couldn't get off if the car didn't stop.

I got in and pushed the button for the top floor. As the car started up, I climbed onto the brass handrails, one foot braced against either wall, and pushed open the emergency trap on the ceiling.

I stuck my head through the opening and looked around. Cyphre was not on the roof of the car. Greased cables and spinning flywheels left no place to hide.

From the fourth floor, I climbed the fire stairs to the roof. I searched behind chimneys and air vents, the blistered tarpaper buckling underfoot. He was not on the roof. I leaned over the cornice ledge and looked down at the street, first up Seventh Avenue; then, from the corner, along 42nd Street. The Sunday night crowds were sparse. Only whores, male and female, lingered on the sidewalks. Louis Cyphre's distinguished form was nowhere in sight.

I tried to combat my confusion with logic. If he was not on the street or the roof and didn't get off the elevator, he must still be somewhere in the building. It was the only possible explanation. He was hiding somewhere. He had to be.

During the next half-hour, I went over the entire building. I looked in all the restrooms and broom closets. Using my skeleton keys, I let myself into every dark and empty office. I searched Ira Kipnis' place and Olga's Electrolysis without luck. I poked through the shabby waiting rooms of three cut-rate dentists and the closet-sized establishment of a rare-coin-and-stamp dealer. There was no one there.

I returned to my office feeling lost. It didn't make sense. None of it made sense. No one can vanish into thin air. It had to be a trick. I sank back into the swivel chair, still holding the Colt Commander. Across the street, the unremitting march of the day's news continued: . . . FALLOUT OF STRONTIUM-90 IS FOUND HIGHEST IN U.S. . . . INDIANS WORRIED OVER DALAI LAMA . . . By the time I thought to call Epiphany, it was too late. Tricked again by the greatest Trickster of them all.

48

THE ENDLESS RINGING STRUCK THE same note of despair as the lonely voice of the Spanish sailor in Dr. Cipher's battle. Another lost soul like me. I sat for a long time with my ear to the receiver, surrounded by the desolate, trash-heap wreckage in my office. My mouth was dry and tasted of ashes. All hope was gone, abandoned. I had crossed the threshold of doom.

After a while, I got up and stumbled down the stairs to the street. I stood on the corner of the Crossroads of the World and wondered which way to go. It didn't matter anymore. I had run long and far enough. I was all through running.

I spotted a cruising cab heading east on 42nd and flagged it down.

"Any special address?" The driver's sarcasm broke a long and moody silence.

My words sounded far away, like someone else speaking. "Hotel Chelsea on 23rd Street."

"That between Seventh and Eighth?"

"Right."

We turned downtown on Seventh, and I slouched in the corner and stared out at a world gone dead. In the distance, fire trucks howled like raging demons. We passed the hulking columns of Penn Station, grey and somber in the lamplight. The driver didn't speak. Under my breath, I hummed a Johnny Favorite tune popular during the war. It was one of my biggest hits.

Poor old Harry Angel, fed to the dogs like table scraps. I killed him and ate his heart, but it was me who died all the same. Not even magic and power can change that. I was living on borrowed time and another man's memories; a corrupt hybrid creature trying to escape the past. I should have known it was impossible. No matter how cleverly you sneak up on a mirror your reflection always looks you straight in the eye.

"Been some excitement around here tonight." The driver pulled to a stop across from the Chelsea where three squad cars and a police ambulance were double-parked. He flipped up the flag on his meter. "One-sixty, please."

I paid with my emergency fifty and told him to keep the change.

"This ain't no five, mister. You made a mistake."

"Many mistakes," I said and hurried across pavement the color of gravestones.

A patrolman was talking on the desk phone in the lobby but he let me pass without a glance. ". . . three black, five regular, one tea with lemon," he said as the elevator door slid closed.

I got off at my floor. A wheeled stretcher sat in the hall. Two attendants slouched against the wall. "Why all the rush?" one of them complained. "They knew they had a stiff on their hands the whole time."

My apartment door stood wide open. A flashbulb popped inside. The smell of cheap cigars filled the air. I strolled in without a word. Three uniformed cops paced around with nothing to do. Sergeant Deimos sat at the table with his back to me, giving my description to someone on the telephone. Another flashbulb went off in the bedroom.

I had a look inside. One was enough. Epiphany lay face up on the bed, wearing only my dogtags and tied by her wrists and ankles to the frame with four ugly neckties. My hammerless Smith & Wesson protruded from between her outspread legs, the snub barrel inserted like a lover. Her womb's blood glistened on her open thighs, bold as roses.

Lieutenant Sterne was one of five plainclothes detectives watching with his hands in his overcoat pockets as the photographer knelt for a closeup. "Who the hell are you?" a patrolman asked behind me.

"I live here."

Sterne looked in my direction. His sleepy eyes widened. "Angel?" Disbelief cracked his voice. "That's the guy. Collar him!"

The cop behind me pinned my arms. I didn't resist. "Save the heroics," I said.

"See if he's heeled," Sterne barked. The other cops looked at me like I was an animal in the zoo.

A pair of cuffs bit into my wrists. The cop frisked me down and pulled the Colt Commander from the waistband of my pants. "Heavy artillery," he said, handing it to Sterne.

Sterne glanced at the gun, checked the safety, and set it on the bedside table. "Why'd you come back?"

"No place else to go."

"Who is she?" Sterne jerked his thumb at Epiphany's body.

"My daughter."

"Bullshit!"

Sergeant Deimos sauntered into the bedroom. "Well, well, what have we here?"

"Deimos, call downtown and tell 'em we've got the suspect in custody."

"Right away," the sergeant said, strolling from the room in no particular hurry.

"Give it to me again, Angel. Who's the girl?"

"Epiphany Proudfoot. She runs an herb shop on 123rd and Lenox."

One of the other detectives wrote it down. Sterne shoved me back into the living room. I sat on the couch. "How long you been shacking up with her?"

"Couple days."

"Just long enough to kill her, right? Look what we found in the fireplace." Sterne picked up my charred horoscope by the remaining unburned corner. "Want to tell us about it?"

"No."

"Doesn't matter. We've got all we need, unless that's not your .38 stuck up her snatch."

"It's mine."

"You'll burn for this, Angel."

"I'll burn in hell."

"Maybe. We'll be sure and give you a head start upstate." Sterne's shark-slit mouth widened into an evil smile. I stared at his yellow teeth and remembered the laughing face painted on Steeplechase Park, a joker's grin expanding with malice. There was only one other smile like it: the evil leer of Lucifer. I could almost hear His laughter fill the room. This time, the joke was on me.

The author acknowledges with thanks a fellowship grant from the National Endowment for the Arts, which made it possible for him to begin this novel.

A condensed version of this novel originally appeared in *Playboy* magazine.

Cover design by Andrea C. Uva

ISBN: 978-1-4532-7113-1

This edition published in 2011 by Open Road Integrated Media
180 Varick Street
New York, NY 10014

www.openroadmedia.com